Girls From Da Hood 14

Girls From Da Hood 14

Treasure Hernandez

and Ms. Michel Moore

www.urbanbooks.net

Urban Books, LLC
300 Farmingdale Road,NY-Route 109
Farmingdale, NY 11735

ISBN 13: 978-1-64556-117-0
ISBN 10: 1-64556-117-8

First Trade Paperback Printing December 2020
Printed in the United States of America

10 9 8 7 6 5 4 3 2 1

Distributed by Kensington Publishing Corp.
Submit orders to:
Customer Service
400 Hahn Road
Westminster, MD 21157-4627
Phone: 1-800-733-3000
Fax: 1-800-659-2436

All the Way In

Treasure Hernandez

Chapter One

Sonya, Book Bag Bandit

I hated the people God chose to make my family. I hated even claiming them as my family because not one of them was successful. Every last one of them was stranded on a welfare check doing dirt ball bad—and here I was born dead smack into absolutely nothing. I hated my aunt's house and everything in it because, to me, it represented failure and everything I *didn't* want to be. The empty wrappers, liquor bottles, and full ashtrays of smoked cigarettes reminded me every day of the life I didn't want. The only reason I even bothered to come here—I call it "here" because I refuse to call it home—was on the strength of my little brother Devin. If it weren't for him, I would have stopped putting up with my aunt's hellhole long ago. Every night, I would lie with Devin on our pallet of sheets and old blankets, which we spread across the floor. I would lie there staring up at the ceiling, trying to figure out a way I could come up with enough money to move my little brother out of that dump and into a place that was at least clean. That was all I cared about . . . not clothes, shoes, or even sleep. I had to get us out of there by any means necessary.

I would kiss Devin on the forehead while he slept. I'd look at his little innocent face for a minute, trying to find the inspiration I needed before I hit them streets and, hopefully, turn up something.

Cuzzo and my aunt were the only two that beat me to the kitchen every morning. As soon as I hit the door, there she sat, legs crossed, in her favorite weathered blue nightgown, sipping coffee while pretending to be knee-deep in God's Word. I swear if there were a back door or any other way out of that house other than going through the kitchen, I damn sure would have utilized it. The only way out was through the area where she diligently sat perched. It was almost like she was waiting to start messing with me.

I would take a deep breath and prepare for the bullshit. "Mornin', Auntie," I would say, heading for the kitchen sink to wash my hands. Even though her place was a mess, Lord knows you better wash your hands before touching anything in her kitchen. Then I would fix myself a simple bowl of grits, and nothing more because I hated eating her food. Auntie was one to make sure she let you know it too . . . that you were eating *her* food and living in *her* house. Her "four walls" are what she called it.

The reason I hated eating her food was that she always held some type of opposition. You were eating too much, or she was complaining that you thought you were too good for her cooking. I kept it simple so that I could keep it moving. She never would acknowledge my morning greetings. Instead, she would give me an evil understare as she sipped her coffee. I'd be sitting across from her, thinking, *Here we go*. And sure as shit, she would start.

"When are you going to get yourself together, Sonya? This is supposed to be your senior year, and I'm sure you won't be walking across the stage in June."

"Auntie, I wish you would stop with all the graduation talk. School ain't never been for me." I was trying to hurry up and finish my grits so I could get the hell out of there.

"Well, I'ma tell you one thing. When school lets out, if you don't have a job, you won't have a roof over your head neither. Are we clear on *that* part?"

Her fat ass irked me. I scooted my wooden chair back from the small table and stood up. I wasn't trying to hear her gibberish, not this morning. Besides, even if I were to graduate, there wasn't a single cent set aside for me to go off to college, so what was the difference? The way I looked at it was I couldn't do any worse than the rest of them.

As I washed my bowl, Auntie spat, "I'm not taking care of no grown-ass woman." That's funny because *she* didn't even hold a job. She was making it off them checks the government sent her wide ass twice a month for my brother and me, not to mention her own flock.

"There goes my baby," Auntie proudly announced, as her eldest son entered the kitchen running late. Cuzzo was younger by a couple of months.

Hugging and kissing his mother before taking a seat across from her, he smiled. "Mornin', Ma."

Auntie scrambled to her feet in a rush to get to the stove. She packed his plate full of bacon, eggs, and french toast. She set the plate down in front of him, then rushed over to her bedroom, where she kept the good cereal under lock and key. "Here you go, baby," she said, setting the Frosted Flakes in front of her favorite child.

"I'm out," I said over my shoulder as I made my way through the kitchen, strapping my book bag to my back.

"Wait up, girl. I'ma walk with you," Cuzzo insisted. He took a long gulp of milk while trying to stand.

But Auntie forced him back down into his chair. "Finish your food, baby," she ordered while rolling her eyes at me.

"Yeah, Cuzzo, I'll see you later. Finish eating." I kept moving to the front door. Deep down, I knew Auntie didn't care for me. I didn't know if it was because I was gay or something else. Nevertheless, she felt like I was going nowhere fast, and she was determined not to let me take Cuzzo with me. Which was good, considering I always had things to take care of that were a one-man job.

I slammed the front door and took in a deep breath of fresh air, relieved to be leaving that house. Quickly, I tucked my hands deep inside the pockets of my black hooded coat and started down the block. We lived on West Grand, one block away from Davison. Every morning, I would leave the house with my book bag strapped to my back, but instead of going to school, I was on my way to pull yet another caper. It was easy enough, and it was just the way I liked my money—fast. Most people would try to tell me that what I was doing was wrong, but you know what? Fuck you and fuck them too 'cause I don't believe in right and wrong. Nah, I believe in what's necessary and what's not. And me trying to change my little brother's living situation was *extremely* necessary.

Nearing the BP gas station, I locked eyes on the well-dressed, half-breed dude standing at the rear area of a pearl-white Lincoln. He was watching the meter on the pump with his back to me . . . straight slipping. I had to get him. I picked up my step and pulled my hood over my head. I quickly checked the scene. Approximately three inches of fresh snow packed the street, so the traffic moving down Davison was at a minimum and at a snail's pace. I crossed the parking lot while clutching the handle of my gun. The meter slowed, then stopped at twenty dollars.

The man shook the last of the gas from the pump and placed it back on its hook. When he turned around to screw the cap on his gas tank, his nose touched the cold steel of the barrel of my gun. I could see the fear in his eyes. It was like I was looking at his soul. He slowly raised his hands above his head, while back stepping into the pump. "Please, don't shoot me," he begged for mercy.

"Shut the fuck up and walk your ass around the back of the station," I ordered through clenched teeth. I looked around my surroundings to make sure no one was watching us. "Move, nigga," I snapped, waving the gun toward the alley.

"Okay, okay." The man started sidestepping for the alley while keeping his hands high and eyes married to the gun.

Once we reached the alley, I ordered him against the wall while I slid out of my book bag. "Here, put everything in the bag," I demanded, tossing the bag to his chest. The man hurriedly removed everything from his pockets, stuffing his belongings inside the bag.

"Everything—clothes, drawers, socks. The whole nine. I want it all and hurry the fuck up."

"It's too cold. Let me keep my clothes at least. You can have everything else."

"Strip." I held his ass at bay while he stripped down. Within seconds, he was standing there ass naked, ashy, and shivering. Pneumonia would *definitely* be in his future.

"Hold up, playboy. Put the ring in the bag too," I ordered with an attitude.

"Come on, not my wedding band," he pleaded. "My wife will kill me."

"Bitch, you can die with it on for all I care. Either way, I guess you gonna be dead, so what's it gonna be? By my hand or hers?" I snapped, then cocked the hammer back to let him know I wasn't bullshitting.

He lowered his hands to his side and started fiddling with the back of the ring like he was trying to get it off, then out of nowhere, the naked fool broke down into a

Barry Sanders stance and hit me with the two-move juke. I started to bang his old ass in his back as he booked down the alley with his feet touching his ass, but I let him go on about his way. That ring definitely wasn't worth catching no body.

I grabbed my book bag from the snow and put it on my back. With a quickness, I cut down the alley in the opposite direction. Even with the three inches of snow, I knew it wouldn't be long before the hook had the entire hood on fire. Once the call went through with my description, every cop in the vicinity would be looking for me. I done robbed so many people at BP, it was crazy 'cause I'd lost count. Every time I made they ass strip naked and put it all in the bag. So many people had the same complaint that the 10th Precinct had dubbed me, "The Book Bag Bandit."

I ain't give a fuck, though, 'cause they all described me as a six-foot, muscle-bound, triple-dark-skinned dude with a deep voice. Of course, I don't look anything close to that description, but I guess fear makes a person see what they want to see. I'm a brown-skinned female with short dreads and a whisper-light voice. But I'll take the name "Book Bag Bandit." At the end of the day, it sounded kind of cool.

I knew my hood like the back of my hand, so shaking the hook was easy. I cut back across Davison, ran past my block, and turned down Pasadena. Then to make sure the cops wouldn't be on my trail after a few houses, I darted between the vacant lots. Thankfully, I was in good shape and not out of breath. I couldn't say that about the first time I robbed someone in the alley. When I ran off, I got winded so fast I thought I was definitely going to get caught. But now that I've done robbed so many, I got my stamina at one hundred.

My slim build was righteous for sprinting, even in the snow. Taking one final look to ensure I wasn't being followed, I climbed the porch of the two-family flat. It didn't matter what time, day or night. Each step served as the doorbell, that's how loud they creaked. Like clockwork, by the time I reached the landing, the door would be wide open. No doubt, today would be no exception. Pops stood in the doorway, scratching at his ashy stomach with one hand and vigorously rubbing his beady head with the other. He looked over my shoulder and then up the street. "Why ain't yo' ass in school, girl?" he asked, slurring and spitting every word.

"The same reason you ain't got your teeth in," I said, brushing past him on my way through the door.

Pops locked the front door using two cross boards, then tailed me into the back room. I could hear his feet scraping behind me. His feet looked like gator boots, that's how badly cracked they were at the heels.

"You don't think I know what you've been doing out there, do you?" he asked, trying to be funny. I tried to shut the bedroom door, but Pops caught it with his big toe. "I know good and well what you up to, Sonya." He slowly dragged his sentence out.

"So, and what? What's your damn point of what you think you know? What you gonna do—turn me in or something?" I didn't give a fuck about his old ass somewhat knowing the score. What was he going to do? Snitch? Naw, he knew that would be bad for his health, especially in the neighborhood where we lived.

"Come on now. Stop all of that bullshit. You know I would never turn my own daughter in, not for nothing in the world. So—"

Yeah, right. For a good shot of dope, you'd turn God in. "All right, so what you want?" I snapped, tired of his games.

Pops pushed up his Coke-bottle Mafia glasses on his nose and squinted with greed. “You know what I need. Give your old man some of that money I know you got . . . just something to get me out the gate. You know, a li’l kick start for the day.”

“What the fuck. Damn. All right, give me a minute.” I didn’t need him sweating my every move because his idea of a “li’l something” would turn into a lot more than what I was trying to give up. Pops released his doorstopper big toe and yelled as I closed the door. “And I don’t want no scraps! Look out for me!”

I took off my coat and tossed it over on the cluttered love seat. As always, I then propped the back of a chair under the doorknob. I cut on the ancient floor-model TV and flopped down beside my book bag, where I searched every inch of my latest victim’s belongings, and all I turned up was sixty-two dollars in cash and an old-ass check stub. I couldn’t believe that shit—all that for *this*. I should have blasted his bitch ass and at least got that ring off him. This lick was a waste of time. I’d been better off just going to school for the free breakfast they’d serve if you got there early enough.

Never again. Next go-around, I’ma pick me somebody that at least looks like they got bread. I fired up a Newport and kicked back, watching the morning news.

“Sonya, hey, Sonya,” Pops desperately called out, harassing me about what was mines, what I’d taken the risk of getting arrested or killed over. When I didn’t reply quickly enough, he jerked the knob violently, trying to get in. Finally, the door cracked some but stopped when the chair’s legs dug into the floor doing their job. That made him even more frustrated as he passed the baton to my mother.

“Open up this fucking door, girl. I ain’t playing with you this morning.”

I hated the sound of her voice. It was my crackhead-ass mother, Mom Dukes, riding shotgun with Pops for a come-up. She and I had a love-hate type relationship. I loved my mother on the strength that she had given me birth, and because she hadn't always been like she was now. We had some good memories, but they were so long ago that I barely remembered them. For the past twelve years, it's been nothing but her smoking crack and nursing a bottle of gin. Truth be told, that's the reason my little brother Devin is slow, 'cause my mom refused to stop hitting the pipe while she was pregnant. And for that selfish reason, I hated her inner soul. Knowing my two, rotten, drug-addicted parents would take the door off the hinges to get to some cash to get high, I stuffed the money I had deep in my pocket. Then I scanned the room before opening the door.

"Sonya, I done told your wannabe-a-boy ass about locking doors in my damn house." Mom Dukes insulted me while barging into the room. She stopped dead center and did an inventory with her eyes. "Yeah, your father told me what you were down here doing."

"And?" I laughed at her, even trying to sound tough or as if she were a decent parent with real rules that mattered.

"And I done told you not to bring no trouble round my domain. You make this your last time, do you understand me? You gonna make my house hot."

"Trouble? The whole damn house is trouble. And this mug been hot since the day you started squatting in this crib." I didn't back down or show her any real respect.

"Yeah, so what, smart-ass? It's mines."

"It's yours until the *real* owner come around claiming this motherfucker. Then you and Pops and all of ya drug-addicted cohorts gonna be back out in the streets searching for another halfway decent bando."

But let's keep it real. I peeped game and always did where she was concerned. Mom Dukes was an extortionist on the low. To shut her up was simple. I peeled a ten off the top of the cash I had stuffed deep inside my pocket. I shoved the money in her palm, and her bitching and fake house rules abruptly ceased. That was more than enough to get her first rock of the day.

"Thank you, baby girl." She smiled and turned on her heels, marching out of the room as if she had not just gone ham on me.

Next, Pops entered the room. He swiftly took Mom Dukes's place, giving me the sad eye. Anxiously, he rocked back on his leather heels, wiggling his stiff toes like he was playing the piano or trying to tap the floor. "Sonya," he swallowed hard, hoping I was still feeling generous.

"What?" I yelled at him while rubbing my fingers through my dreads. "I don't know what you waiting on. I was gonna bless you until you told on me like some damn snitch. So, now, you gonna suffer. So, yeah, bye."

"Baby girl, wait. I ain't tell her nothin'. I swear on God and three angels I didn't. She just worked you, that's all," Pops firmly claimed, following me over to the sofa. "Come on, Sonya. I need to get out the gate before ten o'clock, or you know I'ma be sick. I feel weak already, and my stomach about to bottom out."

"What was you gonna do if I ain't stop by? Then what?" I twisted up my face, waiting for a response.

"I don't know, but you did stop by. So, help ya old man out, will ya?"

I can't lie. I couldn't stand to see my sperm donor like that, scratching his skin until he bled. He was a cold dope fiend and was bold. I knew, unlike my mother, who didn't have to smoke a rock to be okay, Pops needed to push that needle in a vein, or he'd get sick damn near on the verge of death. The heroin had long claimed him and would continue to do so until God called his number. All the treatment and special programs he took part in over the years hadn't helped any. I accepted the fact Pops was a dope fiend, and Mom Dukes was a bona fide crackhead. That's just who they were. Sometimes, I had to remind myself, though. That way, I knew never to expect anything different from each but running game on whoever had the bag. It kept me focused because I know if I weren't the one to go out and get it for them from time to time, it wouldn't be got. In my feelings, I reached in my pocket and felt around.

"I know you peeling. So just how much you get?" he inquired as his tongue protruded through his mouth.

"Damn, nigga, here. Take it." I gave him a twenty from my now almost empty pocket. "Make sure you get something to eat with the rest of it after ya get that pack."

"Rest of what? Shiiid . . . All this going to my arm." Pops tucked the twenty into the front pocket of his filthy track pants and started for the door.

"I hope y'all happy. I done gave y'all half of what I made. That shit foul, 'bout y'all don't give a care. As long as y'all two high, it's all good," I hollered at my no-good parents.

I kicked back and caught the end of some Breaking News Story. Then I heard the voice of OC out in the living room, which was annoying because I had to go to the bathroom, and that meant I'd have to see his ass. Out of everybody around our way, I hated that guy the most. Over the past ten years or so years, he had been my father's main heroin connect. I been wanted to kill OC because I felt like he was responsible for my Pops being strung out. Begrudgingly getting up from the couch, I left the room, heading down the hallway. Once in the front of the house, I shook my head, wanting to slap the fire outta OC's nickel slick-talking mouth.

"Hey, now, baby girl, you showl looking nice and sweet today." He licked his lips as if I were a plate of pork chops and gravy. "What you hiding under all them loose clothes you be wearing, huh? You want me to take you shopping one day?"

Any normal father would step to any grown-ass man trying to push up on his daughter. But, naw, not my damn father. Instead, he stood there like a small child waiting for a piece of candy. I was fuming. Here it was, my father was a mere nothing-ass crumb with a habit, while OC sported minks and gators, slamming Cadillac doors. I could see his old, wrinkled, crooked face smile showing that country-ass gold tooth, while he pocketed the twenty I'd just blessed Pops with. His disrespectful ass was most definitely on my list. But it was going to take some serious planning and lots of balls. However, I was down for it.

Chapter Two

Melody, Money Mel

I was depressed. I felt like my life was going to end. And for me, it was. When my mom told me that we were moving to Detroit, it seemed like the end of the world because all I knew was Chicago. I loved home and wouldn't trade it for nothing in the world. That's where all my friends were, my existence, and most importantly, my hustle . . . how I made money. But when you're 16, none of that matters. When my mom accepted the job offer at Ford Motor Company, what she really meant was that "we" accepted the offer; her, my two sisters, and me.

I tried everything to keep from leaving my birthplace. I even got my uncle to agree to let me live with him and his wife, but no such luck. My moms wasn't buying it. When the U-Haul was packed, my black ass was included. In the weeks leading up to the day we were to leave, she kept talking about us having a better life waiting for us in Motown. But to me, that was all a bunch of bullshit. In all honesty, my life was fine just the way it was back at home. I knew off the bat that I'd hate Detroit just on the strength of it not being the South Side of Chicago.

My mom rented a three-bedroom lower flat on Waverly off Dexter. It was dead smack in the heart of the hood on the West Side of the city. The house came with worn-out wall-to-wall carpeting, an old stove with a nonworking oven, a refrigerator, and roaches. Big-ass roaches neither my siblings nor I had ever seen before. I was disappointed and confused. Back home, we were living rough, true enough, but our new house and the neighborhood it was in were like staying in a third world country.

"Mom, are you serious right now? *This* is what you dragged us all the way from back home for—for *this?*" my oldest sister whined as we all took our first tour of the interior of the house.

"This is kinda messed up. I'm just saying, we was doing way, way better in Chicago," my youngest sister added her two cents, avoiding even touching a wall with her shoulder.

"Okay, y'all, settle down and quit y'all bitchin'. This is just until I can save a few paychecks. This is temporary but necessary. We won't be in this house for long. But until we move . . . welcome home." Mom spoke in an assuring but stern voice.

"I mean, they are kinda right. This is wrong all the way around," I put my two cents in as well.

"Look, 'Ham,' I need you, of all people, to stop complaining and make due until I turn things around."

Ham was my nickname. I was told I had temper tantrums as a baby, and my moms started saying I was always going "ham." So, that title came to stick with family members.

That plea from my mother changed my perspective. I was the first to step in and at least *act* like things would get better with time. Deep down, I knew my mother needed me there with her to help with my sisters, and that was cool because I loved all of them. Our new digs was just gonna take some getting used to. For the most part, we were all close, always had been, and I guess that's how our mother wanted to keep us. I knew all she wanted was a fresh start, not just for herself but for the entire family. And I had her back.

More than anything, my mother wanted me to finish school. I had been held back twice already, and I was going for a third. I was 16 years old and still in the eighth grade. My younger sister and I were in the same grade. And the oldest was in high school. Moms was hoping that I'd do better being in Detroit and away from Chicago, but I gave up on school when my dad died. He was killed gambling in an after-hours joint. Some lame couldn't stand the loss and probably all the cash shit my father would talk while taking loot off of them. *"I now pronounce you broke."* He would taunt them after he broke the next man's bank. I miss the shit out of that old, slick fool. Even though I was a girl, I was his favorite child. We were best friends and did everything together. When he passed away, it kinda left us fucked around, so school wasn't nowhere on my mind.

I found my true calling seven years ago down in Teri's basement. She was an old, free-spirit type woman who lived two blocks over from me back in Chicago. For some reason, Teri took a liking to me. She said that I reminded her of her late husband. He was like me, an occasional Muslim when it suited him, but still infatuated with the streets. Rumor has it that man had to be the slickest Negro God ever created. Legendary, he was the coldest to ever play the "two-finger dip" game in the South Side of Chicago.

Teri saw something in me, I guess, so she blessed me with the game on how to dip. The dark-haired woman had a mannequin set up in her basement. It was fully clothed and rigged up with buzzers that went off at the slightest touch. The object was to pretend the dummy was a victim, and you had to pick wallets and other hidden trinkets from various pockets without setting off the buzzers. Every day after school, I would go straight over to Teri's and down in the basement to practice on that damn dummy. For three months straight, I practiced. Sadly, every time I went for one of the wallets, the buzzers would sound off. That infuriated me. But at the same time, it encouraged me to try to go even harder to get the game down packed.

Teri would say, "You don't get a second chance in real life. Now, let's get it right this time."

She would demonstrate with ease how to pick the dummy, clipping one of the wallets, removing the money, then return it to the pocket. Her expertise had me mystified. Finally, one day after *millions* of tries and *countless* hours, I successfully clipped my first wallet. I was struck to see that the mannequin didn't snitch me out.

"I did it, I did it," I excitedly called out for Teri. I wanted to show her that I had mastered the art of pickpocketing. Impressed, she made me do it repeatedly until she was satisfied that I had it down.

She smiled through the cloud of smoke from her cigarette. "It's time to put all that practice to work. You ready, Melody, or what?"

Damn, I couldn't wait. The deal was since Teri blessed me with the game, I owed her 20 percent off the victims that I picked for the next six months. I wasn't tripping, though. For the art she had given me, I would've agreed to two years. I was just ready to put what I'd learned into play.

The next morning, I skipped school. I started out riding the train. I'd brush up against people picking they shit left and right. Teri showed me how to train my eyes to spot where a victim was holding their prized possessions. I could look at you, and in five seconds, I knew where a wallet, cell phone, or iPod was located. Once I did zero in on that small bulge of wealth, there was nothing that could keep me from clipping yo' ass. Every day when I finished pickin', I would break bread with Teri. She would have a nice dinner spread waiting on me. We'd eat and then count our chips, and I'd dip. She'd keep all the credit cards and IDs. All I wanted was cash. And initially, that's how I traded in the nickname "Ham" and became "Money Mel."

Blessed with a skill, I didn't leave Chicago empty-handed. I took my show on the road. For the first two weeks in Detroit, all I did was learn the city. As soon as my mom dropped us off at school, I'd wait until she pulled off. Once I made sure she was well out of sight, I would cross the street and wait for the bus to take me downtown. Once at the main transit terminal, I would ride east to west, picking the early-morning passengers for their lunch money and whatever else I could clip.

One morning while I was riding the Woodward bus, I scanned the seats looking for a victim before I sat down. I spotted a gorilla knot bulging out the front shirt pocket of a heavyset, no-neck man. He was too lost looking out the window to notice that I had slid in the seat beside him. I folded my arms high across my chest and assumed the two-finger dip position. I scooted so close up on the man that he looked over at me with a look that said, "Damn, girl, you ain't got enough room?" I kept my head and eyes straight to the front of the bus. I didn't care how his big ass was feeling. I had my seat, and I wasn't moving until I got that knot up off him.

Every time the bus rocked and dipped into a pothole, I would inch closer up on him until my position was just right. No-Neck kept breathing hard and looking over at me with his eyes bucked like "Get up off me." When the bus rocked again, I leaned into him, and that was all she wrote. *Got 'em.*

Ole No-Neck got frustrated by the closeness. "Fuck it, I'ma move. Excuse me," he yelled, trying to get into the aisle. "Move the fuck outta my way. You young people are the worse. Y'alls' mommas raising y'all like animals." He rolled his eyes on the way to an empty seat.

That was my cue. "Sorry," I smiled, letting his insult roll off my animal back. I pulled the cord and got up, walking to the rear door while keeping eyes on No-Neck in case he realized he'd been hit. Out of all my times of clippin' folks, I could count on one hand how many times I got caught with my hand in the cookie jar. Twice, but never did I stick around long enough for the police to show up. If a victim caught me dippin', I would flip the script. I had to because shit could get ugly—quick—and Teri taught me not to allow the victim to pump they self up. Lastly, I was to remember, in most cases, that they were just as scared of you. So, when they screamed, I'd scream louder. Shit, I would play crazy . . . whatever the situation called for, as long as it was good enough of a diversion to get up out of there.

Once off the bus, I darted around the corner, then sprinted up the block to watch the bus through a parking lot. After patting myself on the back, I counted my earnings as the bus faded into traffic. *Yeah, not bad, fat boy. Yeah, not bad at all. This so-called animal got down on you for $300. God made suckers so us hustlers could survive.* Content with myself, I tucked the money in my pocket and crossed the street. I was starting to feel like moving to Detroit might work out.

Chapter Three

Two of a Kind

The parking lot of Atlas grocery store was packed with customers. It was the first of the month, and everyone had their government money—my damn favorite day. For me, it was like my birthday and Christmas put together, only better. The first is when I did my best pickin' because everybody had money to lend, not spend. I dubbed the first as the official two-finger dip holiday. It was the only holiday that came twelve times a year. Ready to get it going, I stood outside the entrance, just peeping everything out before I started moving. Everyone had turned out to spend their food stamps in groves. They pushed carts packed to the hilt with generic items, everything from soap to dog food-size bags of cereal. Jitney cabs lined the exit, soliciting folks in need of a lift, while random teens helped exiting customers with their bags. I was no different. I fell right in with them . . . only I wasn't accepting tips. I was on another mission, bigger than the scraps they'd probably offer.

"Nah, that's okay. Keep your money. I'm just out here helping, doing God's work," I'd tell them when they offered a tip. I'd lie, of course, helping myself to their choice items as we walked to their car with the bags. By the time we reached the trunk, I would have all the tips I needed. I would wave them off, then return to my post with the pack of thirsty teens wishing for that one big tip.

After a twenty-minute dry spell, an old man came scooting out of the store, pushing a buggy. *Jackpot!* It was easy to see his old ass had a vault in his back pocket. I could practically see the bills screaming from his wallet. Ready to make my presence known, I yanked an anxious boy by his shirt. "Fall back and chill out. I got this one."

"Come on, Pops." With a reassuring smile, I grabbed the two bags from the basket and waited for him to walk around the rail. "I got you, Pops." He just smiled back from behind the big blue blockers he wore on his face. He was happy to see a pretty young girl's face offering to assist him. He had to be pushing 70, but I didn't care. That wasn't gon' save him or his first-of-the-month windfall. "So, okay, where you at, dear?" I asked once I had him in the solitude of the closely parked cars.

"It's a grey Crown Victoria, with a dent on the side door. It should be around here somewhere."

"Okay, then, there it is. I see it." He had parked near the alley, which was perfect for what I had in mind next. As we approached the trunk, I went into my spiel about not wanting a tip, all the while I was angling myself for the clip. Not thinking anything was strange, he popped the trunk so I could put his bags inside. I did that while checking each side of the vehicle for any passersby. Luckily, the coast was clear. When the old man reached upward to shut the trunk, that's when I made my move. *Oh, hell yeah, this like taking candy from a baby*. As my hand reached for my prize, the sight of a huge pistol stopped me. My eyes widened, and I shook with fear as it was aimed dead at my face.

"Both y'all jokers move to the alley. And hurry the fuck up." It sounded like a young person about my age who ordered me and who was going to be *my* victim to be quick in our actions. It was hard to see his face, but I could tell he was talking through clenched teeth. "Hurry the fuck up before I make this thing sing. Move," he snapped, waving the gun barrel toward the darkness of the alley.

I was terrified. His tone was one that meant business. I was confused about what was truly going on; yet, whatever this person was after, I damn sure wasn't about to be the one to deny him. Doing as demanded of me, I started for the alley with my hands to the sky, praying not to get shot. Stubbornly, the old man wasn't going for it.

"You young punk. I wish to hell I would let you take something off me. Don't let these glasses fool you." Ready to battle, he snatched off his blue blockers and bounced back into a boxer stance as if he had a death wish.

"Look here, old man, don't make me shoot you in the stomach. Now, I said, get yo' ass to the alley—now!"

Fearing no man or beast, he bent down and pulled up his creased pants leg. I was ready to piss on myself when he revealed an ankle holster with a .38 Special tucked inside. This evening was gearing up to be the most dangerous one I'd spent on the streets of Detroit since moving here. I was a nervous wreck, but strangely still had a thirst and desire for the old man's wallet. Seeing the diversion of a surprise second weapon making its untimely presence, I found a bit of courage. I reached over, making my move for the wallet, hoping I could sprint away while the two of them argued about who was going to shoot who first. In theory, it may have sounded like a halfway decent plan, but as luck would have it, things didn't go that way. The old man whizzed around, focusing on me now. Not only had some random dude caught me slipping . . . but also, now, the old man had caught me with my hand in the cookie jar. I was busted and stunned. There was no way possible that this situation could get any worse. But in mere seconds, as I held his wallet tightly, it did just that.

"Oh, so I get it. What's this, a setup, or something? That's all right, you wait yo' ass right there too," he ordered with certainty as he bent over, reaching for his gun. "Yeah, I got something for both you and your sneaky li'l girlfriend."

This was it. I knew I was well on my way to either going to jail or hell. Tears formed, knowing my mother would have to receive a fucked-up phone call about my whereabouts. *God, please, please, please, get me outta this. If you do, I promise I will change my ways*. I hoped the man up above was listening to me blatantly lie about my future intentions but would help me out anyway. I was elated when my prayers were somewhat answered.

A thunderous blaze erupted. The old man was hit square in his ass. I could hear him screaming out that he'd been shot as I fled the scene. Wisely, I'd made a run for it. There was no need for me to stand idly by and wait to see if the mysterious gunman would make me his next target.

I barreled down the deserted, litter-filled alley, and my heart raced. I never had asthma before, but at that moment, I was struggling to breathe. I wheezed while praying that I didn't take a slug in the back from either of the two persons in possession of pistols. Nearing a dilapidated garage, I was going to duck behind the half-standing structure to catch my breath. Yet, shockingly, I discovered I was not alone. I glanced over my shoulder and suddenly found the energy to pick up my pace. As I ran full speed down the alley, ole boy was on my heels, gun in hand. There was no way I was going to be shot in an alley left to bleed out and die or maybe raped. I had to get out into the open, even if it meant the police seeing me.

Intent on living to see the next day, I hopped the next gate into someone's backyard. Just as I thought I was home free—I was proven wrong. The shooter must have had horse in his blood because he cleared the gate with no hands right behind me. At that point, I was done. I couldn't go on. I was exhausted. My only option was to hope for a miracle.

I stopped dead in my tracks and quickly turned around. With my hands reached up to God, I begged for mercy, taking a few steps back. "Please, don't kill me, please, please."

"Kill you? Naw, I ain't on that tip right now," he said, tucking the gun in his waist. Then he removed his hood.

My heart skipped two beats. I was shocked all the way around, not expecting what I was seeing. It was then that I realize that he was actually a *she*. The oversized clothes were just a front, although her voice still remained on the deep, raspy side. "Damn, thank you," I stammered, not knowing what else to say or do.

Momentarily, she paused, then looked around like, "You hear that?" Police sirens filled the air, and it was apparent that they were getting closer. "Come on, girl, we gotta get outta here before they box us in," she urged, pulling on my shirt.

Say what? Huh? We? When did I become a we? Girl, I don't know yo' crazy ass. I don't even know why you following me in the first place. I stood there with a blank expression. But since this female did have that big-ass gun and had just shot the old man, I guess the loon was running shit. So, also taking into consideration I didn't want to get knocked, I took off running full speed toward the street. My new partner in crime, of course, was trailing close behind.

Oh shit. My heart sank as a Detroit police car roared up the block with its lights flashing. I took a deep breath and said my prayers. I just knew we were on our way to jail, but God had other plans. The squad car blew past. I glanced over at her as to say, "Damn, that was close."

Committed to getting all the way out of Dodge, we jogged side by side for several blocks. With her now taking the lead, she cut down the alley and came out through a vacant lot. At that point, I was all turned around, not knowing the neighborhood that well. I was exhausted as she practically dragged me by the arm up the stairs of a seemingly abandoned dwelling.

"Yo, sis, hurry up, hurry up. We gonna be good now," she happily announced, closing the door behind us.

We entered a kitchen, and I leaned against a filthy, plate-filled sink with my face buried in my arm, gasping for air and licking my dry lips. I looked up to see this girl peeking out the kitchen window into the yard.

"So, wow, I think we shook 'em," she said, releasing the curtain and turning to face me.

Only then did I realize that I'd followed this nut right into a death trap. That weird hunger I had seen earlier back in the alley had returned to her eyes as she smoked me over. I stood up and pleaded my case like a habitual convict fighting a murder case. "Look, seriously, I don't want any problems. If it's the money you want, it's yours," I said, extending the wallet as a peace offering and bribe to live.

"Sonya, is that you in there?" a voice asked from the front part of the house. Then a nappy-chested old man turned the corner, coughing, not even bothering to cover his mouth. Confused, he looked me up and down and then over to who I was guessing was Sonya.

"Hey, girl, who in the hell is this?"

"Damn, why you wanna know? You bugging."

"'Cause she's in my damn house, that's why. Ya ass out there up to no good. Whoever y'all running from betta not show up here blowing my high," the old man snapped as if he were proud of his raggedy surroundings.

"Look, not now, Pops. Fall back with all that bullshit. Ain't nobody chasing nobody."

Pops? You mean to tell me this snaggletoothed nigga is her daddy? I swear I thought that this dump was abandoned. And here, his old ass has the nerve to be bitchin' about "his" house. I was more than ready to just get outta here. I glanced over at the door as I slid the stolen wallet into my pocket.

"Hey, what's going on out here?" A wide-bodied woman stepped into the kitchen, joining the conversation.

"Your wild-ass daughter and her little hoodlum sidekick is running from some damn body. You know, with her, it's always something."

"What's going on, Sonya?" her mom asked, reeking of alcohol.

"It ain't nothing, Ma. You know them cracker police be messin' with us for no reason."

"And who the fuck is you?" her mom snarled at me.

Hesitantly, I said, "Umm, my name's Melody."

"Where the hell you from? You ain't from around here."

"Naw, I'm from Chicago."

"Yeah, well, Chi-Town. Keep up running with this no-good daughter of mine, and you two gon' be cell mates."

"Look, let me stop all this fake shit. Here, now go somewhere and get the fuck on," Sonya interrupted in a loud tone that would have my mother slapping my face. Handing what looked like a twenty to her father, she told her parents to split it. I could tell that she was embarrassed by them. Who wouldn't be? Yet, I played it like it was all good. I mean, it was because now I saw why this girl kept that dead, cold, blank hunger in her eyes. My level of understanding would be zero too if I were living in circumstances like hers.

"So, I guess your name is Sonya, huh?" I blurted out, feeling a little bit more at ease, seeing as we were not alone. "My name is Melody. Well, Money Mel," I boasted, trying to make small talk and sound supercool.

"Oh yeah, Money Mel, huh?" she laughed, seeing I was trying to brag on myself. And not to be outdone, she was eager to do some quick bragging about her own rep as she turned her back on me. "Well, they call me the Book Bag Bandit."

"Oh, snap! Are you serious? Oh my God, I seen that shit on the news the other day." I put the side of my fist in my mouth, then stopped and laughed. "That's some official shit, making people rob they self." It was all making sense now. That's why she was carrying a book bag. "I'ma call you 'Bags.'"

Sonya thought for a second. "I like that." She nodded and smiled. "I gotta give it to you too. I watched you working all day, Money Mel. You must have clipped every bit of ten people before the old guy."

"Yeah, that's what I do," I proudly smiled.

"So, where you learn how to pick at?"

"Back home in Chicago; the South Side. That's all we do in my area. Picking pockets is bigger than the dope game. We call it two-finger dippin'. You slippin', yo' shit missin'."

"I like that." Bags nodded, then raised her shirt. "But here in Detroit, we flash this burner and make a nigga drop down. But for real, for real, I think we could make some noise together if we link."

I squinted at her, like, "I'm listening, go ahead." I nodded and watched as Bags did the math in her head. The way the sirens were still flying past, I was not trying to see outside anytime fast. After nearing twenty minutes of Bags running down her potential game plan, I was in total agreement. We'd make a great team. And to show my good faith and willingness to link, I made a financial gesture. "Look, I ain't never been no stingy type hustler, so here, take half of this," I said and handed my new partner the wallet I'd just clipped.

"Naw, Mel, I can't take your money. That's yours. You earned that shit for real, though." She backed away as if the wallet were poison.

I could tell she was a female with pride, even though she was dressed like a dude. And truth be told, I felt her vibe. I didn't want anybody to give me jack shit just on some pity tip. Instead, I'd rather take it. That way, I would feel like I earned it, stolen or not. "Look, me and you a team now, right? So, one day, I might not make nothing out in these streets, and you might make all the loot. So, when that day comes, just return the favor."

"Dig, that's real. I appreciate you, 'cause you already see I got them two begging motherfuckers in there that be on my head." Bags nodded toward the front part of the house.

"All right, then, take your half, family," I said, extending my hand to seal our friendship.

We kicked it around Bags's people's crib until the police stopped circling the hood. I was feeling my new friend and wanted to ask her all types of questions, some more personal than others. But I pumped my brakes. The bottom line was she seemed a little crazy, especially since I witnessed Sonya had no second thoughts or remorse about pulling the trigger. I didn't mind breaking bread with her 'cause I felt she would be loyal. And despite all of the news reports claiming hundreds of citizens had been robbed, it looked like the infamous Book Bag Bandit really needed the money.

Chapter Four

Sonya

The next day, I woke up with money on my mind. I kissed my little brother, listened to Auntie belittle me for a few minutes, then I hit the door. Today was going to be an excellent day to make money—I could feel it. Auntie couldn't even ruin it. I refused to feed into her negativity. It was early Sunday. That meant plenty of money would be on the streets, mostly churchgoing people. Shit, I didn't have no picks when it come to me and mine, and from the looks of it, neither did Money Mel. I ain't never been no friendly type hustler. I did my dirt solo. But she was on some real shit when she bust down with me yesterday with that wallet. We could and would definitely get some money together.

I was on my way to holler at Mel. I wanted to see how much hustle game her cute li'l skinny ass was sitting on. I climbed the steps up the front porch to the house I walked her to last night. From the looks of the outside of her crib in the daylight, she wasn't in no better shape than I was. I pushed the doorbell twice and waited.

"Yeah, who is it?" the voice of a female asked from the other side.

"Uh, it's Sonya. Is—" Before I could fully finish my response, the door swung wide open. I was stuck. There stood a redbone leaning against the door frame lookin' good enough to eat. I was like, damn. She was all of that. My eyes stared at her pretty little feet, up to her petite yellow thighs, past her perfect C-cup breasts, and stopping on her angelic face. She was beyond beautiful.

"Yes, can I help you?" she frowned with a hint of attitude in her voice.

I had to swallow and clear my throat. She was so fine. "Yeah, uh, is Melody here?"

"Yup, hold on," the mystery female seemed puzzled, leaving the door slightly cracked.

I watched through the crack, lost in the sway of her hips. The way she had those peach boyshorts cutting up in that ass, I was in a trance when, out of nowhere, Melody popped up in the door with a big-ass smile on her face.

"You ready?" she asked, cheesin' hard.

Hell nah, I thought. I wanted to know baby girl. But Melody pulled the door shut and stepped out on the porch while putting her arms into the sleeves of her flannel. I tucked my hands into my pockets and followed her down the porch. "Yeah, so what up, doe?"

"You up early, ain't you?" she asked over her shoulder.

"If you saw my house, you'd know why."

"Huh, wait, hold up. I saw your house yesterday evening, didn't I?"

"Nah, that's my parents' crib. I live with my auntie, and a bunch of other supposed kinfolk," I remarked with a long sigh. I hated even thinking about that house. But the thought of baby girl who'd just opened the door brought a grin back to my face. "But, yo, who in the hell was ole girl that answered the door?"

"Slow your roll. That's my sister." Melody got all short with a nigga and serious. "And check this here out." She paused, stopping to face me. "Bags, if we gon' be gettin' money together, my sisters are off-limits. We clear?"

Did I just hear her say "sisters"? You mean to tell me there was more than one of her running around, and she blockin' me from getting one? "Okay, damn. I got you. Stop bugging out so early."

"Melody, where are you going?" A woman emerged from the front door and yelled from the porch.

"Dang, I'll be back in a few," Melody hollered back with an attitude.

"Who's that?" I asked.

"My moms."

Damn . . . Melody's mom could get it too!

"So, okay, Bags, where we going? What's the deal?"

"I was thinking we'd hit the streets. Then maybe hit the mall afterward. I want you to show me that two-finger shit."

"I got a li'l something else I wanna work on these lames in your city anyway. You ever heard of 'tilling'?"

"Nah, girl, what's that?"

"I'ma put you down. By the time we get back, we should have no less than maybe five, six hundred," Melody confidently blurted out.

"Five, six hundred?" I inquired.

"Yes, dollars, homegirl. So what's the most amount of money you ever had at once, in one day?"

"Maybe two or three hundred."

"Well, stick with me, and by the summer, you'll be sitting on some Gs."

And for some reason, I believed her. I knew her weasel-lookin' ass had some game running through her veins. I could really use the money, especially before the summer hit. I could maybe get a car. Shit, I would give my left eye just to show Auntie's ass up.

We turned into Sonya and Melody as we bent the corner onto Dexter. I waved a Checker cab to the curb, but Melody told her to move on.

"Whoa, wait, hold up. What you doing? That was our ride to Northland Mall."

Melody pointed to the bus stop. "Naw, sis, *that's* our ride."

"Dang, I would've paid for it. It ain't no thang."

"It's not about that. How much money you got on you right now?"

"About a buck eighty. Why?" I said.

"That's all the bread you made yesterday and probably your entire life savings. Now, ask me how much money I got on me right now."

"How much?" I asked with my face twisted.

"Two dollars, enough to catch the bus. That's how much I come out with every day. The game is 'bout turning nothin' into somethin'."

"Okay, yeah, I feel you. You right."

While we waited at the bus stop, we talked about any and everything. Soon, we saw the Dexter Providence bus coming up from Fullerton Way. It rocked and dipped into the many potholes hugging the curb until reaching us at the stop.

"Hey, when we get on, don't sit next to me," Melody whispered over her shoulder as we waited for two elderly women and a man to step off.

"Hey, girl, it's not a school day." The bus driver turned in his seat and snarled after Melody slid her school pass through the swipe.

"But I'm broke, and besides, I'm going to do some homework, so it's kinda school day for me just the same," Melody nonchalantly announced, keeping her stride.

"So, wow, I guess you too?" The driver snapped at me, thinking I was about to repeat the same excuse. But I didn't. I grilled the shit out of his lopsided fade ass and fed the meter a dollar.

I couldn't help but smile as I walked past Melody. She was already seated next to a young woman and wasn't wasting any time. Like a hawk, I watched from the rear of the bus as Melody made the clip. All in one smooth motion, she removed the woman's wallet from her purse and slyly tucked it inside her coat pocket. The girl had skills, and she was so bold with her shit that she even had the nerve to spark up a conversation with the woman. She smiled and snickered at whatever she was saying as if they were best of friends.

We got off on Greenfield and Eight Mile Road. Then we walked the rest of the way across to Northland Mall.

"How many ten-dollar bills you got on you?" Melody asked as we cut through the parking lot.

"Uh . . . let me see . . . six," I said.

"I'ma show you how to turn sixty into six hundred. Give 'em to me."

"So, what you want me to do?" I asked as we entered Target.

"Just follow my lead." Melody pulled out an ink pen and told me to give her the hundred-dollar bill I had. We stood over by an application booth. I watched over Melody's shoulder while she scribbled some numbers on the back of the hundred. Then she handed it back to me, tucked the pen back into her pocket, and started for the doors leading out into the mall area.

I didn't know what that girl was on, but I was down for whatever. As long as we came out with that thousand dollars she promised, then . . . *bingo!*

"You say I need some new pants, right?" asked Melody. She stopped in the center of the mall.

"Yeah, at least two pair."

"All right. Well, we gonna start with one pair. You see that store?" Melody nodded at the Sun's 2 sign.

"Yeah, what's up?" I asked, looking at the store.

"I want you to go in there and buy me some pants. Use that hundred to buy them. Get size 7–8."

"Then what?" I asked.

"Then you watch me work. Go ahead. I'ma wait out here for you."

"All right." I let out a deep sigh, then headed for the store. One of the sales representatives greeted me. Ole girl looked like she needed to be in somebody's magazine modeling something, but instead, she was there blessing the store and its customers with her beauty.

"How can I help you?" she asked, smiling.

"What new jeans do you have?"

"Uh, let's see." She turned, leading me over to a wall full of denim.

"How about these? We just got them in last week." She unfolded a pair of crispy jeans and handed them to me. The tag read thirty-seven dollars.

"Let me get these in a 7–8," I said.

"Would that be all?"

"Yeah, that's it." I followed her over to the register. With confidence, I paid for the jeans with the hundred-dollar bill. She gave me my receipt with my change, and I was on my way.

Stepping out of Sun's, I didn't see Melody anywhere in sight. Then out of nowhere, she peeked from inside the jewelry store. "What'd you get?" she asked.

"These here," I said, trying to hand her the bag.

"Hold on to them. I'll be right back. Wait for me down in the food court. Matter of fact, give me another right quick," she said, holding her hand out, wiggling her finger impatiently. I handed her a twenty. She scribbled some numbers on the bill, then gave it back to me.

"Use this to get something to eat," she instructed before setting out to do whatever it was she came to do.

I wanted to watch the lick when it went down, but I didn't want to blow up the spot either, so I did what Melody said. I waited down in the food courts. I bought a number one from McDonald's. A few minutes later, Melody came bopping with a Sun's 2 bag in her hand. She nodded, stepping to the counter of McDonald's.

"Can I help you?" asked the same young man who had served me. I was eating my food and watching the scene at the same time 'cause I knew Melody was about to put some shit in the game.

"Yeah, let me get a number two," she said, looking up at the menu.

"That'll be three dollars and twelve cents." The man drummed his fingers on the register, as Melody peeled through her wad.

Fuck she get all that money from? I thought.

"Here you go." She handed the man a five. When the man counted Melody's change back to her and tore the receipt from the register, Melody went on one.

"Whoa, whoa, hold up. Where's the rest of my change?"

"Let me see," the man counted it back. "Yeah, that's correct. You ordered the number two, which is two dollars and ninety-nine cents, plus tax."

"Since when is tax fifteen dollars?" yelled Melody.

"Excuse me, but I'm lost."

"I know the fuck you is lost. I gave you a twenty."

"No, I'm pretty certain you just gave me a five, miss."

"You gonna tell me I didn't give you a twenty? What, you gon' take my shit? That's what you doing?"

Melody was loud enough to where the manager heard her and came out of her office to see what was going on.

"Is there a problem, young lady?"

"Yeah, and it's gonna be a problem if he don't give me my correct change."

"She's mistaken. She believes that she gave me a twenty. But I only took a five from her," the cashier informed the manager.

"My momma just gave me that twenty. Matter of fact, my phone number is on the back of the bill. It's 313-893-0043."

The manager punched in her code and thumbed through all the twenties. Sure as shit, there sat the bill I had just used to pay.

"I am so sorry, young woman. I assure you this will never happen again." The manager handed Melody the entire twenty back and told her the meal was free.

She came over and took a seat across from me. I was holding my side from laughing so hard because her slick ass had convinced me too that she really paid with a dub—that's how serious she was at that counter.

"I don't pay for nothing," she said with her eyes bucked as she bit into her double cheeseburger.

I couldn't front, this girl had old-school game. And I was going to ride her coattail all the way to the bank. We stayed out at the mall all day, burning up damn near all the stores.

Chapter Five

Melody

In the two days that Bags and I had been hustling and working the tills, she had $2,300. I knew the exact amount because she counted it every chance she got like a bill was going to slip out of her pocket and take off running. Despite my advice, she was still carrying all her money on her at once. And after seeing her aunt's crib, I couldn't blame her. I was sitting in the front room on a stained, soiled sofa and waiting on Bags so we could do our one-two. She'd been picking me up since we started hanging, so I figured it was my turn.

"What, you too damn good to sit down and eat my breakfast like the rest of us?" I could hear her aunt cutting into her ass. So far, everything Bags had told me was one hundred. There the ole lady sat, perched centerfold, watching everything, me included, her broad face twisted up in disgust.

"Nah, that ain't it. I got somebody waiting on me," Bags said calmly. She wasn't trying to stir her up bitchin', but the ole auntie was set on doing so anyway. She reminded me of my grandma back in Chicago. The day wouldn't be off to a good start unless she pitched a bitch.

"I see you got on new clothes every day the week," Auntie said, looking Bags from head to toe.

"Yeah, I got 'em off the clearance rack."

"I'll bet to hell ya did. But I'ma tell you one thing. Ya ass get caught stealing, ya better have bail money, 'cause I won't be down there to get you."

"Oh, trust me. I know," Bags said, being smart. She tossed back the rest of her orange juice, then rinsed the glass.

Bags nodded at the door. "I'ma catch you later."

Her aunt was staring a hole through Bags's back as she slid into her new jacket.

"You ready?" she asked, stepping into the living room.

"Yeah, let's make it," I said, following Bags to the front door while shaking my clothes on the low. I wasn't trying to take nothing extra back home with me. We had our own roaches. Plus, her aunt's crib was a different kind of dirty, that "no thanks, I'll stand" kind of dirty.

Bags let the door slam as we stepped on the porch. She looked at me like, "I told you." As we stepped off the porch, her uncle Tony was on his way in.

"Damn, Unc. You look tired as hell."

"It's called work," Tony said, brushing past us.

"Nah, it's called stupid," Bags mumbled. I could tell Tony had just ruined Bags's mood by the way her face was all balled up.

"You straight, B?"

"Yeah, I am. I just can't wait until I get enough bread to where I ain't never gotta come back to this house. Enough to move my little brother and me far away."

"We gonna get that money up. Summertime, remember?" I stuck out my fist for a pound, to which Bags pulled back a smile and hit rocks with me.

"So, what's up? Where we going today?" I asked, ready to turn into Melody.

"I say we finish burnin' up the city. Gotta get it while the gettin' is good."

"You know what you know, 'cause soon, that's how it's gon' be . . . burnt up. Each store is a one-time deal. Then it's over."

We caught the bus going west. We had been mainly working the East Side, and I didn't want to risk somebody seeing us running the same trick twice. So, I thought we'd hit up the West Side. Bags kept to the back of the bus while I set my sights on my money the red-faced nigga with dreads was holding for me in his left pants pocket. He looked from the window as I took my place beside him. He did what a million other people did right before they got picked. He looked down at all the empty seats as if to say, "Damn, girl, why you all on me?"

You know I wasn't stuntin' that nigga and his feelings. The quicker he played victim, the quicker I could give him all the space his heart desired. Soon as he returned to looking out the window, I assumed the two-finger dip position and waited for the first rock of the bus. Got him. I locked on the wallet and waited for the next rock. I pulled the wallet out, but it was hooked to a chain.

"Hold up, little bitch. I know you ain't got yo' hand in my pocket!" The dude stood up towering over me, ready to swing.

"Nah, it was falling, so I was just helping you out," I claimed. I was thinking about snapping crazy on his ass, but there was only one problem. He looked like he would beat all the shit out of me. I tried to stand up so I could move, but the dreaded beast yanked me by the arm.

"Girl, I ain't done with you." Not caring if I were a female or not, he took a wild swing. Thank God, I ducked and sidestepped right into a seat. But I was trapped. He held his hand cock back like he was trying to decide where it would hurt the most. He was in midswing. Yet, he never made it because Bags blew his shit clean out in the name of Jesus. The guy folded up and was out cold.

Bags put feet all upside his head, while I got what he'd unknowingly been holding for me.

The bus driver pulled the bus over and picked up the phone. I had to pull Bags off the dude 'cause she was about to stomp him blind.

"B, I think he's calling the police. Let's go," I begged, pulling her by the arm.

"Yeah, keep the change, bitch," I hollered at ole boy on our way to the back of the bus.

"Yo, open the fuckin' door," Bags yelled at the driver. She was jerking and kicking at it. However, the driver had it locked.

"We gotta wait on the police to get here," the driver yelled.

Bags wasn't trying to hear that. She pulled her trusted, never-leave-home-without-it pistol from her waist. People on the bus were getting low in their seats as Bags made her way up toward the driver.

"Oh, Jesus," one churchgoing woman closed her eyes and prayed.

"Look, if you don't open this door, and I mean right *now,* I'ma dust yo' ass." Bags stood back and cocked the hammer.

I guess the driver wasn't ready to die. Quickly, he grabbed the lever and opened both doors. I got off the back, while Bags got off the front. She nodded for the strip mall across the street. "We need to split up. Meet back here when it calms down."

We dodged the oncoming traffic in a hurry to get away from the scene. I went one way, and Bags went the other. I guess the driver was scared enough because he said fuck waiting on the police. He pulled away from the curb as soon as the traffic cleared up.

After dipping in and out of vacant lots until the coast was clear, we met back up at the strip mall. Bags was waiting for me in the parking lot right outside the Laundromat.

"Fuck you laughing at?" I asked, out of breath.

"Yo' scary ass. That nigga was 'bout to beat the sleeves off you." Bags continued riding me.

"That asshole wasn't gon' do nothing except what he did."

"And what's that?"

"Get knocked the fuck out."

"I already know. I'm just fuckin' with you. I wasn't gon' let him get off on you."

"Anyway . . ." I wanted to switch the subject. "We haven't hit this spot yet. It's as good a place as any."

"Cool with me. Where you wanna start?"

I looked around, then at the Dollar Store beside the Laundromat. "We can start here."

"All right. I'm 'bout to kick it off then," said Bags. She started for the Dollar Store while I fell back. I ain't like the way that shit on the bus had played out. Bitch-ass nigga had a purse hook. Where the fuck a grown-ass man do that at? Anyway, he fucked up my record, but whatever. I scanned the parking lot in search of somebody I could redeem myself on. I zoomed in on a woman coming out of Rite Aid. The way she was holding her purse, I knew she had something of value in it.

"I see you back on your shit," Bags said smiling, as she emerged from the Dollar Store.

I had just finished clipping ole girl. "I had to get my mojo back; plus, she was holding."

"What she have?"

"I don't know. Here, count it up and meet me at the Chinese restaurant."

"All right. I went through the line with the yellow bone cashier," said Bags.

I walked to the back of the store and picked up a bottle of dish soap and a roll of toilet paper, then stopped at the cashier's drawer Bags told me she went through.

"Woo woo woo. Baby girl, you slippin' on my change," I said calmly at first. But ole girl looked at me like I had lost my mind.

"Let me see," she said, snatching back the change. "No, that's right," she said, trying to hand me back the money.

"Look, skunk meat, if you don't get the rest of mines, we gon' have some problems."

"Unt-unn . . . Girl, did you hear what she called you?" the other cashier said, all in my mix.

"Yeah, I heard her, and she 'bouts to get fucked around if she keep slippin'."

"Bitch, I will slap two perms in that nappy shit of yours. Get my mothafuckin' money out of that drawer."

"I got yo' bitch," she snapped while coming from behind the counter, hands open, like . . . "What's up?"

"What seems to be the problem?" The manager came flying up, trying to get between us.

I ran down my spiel about her not giving me my correct change. "My number is on the back of the bill. My momma makes me write it on all my bills."

The manager popped the drawer; then, of course, cashed me out.

"But I know what she gave me." I could hear ole girl saying as I pushed the door open.

"Yeah, me too."

Bags was at the counter, getting our order when I walked inside the Chinese restaurant.

"You get that?" Bags asked over her shoulder.

"What kind of question is that?" I slid into one of the booths and took my jacket off.

Bags spread the sweet & sour chicken, pepper steak, shrimp fried rice, and egg rolls across the table. As we sat there, an old man came inside the restaurant. After giving us the side-eye, he cut into us, claiming he had a business proposition if we were interested. We looked at each other, hoping he was not just some random old perv trying to buy some cheap pussy. If so, we were not selling. He went into his pocket and took out his wallet. He pulled out a business card. "I met a thousand of yous. Call me when you ready to make some *real* money. Not like the piddly sums you make running games at the Dollar Store."

We both looked at him, shocked that he knew what we did.

"Yeah, I was in there and saw the scam you ran." He handed each of us a business card, then walked out.

All day yesterday, while we was out killin' the till, the only thing I could think about was the old man and what he said. His words lived in my head . . . *"I met a thousand of yous."* He had me feeling like the typical hood rat, like "What you doing ain't nothin', slick." I kept looking at his card: *Mr. Brooks,* it read. I knew money when I saw it. And I was certain that old guy was holding it. I could feel it in my soul.

I wanted to get up with his old ass and see what he was talking about as far us working for him. Who knows, it could be our shot at some real money. But my homegirl was on some scary shit. Melody thought that he might be trying to lure us somewhere and kill us. I'm not saying that's not what he was on, because I didn't know his ass either. But I ain't never been one to get caught slippin'. I prided myself on that. Besides, that's what and where my pistol came into play. It ain't let me down yet. I said fuck what Melody's shook ass was talking about. I wasn't about to miss my lick. I'm an opportunist, and chances make champions, feel me? Them little burn-out licks that she had us on were straight. The shit was game to me. Yet, they were also one-shot deals. I needed something more stable to come all the way up. So I called the number on the card, throwing caution to the wind.

"Okay, so you comin' with me or what?" I asked. I had just hung up the phone from talking to Mr. Brooks.

"I'm tellin' you, B, I don't trust that man. He's creepy as hell."

"Look, girl, I don't trust him neither. But I'm sayin', trust me." I upped the gun from my waist and continued. "I'm not gon' let nothin' happen to us. No matter what, we coming up out on top. Period."

"Okay, but—"

"But what? Dang, Melody, we done robbed damn near every store in Detroit in less than a week. What we gon' do next? Go back to digging in random niggas' pockets and might get killed behind the bullshit?"

"I'm not complaining. Shit, the games been good to me. But you might be right."

"Might be right? Girl, I *know* I'm right. We not growing if we keep running in circles. It's time to do something else 'cause we damn near grown. What we gon' do, pick and rob for the rest of our lives?"

"Shit, back in Chicago—"

I finally snapped. "You don't get it, do you? Nigga, you *ain't* in Chicago no more, so stop talkin' 'bout that 'back in Chicago' shit. This is Detroit, the city of playas, hustlas, pimps, and gators."

"Yeah, I know." She dropped her head.

"Then *act* like you know. The only way we gonna come up is if we level up. We gotta stop playin' out here." I was so mad that I had to stop and fire up a Newport. I really fucked with Melody the long way, which is why I wanted us to make the possible come-up move together. But she wasn't on it like I was. My ribs were touching, and I was down for whatever to get at a dollar. I was tired of just surviving. I felt like it was time to get over. "I know what it is. Yo' ass is spoiled. You don't have to be out here doing what you doing for real, and that's why you playin'. But me, though, I'm dead-ass serious."

The front door opened. Pops stepped inside, smiling, with LC dead on his heels. They stopped in the living room, where they always did their exchange. LC had a black diamond mink draped over his shoulders. He wore big, black, block gator boots. He stayed casket clean, and that's precisely where his ass was going to be soon. I hated that old bitch nigga. In fact, so much so that I forgot what Melody and I were just talking about. I stubbed my square into the ashtray, then grabbed my jacket.

"Come on, we out," I announced, standing up from the sofa.

"Hey, Miss Lady, I ain't seen you in a while. You been all right?" asked LC, looking me up and down.

"You hear LC talkin' to you, Sonya?" Pops butted in, trying to earn brownie points for a possible discount.

"Yeah, I heard him." I still didn't answer, though. I grabbed the door handle and let Melody step out first. I wasn't never with the fake and phony shit. If I didn't fuck with you, we weren't about to do the pretending thing. It is what it is with me.

"What's up with that old-time player back in there? Why you so cold to him?" Melody cut off into me.

"You see that over there?" I nodded at LC's candy-apple red Caddy parked at the curb.

"Yeah, that bad boy is fresh." Melody admired the shiny rims.

"I know. And look where my peoples are living. All the dope my father snorts comes from his ass. He jumping out with minks on his back my peoples helped sponsor. So, yeah, fuck him and fuck speaking to him. Let's just be out."

We caught a cab to the address that Mr. Brooks gave me. Melody could fall back when we got there. She could just linger around outside, and I'd get the true official rundown.

When we arrived at our destination, I did just that. "Just stay here and wait to count our new hustle come-up money." With my pistol tucked in the small of my back, I marched into the building. Sitting behind a huge oak desk in the far corner of the room was Mr. Brooks. With my chest stuck out, I made my way toward him.

"Have a seat." He motioned to a chair.

"No, thanks. I prefer to stand." That way, there would be fewer motions to go through if I didn't like what he had to say.

Luckily for Melody and me, what Mr. Brooks had in mind was *definitely* something we could work with. And certainly something that would get and keep our pockets off of craps for some time to come.

Chapter Six

Sonya

I could tell that Melody didn't care one way or the other if we hit the lick. She was on some real shook shit thinking that it was all a setup and that Mr. Brooks was rocking us to sleep. I was tired of hearing all that scared talk. I was not about to let her blow them twenty-four stacks promised. I mean—damn, all we had to do was move some punk-ass vehicles from one spot to the next. Since Mr. Brooks was part owner in the Ford dealership, what could go wrong? Besides, we even had the keys, so how hard could it be? That loss would be between him and his partner that he had come to hate.

No longer in the mood to baby Melody, I gave it to her raw. "If I have to stay up all night and transport the vehicles one by one, I will. And if so, no matter how close we are, you ain't gettin' no parts of the cash." Having thought about having half of twenty-four racks versus none snapped her back to reality.

"I'm in," she said. My hustle buddy was back.

Dressed in black and Jordan sneakers, we worked all through the night. Moving the Navigators first, then the Expeditions, we were on a roll. Styling in a few Mustangs, the task was close to being completed. It was a little shy of three in the morning, and we were exhausted. We'd made eleven trips in total between us and had one more truck to move before calling it a night. I was riding shotgun with Melody as she pushed the stolen, fully loaded F-150. Floating down East Jefferson, we were soon right back at the dealership ready to get it in.

"Okay, Melody, last one. Then we home free." I grabbed the door handle and jumped down out of the truck and confidently walked across the lot, keys in hand. Then I pushed the alarm button as I cut across the grass, seeing Melody pull off.

Hurriedly, I slid behind the wheel of the midnight-blue Mustang, cranked the engine, and backed out of the space. After pulling out into traffic, my heart sank. A Detroit police cruiser drove by on the other side of the road. Seeing how late it was, the officers were, of course, suspicious. The driver and I locked eyes. It was easy to know what was about to take place as the car hooked a hard U.

I weighed my options. If I just hoped and prayed they weren't focused on me and were suddenly headed somewhere else that required a swift change in direction, I'd be a fool. Without delay, I exercised Plan B. I floored the bitch, putting the high-performance engine to work.

I could see the cops' light flick on in the rearview mirror. I had them by a good enough distance, though, because they weren't prepared for a full-blown pursuit that I was willing, able, and prepared to take on. For the cops, them catching me was just them doing their job. For me, getting away meant me keeping my freedom and collecting that huge cash payout from Mr. Brooks.

I gripped the wheel with both hands and punched it down a random side street. I busted a sharp left and gunned it down a few blocks over. I assumed the cops thought I would try jumping down on the freeway so I could punch the Mustang wide open. However, I didn't. I couldn't risk possibly having not only the Detroit police on my ass but also the Michigan State Police as well. Instead, I played it smart and cautiously doubled back in the direction I'd come from. After ducking and dodging here and there, I ended up near the old, abandoned Packard plant. I couldn't go to jail, not tonight anyway, was all that stayed on my mind. All I had to do was make it back to the collision shop. And I would. Taking a few more back roads, I knew I was home free. I made the last turn down the dimly lit block. Thankfully, I could see Melody parked across the street, waiting. I hit the horn and flashed her a huge smile. She pulled behind me, and the garage door to the collision shop flew open.

Earl was on edge from all the sirens he'd heard. He waved us both in. Then he stepped out and looked up and down the block before snatching the garage door closed. I could easily see why he was so cautious. He had well over a million dollars' worth of stolen cars and parts inside his chop shop. They had everything from air bags, door panels, rims, bumpers, engines, seats, etc. Melody jumped down from the F-150. After stepping out of the Mustang, we both joined the musty, shady-looking king of the illegal castle near his office door. He wore a soiled wife beater and muddy, oily jeans but had to be making money by the boatload.

"Yeah, so, these are the last two on the list," Earl acknowledged, marking something onto a clipboard which he clutched diligently. Slowly, he walked all around both vehicles, inspecting them for damage, then checked the interiors just as he'd done the others.

"Man, they all perfect, so what up, doe? Is we good?" I snapped, ready to get to the good part . . . leaving from that hot box building of felonies.

"Yes, we're good. I'll pass the word along," Earl said, not taking his eyes from the clipboard.

"Well, let us out then," Melody insisted, who was jumpier than I was.

"And look, I don't know what you doodling on ya li'l pad and whatnot, but all them shits were straight when we brought 'em up in here," I made it clear stopping at the door. "So, I don't want no bullshit."

"For two females, y'all both mighty feisty. Now, damn, I said that I would pass the word, so relax. You'll get paid." He pushed the door open while keeping his eyes on me until the door closed.

"What happened back there?" Melody asked as we started walking down the block.

"Let's grab some Coney Island and go chill at my crib until daybreak when it's time to get cashed out. I'll tell you then. But just know your friend is the shit."

Chapter Seven

Melody

I woke up to Bags's musty-ass daddy leaning over me in a two-finger dip position. The old bastard was trying to clip me in my sleep. He would have had me too if it weren't for the screaming stench rising off his body. I squinted up at him and pulled my coat all the way off my face. "Bags, man, get yo' daddy before I break his old-ass hand."

Bags sat up and laughed after peeping the move. "What, I ain't tell you? You gotta sleep with both hands tucked in yo' pockets 'round here."

"And one eye open. It's all fair games . . ." Pops slurred, still holding his position as if he couldn't get socked in the mouth.

"Pops, leave my girl alone."

"Hey, Sonya, give yo' daddy some more of that money you holding. I know you got some 'cause I can smell it."

"Here, man, damn." Bags handed him a few bills, then stood up from the sofa as he bolted out of the room to go cop a morning blast. "So, you ready to help out or what?" she asked me.

"What time is it?"

"Almost seven. But by the time we make it over the way, the spot should be open."

"Yeah, okay, let's go." I stretched and yawned, then stood up and slid into my lightweight jacket. I wanted to wash my face and at least brush my teeth, but since dealing with Sonya, I'd let my hygiene fall way off. Wiping the sleep out of the corner of my eyes, I promised myself that I was going to take a long, hot bath later on. I'd barely been home as of late, and my mother and sisters had threatened to disown me if I didn't fly right. Nevertheless, thankfully, I would throw them a few dollars to keep them quiet.

The address where we were to meet Mr. Brooks was in view. When I opened the door of the greasy spoon diner, our eyes met his. There sat Mr. Brooks with his leg crossed, sipping coffee while reading the paper.

"Morning, young ladies," he smiled, putting the paper down, waving for us to come over and sit. "Have y'all ate breakfast? They have some great food here."

"Naw, not hungry," Bags replied, ready to cut to the chase.

"No problem. I understand young people, such as you two, don't wanna slow down. But you know that they say breakfast is the most important meal of the day."

"Look," I spoke up, "with all due respect, fuck breakfast. We just need what is due us; nothing more, nothing less."

My words did not move Mr. Brooks. With a grin, he took another small sip from his coffee. Then he reached down beside him, grabbed two brown paper bags, and pushed them across the table, one to each of us.

"I believe that's what I owe you." Mr. Brooks released the bags and sat back. He was amused, watching us fight the temptation to open them.

"Just as I thought. You gals did well, except the police chase, of course."

Both our eyes opened like saucers. How did he know about the chase?

"No need for an explanation. No harm, no foul. So, are you girls interested in making some more money, or what?"

"When do you need us?" Bags wasted no time speaking up.

"In a couple of days. I'ma give ya some time to enjoy ya earnings. Maybe get your hair and nails done, but I'm going to tell you, the next job won't be moving cars. Y'all still down?"

"Whatever it is, it's fine as long as we keep getting cashed out," assured Bags.

"Give me a call in two days, and I should have everything lined up."

"Thank you, Mr. Brooks." Bags slid out of the booth respecting the fact the old man had kept his word.

Mr. Brooks raised his cup of coffee in salutation.

I slid out of the booth behind Bags and started for the door. As soon as we got outside, we ran to the back of the alley, pulling and tearing at our paper bags.

"So, what you 'bout to do with all that money?" I asked.

"I'm 'bout to hit the car lot and do a little shopping," Bags said, excited to be all the way up.

"All right, sis. But let's not forget about your goal."

"And what's that?"

"Getting yo' own spot and moving your li'l brother out with you. Remember that?"

"Yeah, no doubt. Fuck my auntie. That's at the top of my list." Bags nodded, still with her face buried in the paper bag.

"Well, me, I'm 'bout to catch a cab home and climb in bed after I take a bath. I'm still exhausted from last night."

We parted ways with much different agendas for our blessed windfall. Like night and day, one thing we had in common was a thirst for making money. So, no matter how we moved spending cash, at the end of the day, earning it was king.

Chapter Eight

Sonya

I couldn't wait to see the expression on my auntie's face when I pulled up in my new car. Sure, it wasn't a brand-new vehicle off the lot like those I was pushing the previous night. But it was still brand-new to me and better than anything Auntie was driving.

"Fam, this your car?" Cuzzo smiled.

"Oh, yeah . . ." I shrugged, playing it like it was nothing.

Cuzzo went to check the vehicle out while I finished frontin' on my new phone. And, of course, waiting on Auntie to show up to bug out. Under a minute, I saw a solar eclipse appear at the front door. I turned all the way around, and there she stood, arms folded, her expression stank. I plastered a wide grin across my face, knowing it was about to be on. "How you doin', Auntie?" I taunted.

By that time, my whole family was out there riding my jock except for her. The kids wanted me to take them for a ride. "None of you is getting in that car," she warned. "I'd bet my life that car is stolen."

I reached in the glove box and produced the bill of sale. Even when I waved it in her face, she was having no part of it. "Please, anyone can forge one of those," she said.

To make her even more heated, I dug in my pocket and pulled out all of my remaining money. I licked my thumb and peeled off three hundred-dollar bills. Playing the big-shot role, I tried to hand it to Auntie.

"I don't want no drug money from the likes of you. You keep that shit from around my address and away from my kids."

"Are you serious right now? You, of all people, turning down money? Imagine that. You funny as hell right about now."

"Am I?" She posted her hands on her hips.

"Yeah, Auntie, you live for money, no matter what. You think everyone in the family don't know how you cut?"

"And just how am I cut? You tell me what my no-good family has to say."

"Whatever. I'm not gonna rat nobody out."

"Look, girl, why don't you take that money and find yourself an apartment? Maybe one with that girl you been running around with the last few weeks or so. It'll be best for all of us because Lord knows that you're not going to change."

"What's that supposed the mean?"

"Look, I done put up with enough of the crazy hours you insist on keeping, skipping school, and all. And to top it off, you running around here don't know if you wanna be a boy or a girl."

"Wow."

"Yeah, wow. So just go," Auntie repeated, not backing down one bit.

"Okay, that's fine. But I'ma take Devin with me." I bossed up, prepared to do battle.

"Oh, hell naw. I'm not about to let you destroy that kid's life like you done did yours."

"And I'm not going to leave him in this dump to be mistreated."

"You watch your fucking mouth." Auntie took a step closer. "For close to seventeen damn years, your rotten ass done lived under my roof, ate my food, drank my water, and whatever else. So, for you to stand up here in my face and call my house a dump takes a lot of nerve. Devin is mine. I got paperwork that says so. Your sorry-ass mammy ain't want him or your ungrateful ass, remember? So, I took y'all instead of letting the State take you."

"And you ain't never let me or my brother forget it," I fired back, elated I no longer had to hold my tongue. The money I'd made the night before in my pocket had made me brave. I was standing there close to punching ole auntie dead in her shit. How dare she! Making it seem like we were eating crab legs and steak and wearing the latest fashions at her expense. That woman knew like I did that was the furthest thing from the truth. In fact, my brother and I were sleeping on the floor, eating Focus Hope and mayonnaise sandwiches. So, I wasn't going to stand there and allow her to pat herself on the back too much, because we had earned our keep with the checks she was receiving monthly.

"It's my house, and I don't have to explain any of my damn actions."

"Look, Auntie, if it's about them checks, you can keep all of them. All I want is my brother and—"

Auntie laughed, walking toward the house. "Sonya, you must didn't hear me when I said Devin is mine. And if a check comes along with him, so be it," she hissed, climbing the steps going onto the porch.

"Fat bitch, I'ma get my li'l brother sooner or later, you'll see. Trust and believe, I don't give a fuck what you think." I jumped in my car and roared off. I didn't give a shit about any of the measly belongings I had at Auntie's. I'd deal with them and her later. In the meantime, I got a room. Within hours I was kicked back in the motel room lying in bed watching television.

I can't lie, today was the best day of my life, and I didn't want it to end. I had a feeling that if we kept doing jobs for Mr. Brooks that there would be plenty more good days to follow. I spread my money out across the bed and counted it. I had somehow run through $10,000, just like that. I knew I had to make more moves to come back up. And Mr. Brooks was the solution to doing so. Maybe he could even help me find an apartment. It wouldn't hurt to ask. After all, we were kinda in business together.

Chapter Nine

Mr. Brooks

The inside of Sal's 24-hour Check Cashing was packed to the hilt with Friday's check cashers. It was always like that on any given Thursday and Friday, which is why my partner Sal asked me ten years ago if I would be interested in franchising his existing store. I agreed. I was always looking to clean up some old money I made during the '70s heroin rush. Sal's was just one of the many ventures I went into after I left the streets alone. For ten years, we've done good strong business, but also for those ten years, I was plotting the day we'd cash out on our $3 million insurance policy. We were in such good standing that the insurance company that was covering all our stores allowed us to put the maximum amount on our insurance.

"I'm telling you, Sal, these two females are perfect for the job. They're eager, hungry, and most important, they listen." Sal and I were in his office overlooking the lobby area.

Sal turned from the window and faced me. "I have never questioned your judgment, Brooks. But you left one thing out, which I feel is more important."

"What's that, Sal?"

"Loyalty. What if they get caught in the process? Are they going to be solid or snitch?"

"I understand you, I do. And, yes, I have thought about that. Remember, even if they were to get caught and tell, they wouldn't be able to implicate you because they don't know you. Trust me, Sal. I've thought out every angle."

Sal walked over to his desk and reclined in his plush leather chair. He put his feet up, and his eyes went to the ceiling. It wasn't that I needed Sal's permission to go ahead with the job. I was just really allowing him to go along with it because he'd put a lot into the stores over the years, so I could understand his hesitation.

"They both really hungry, Sal. And one of them is slick as all outdoors. Goes by the nickname Bags and dresses like a boy."

"Bags?" he quizzed.

"Yeah, between Bags and the other girl, I think they can take it." I pushed the issue.

"Well, you know it's a one-shot deal. If they blow it, we'll have to find new insurance, and we'll have to wait for years before we can try again."

"I know. And I'm betting on black. We good, Sal, trust me."

Sal took his feet down from the desk and rested on his elbows while rubbing the stressful decision away from his face. "All right, old friend. Then I'm riding with you."

"Good, 'cause I'm getting ready to meet with them and tell them all about the job." I stood up and walked over to the minibar to pour us some scotch.

"Here," I said, handing Sal his drink. I sat on the edge of the desk and tried assuring my buddy that everything was going to go down smoothly, and by this time next week, we'd be $3 million richer.

"I hope you're right," Sal said, then tossed back his glass.

I finished my drink, then grabbed my sports jacket. "Just take the week off and go down to the condo we have in the Caymans. Let me handle this. By the time you get back, I'll have your end, and it'll be business as usual."

"I think that I just might do that," Sal said, walking me to the door.

"Good, I'll have my agent set it up." I patted Sat on his back, then stepped out of the office.

I climbed behind the wheel of my Lincoln parked at the curb. Then I turned on the oldies but goodies and drove off. I knew Sonya and Melody could handle the take. Sal's ass was just scared. I was putting him on a plane first thing in the morning because I didn't need him worrying too much and messing things up. Out of that three million, them silly females weren't going to see a fraction of that. They wanted to be slick, grown, and in the game like real movers and shakers. Well, I was gon' teach them the meaning of playing with the big boys. It's a man's world, and they will soon discover that.

Chapter Ten

Sonya

I had hollered at Mr. Brooks over the phone. He wanted me to meet him at the breakfast spot so we could go over the next job. I didn't care what his old ass had lined up, as long as the job was paying like the last one. The fool could have said to kill the pope, and it would have got done. I swung past Melody's crib so that we could go together, but she was on some, "Nah, I'm straight" type shit. That girl was really starting to get on my nerves with that scary shit. She kept pressing the issue that we "really don't know Mr. Brooks and his true intentions." I wasn't having it, though. Unless her skinny ass could pickpocket me another $12,000, "we" were on our way to see Mr. Brooks 'cause I needed some more fuckin' money. Unlike me, Melody had saved the bulk of her cash.

When we got to the restaurant, I noticed we'd beaten Mr. Brooks, so I parked at the curb two spaces up from where he'd always pull up at. Melody was giving me the silent treatment because I literally had dragged her ass out of the house by the arm.

"You know what? Just wait in the car. I'ma go in and holla at the old guy. If he asks, you got a cold, and that's the reason you ain't come in."

"All right, whatever," Melody dryly replied, staring out the window.

I didn't know what was wrong with Melody. She was moody, acting like we had a bunch of other thousand-dollar licks lined up. I don't know what she was going through, maybe her period or something like that. But long as she was out there going through it when Mr. Brooks pulled up so he could see her, that was all I cared about.

"Well, I see you've done some shopping. I hope you've put a little something to the side." Mr. Brooks came inside the restaurant, immediately taking notice of my new outfit and that my dreads were retwisted.

"Oh, yeah, I most definitely did that." I wasn't lying about the li'l something. I only had $800 to my name. I had spent fast and hard.

"Hey, I just noticed something. Where is Miss Melody?"

"She's out in the car. You must didn't notice coming in. She's coming down with a cold, and I didn't want her bringing it in here while people ate," I played it off.

"Okay, then. But I hope our girl is feeling better and soon because I have another job if you're both interested. It's paying $50,000."

Mr. Brooks watched the lump slowly travel down my throat as I swallowed. I know he didn't just say fifty of them thangs. Once Melody heard how much we were walking away with, I just knew her ass was going to drop that bitchy attitude and get on board with me. "Fifty racks?"

"Yeah, that's correct. However, I must tell you it's not as easy as the last job. And it calls for some real guts and courage."

"No problem. What is it, when is it, and how do you want it done?" I eagerly begged to know the particulars.

"Okay, look. I own a check-cashing spot over on the West Side. It's one of those 24-hour joints."

"Yeah, I know places like that."

"Well, I want you girls to knock it off."

"Say what?" His words threw me off.

"Yes, and there won't be any help as far as the inside goes. The workers won't know what's going on, so it'll be an actual robbery."

"So, how are we going to get in the back? Don't they have bulletproof glass and all of that? I'm confused."

"Yes, it's all of that and a locked door. But your advantage is I also have keys to the entrance door leading to the back." Mr. Brooks slid a manila envelope across the table. "I want y'all to hit the place Monday right around noon. That's when the money wagon makes its primary drop for the week. Like I said, this job takes real guts. So, take a few days and see how you want to do it, but let's get it done. If not, I can easily get someone else to earn that 50K."

"Naw, we down. But what if someone innocent gets in the way?"

"Hopefully, that won't happen, but if it does, I understand casualties. Just get the money out of there. That's all I truly care about in the long run. So, that's a yes. Can you handle it?" Mr. Brooks awaited my reply.

"Robbery is my specialty—period. I got this."

"Good. After the job is done, I want you to drop the bags off here to the waitress. Wait for me to give y'all your portion. Don't try to open them bags because they're rigged with ink. You need a key to open them. Just follow the instructions inside the envelope. Memorize them, then burn the paper."

I slid the manila envelope into my jacket pocket. "No problem. I understand. Burn the paper."

"Okay, now, Sonya, you and Melody don't let me down. I've got a lot riding on this. And as soon as we're done, I have another big job lined up. You are both gonna be rich in the months to follow."

"Okay, cool. We with that, fa'sho. See you in a few days." I smiled, heading toward the door. *Damn,* I thought, stopping in my tracks. *I was so geeked up from the $50,000 that I forgot my ass is homeless.*

"Is there something wrong, Sonya?" Mr. Brooks called out, observing me stopping.

I turned around and walked back over to the booth. "Sir, I'm having a slight problem, and I was hoping you might be able to help me."

"Anything for you, Sonya. What is it?"

I slid back into the booth and spoke in a low tone. "I'm having some issues with my family, and I need some help finding a place to stay."

"Say no more. After we're done with this job, I'm going to set you up in a nice loft. Do you have somewhere to stay right now?"

"Yes, at least for a few days."

"Okay, good. Yeah, that's not a problem. I have a place that I rarely use. You can stay there for as long as you need to."

"Thank you, Mr. Brooks."

"Don't mention it. I have got big plans for you, Sonya."

Mr. Brooks hit me with a nod and a wink as I left. I couldn't have thanked him enough. Everything that I wanted was coming to pass. Fucking with this old playa was the smartest decision of my life. I was finally about to be set.

"What was he in there talking about?" Melody swiftly asked as I got into the car.

"Wait for it. Wait for it . . . You ready? He talking about us making fifty motherfucking stacks," I blurted out.

"Say what? Are you serious? Doing what?" Melody turned all the way around in the passenger seat to face me.

"Easy pickings, as you call it. Don't sweat it, I'ma do all the work. Just tell me you down," I said, holding my hand out.

"I'm down . . . I guess," Melody said, taking my hand. "But tell me the score."

"Okay, then, I'ma shoot you back to your crib, so I can put you down with the lick." As I drove, I fired up a Newport just thinking about what all I could do with $25,000. My life had gone from shit to sugar since linking up with my homegirl, Melody. We made one helluva team. I just hoped she was down for this next move because it was going to be major.

Chapter Eleven

Melody

I listened to Bags run down the check-cashing lick, and I wasn't feeling it. This idiot made it sound like all we had to do was go in and make a withdrawal, and that was going to be the end of it. She was making it seem like there wasn't no way we could get caught. And from listening to her conversation, you'd think her fool self done robbed twenty of them joints. Yet, I knew better than to just listen to the amount of money we stood to gain. What about what we stood to *lose* if the shit went sour up in there? Sonya, Bags, or whatever name she wanted to go by, was trippin' hard. Somewhere along the way, she'd managed to let that old Negro put a battery in her back and charge her straight the fuck up. I know that the first $12,000 had strings attached to it. But we didn't have to bite. We could just walk away with not only our lives but also our freedom as well.

My new best friend and partner in petty crime wasn't thinking that far ahead. She was gone, and the crazy part is, I'd allowed her to drag me along down the rabbit hole. After all the madness we'd been through, I couldn't leave her out there stranded. She'd saved my ass on more than one occasion. So, even though I had an awful feeling about what she wanted to do, I was gonna ride. I just hoped we got up out of that bitch alive and in one piece.

Over the next few days, Bags had been inside the check-cashing spot a few times. I don't know if she thought she was some professional heist man or some shit, but she claimed that everything was kosher.

"The only thing you gotta do is open the back door." Bags handed me the key.

"I'll do it, but straight-up, if something pops off while we in there, all you gon' see is the back of my head gettin' small."

"Ain't no thing. This lick be cake. Nothing will go sideways."

On the day of the lick, I dressed up like a straight-up clown of sorts. I'd gone to the beauty supply store and bought some wire-framed glasses with a rose-color tint, a cheap, black, shoulder-length wig, and a skull cap.

I applied a dark foundation to my face, neck, arms, and hands. After finishing the application, I was more than a few shades darker. To finish off my disguise, I placed a fake mole above my lip and a fake nose stud in my right nostril. After throwing on an old velour, two-tone tracksuit I'd purchased from the thrift store, I was ready.

Bags looked at my getup. "You crazy. No need for all that costume shit."

"Whateva. I ain't tryin' to see the back of a police car or hearse."

As planned, I slid into the check-cashing place first. I stepped over to one of the stands pretending like I was signing a check, then went to the back of the line. As the line inched closer to the door leading behind the counter, I purposely dropped the piece of paper I was holding.

"Excuse me," I said. I waved the two customers standing behind me to go ahead. I slowly stood back up and scanned the lobby area. Within seconds, it was on. I could see Bags on her way, barreling in through the double doors dressed in black and ready to kill something if necessary. I assumed the two-finger dip position, arms folded across my chest. Trying to remain as if I were an innocent bystander, I casually leaned up against the door, using the key Mr. Brooks gave us. Just like that, the security door was prime.

As I stepped away from the door, Bags pulled her gun from her oversized purse and bolted for the unlocked door. I had to hold all the customers in check so nobody could run out and alert the police. I was standing there with my mom's old .38 Special, trembling like a motherfucker.

"Don't nobody move," I shouted, trying to sound crazy and hoping they all believed me. "Ya won't be cashing them checks today, not at Sal's, so relax." I laid everybody down, then looked over the counter to see what was taking Bags so long. She had the two cashiers hemmed up against the wall with the barrel pressed to the back of one of their skulls. I thought, *Please, give up the money, lady*.

"Where the fuck is my money?" Bags loudly demanded, dressed like a prissy female, floppy hat with her dreads tucked underneath, pressed on nails, and a sundress and pumpkin seed sneakers.

"It's in the vault," the other woman cried out, praying for mercy.

"Open it, bitch," Bags said, gripping them both up and pushing them toward the back and out of my sight. I looked at the clock high up on the wall. We had been in here two minutes too long, and my heart was about to jump right out my chest. *Please, hurry up*.

"Hurry up. I'm not playing around, bitch, so you betta stop stalling."

I could hear Bags in the back going wild. Then I heard the thundering sounds of gunshots ring out. I damn near shitted on myself at the sound. The customers all feared that they were next, so they all said “fuck me” and jumped to their feet, running out the door to escape unharmed. Suddenly, Bags came running out the rear with three big bags at her side. She tossed one into my chest and waved me to come out with the gun. We ran out of the store behind the stampede of everyone else. Wasting no time, we cut down to the alley where the first of three stashed getaway vehicles sat, a stolen grey Chevy Tahoe.

Bags took the wheel. “Close the door,” she demanded in a rush as I stuffed my bag into the rear seat next to the two she’d also thrown back there. We peeled down the alley and came out on a side street. We could hear sirens coming in our direction.

“Fuck,” I mumbled as my heart raced.

“Just relax,” Bags urged as four Detroit police cars blew past in the opposite direction.

I looked in my side mirror, praying to God that they didn’t hit a U-turn. Thankfully, God must have heard my prayers because within minutes, we were getting on the Davidson expressway headed for the next vehicle so we could swap out.

“Stop looking at me like that,” she calmly said, as I was staring a hole through the side of her face.

“What in the fuck happened back there?” I was no fool and knew the answer, but I just didn’t want to believe it.

Nonchalantly, she turned from the road to momentarily look me in my eyes. “Look, Melody, it’s best if we leave everything that happened back there where it’s at.”

I knew damn well what happened. She killed those two women, and for what? They obviously gave up the money. The bags in the backseat were proof of that. I clenched my jaw and balled my fists. I didn’t sign on for being part of a murder case, and that’s precisely what we’d be facing if the police caught us. I just wanted to get out of the truck and do as Bags suggested . . . forget about what just happened back there. *Damn, I wish I was back home in Chicago.*

"Hey, hey! Where are you going?" I asked.

Bags had zoomed by where we had the next car parked.

"First, we gotta shoot this money up to the restaurant."

"Man, fuck that old nigga. That wasn't our plan. He's tryin'a jerk us with that $50,000 shit. Those bags are heavier than a mug. It's gotta be at least a couple of mill, if not more."

"You thinking small," Bags giggled with her eyes straight-ahead focused on the road.

"Look, real talk. If we get jammed up, we're going to need a lot more than $50,000. I say we at least hold it until we see what's what."

"Whatever's in these bags is going to Mr. Brooks. He put us on the lick, Melody. Tell me, when was the last time you hit a fifty-stack lick?" Bags glanced from the road. "Never," she smiled, answering for me.

I couldn't believe this stupid bitch was really sitting beside me talking that loyalty shit to me. Truth be told, Mr. Brooks didn't give a fuck about our black asses. We were just expendable pawns doing his bidding for cheap. If we went to jail, that would be the last time we heard or saw from him. We could say fuck him before he got the chance to say fuck us. I wanted to try to convince her naïve, brainwashed ass, but Bags turned up the radio like that's the end of that. She profile cruised the rest of the way to the restaurant as if she'd not just committed a few murders and robbed a check-cashing spot in broad daylight.

She parked in the parking lot and grabbed all three money satchels. I quietly looked on, wishing this entire thing never happened.

Just as Mr. Brooks told her, Bags dumbly dropped the satchels at the rear door of the building, then jumped back into the stolen truck.

"Okay, so, when we gettin' ours?" I was pissed, and she could tell but didn't care.

"Chill, we'll get it tomorrow. But let's just see what else the old guy has got up his sleeve for us, all right? If we play our cards right, he said we could get rich fucking around with him."

"Or dead," I mumbled, just wanting to break free of all the madness.

Chapter Twelve

Bags

The next morning, just like clockwork, Mr. Brooks was perched in his favorite booth sipping coffee and reading the paper. He smiled at the sight of Melody and me coming through the door. His old ass had better been smiling, because even though I didn't tell Melody that she was right, she was. There had to be at least several million dollars in them satchels. So, yeah, his old ass better be cheesin'.

Mr. Brooks stood up to greet us with open arms. "Waitress, I want you to whip us some of those famous meat omelets deluxe with extra cheese for my goddaughters." Mr. Brooks half-hugged us both, then waved for us to sit first. "Good job, and good morning." He was all smiles. I thought that he might be a little tight about the dead bodies left back at Sal's, but obviously, he could care less. "So, umm, yeah, I see y'all gals made the front page." He pulled a folded morning paper from his seat and pushed it across the table.

I unfolded the *Detroit Free Press* and spread it open so that Melody and I could read it. The headline read: "Two Cashiers Slain." It reported the murder was an execution during an armed robbery. There was a picture of the building and a picture of Melody and me. We both exhaled, relieved that the pictures and descriptions they had looked nothing like us in real life. I couldn't even recognize us. Thank God our disguises had worked. I was sure happy now that I had been extra with my costume.

"So, listen up, young ladies, I'm not going to ask what happened back there. What's understood need not be said. It was unfortunate, but obviously unavoidable. The important thing is that you two made it out alive and with those bags in tow."

"Okay. So, Mr. Brooks, what's next?" I eagerly inquired, having zero remorse for the loss of two human lives whose blood was on my hands.

"Well, first, Sonya, I'm going to give you all your money." He reached down between his legs and came back up with two brown paper bags, one for me and one for Melody.

"There's $25,000 in each. It may be a little more because I didn't count it. I weighed it. So, if it's off, let me know, and if it's over, just keep it. You both earned it."

"Thank you so much," I grinned at the waitress as she spread our plates on the table.

"You're welcome, baby. I'll be back with your orange juice."

"You girls go ahead and eat. And, Sonya, I want to show you the loft if you have time." Mr. Brooks got up from the table and walked over to the vintage jukebox. He put a quarter in, and The Temptations filled the diner.

I hurried and ate my food. I didn't want to keep Mr. Brooks waiting.

"Damn, girl, I guess you 'bout to slide with your godfather, huh?" Melody gave a hard-core, serious side-eye.

"Don't make me fuck you up, fam," I replied jokingly. I slid out of the booth with the brown paper bag clutched in my hands. "I'ma fuck with you a li'l later, cool?"

"Handle your business, girl. I'll see you when you get back around the way. I guess I'ma catch a cab and put this money with my stash. I'm out," Melody said, then darted out the door.

"Are you ready, sir?" I then inquired, making my way over toward the counter where Mr. Brooks and the waitress were talking in whispers.

"Yes, I'm ready. Just let me grab my jacket. Then we can be out."

Once outside, I jumped in Mr. Brooks's vehicle. We were on our way. I held on to my bag of cash as if it might blow out the window, even though the windows were closed.

"You girls did a damn good job yesterday." He paused to light one of his cigars, then leaned back and continued. "Couple of more jobs like that, and you'll be pros. I watched that tape of the robbery. You didn't have to do what you did, but if you felt it was best, then who am I to complain? I'm proud of you, Sonya."

"Thank you." His words of praise humbled me. I hardly heard anyone say that they were proud of me. So, Mr. Brooks telling me that was major.

"That was good work, dear. And if you keep it up, it won't be long until you're rolling in the big bucks. I keep telling you, Sonya, I have big plans for you. Big, big plans."

I was too stuck on him, saying that he had big plans for me. If they could be any bigger than $25,000, then I was all for it. That shit Melody was talking about wasn't hitting on nothin'. Mr. Brooks didn't ever have to worry about me be being disloyal. I was solid and down for the cause.

After a twenty-minute ride in early-morning traffic, we pulled up in front of a boat shop located off the River Walk. As Mr. Brooks parked, he pointed up to the big, red, cursive sign which read: *Brooks Riverboat Rentals.*

Needless to say, I was impressed as my eyes grew in amazement. "Damn, how much stuff do you own?"

"Not nearly enough, sweetheart," he boasted as we got out of the car. Then we entered the building.

"Mr. Brooks, how are you this morning, sir?" a white man from behind the counter respectfully inquired as we approached.

"I'm 67 and at the top of my game. How about yourself, Alex?"

"Business is good, so, of course, I'm good."

"Well, all right then. Glad to hear it." Mr. Brooks grabbed me by my shoulders and pushed me forward. "I want you to meet my goddaughter, Sonya. She'll be living upstairs in the loft until further notice."

"Nice to meet you, young lady." Alex extended his hand across the counter, and we shook hands. I was still tightly holding on to my bag of cash.

"Alex is the owner of this shop," Mr. Brooks said.

"Thanks to you," Alex replied. Mr. Brooks put up the money to open the business, and he was using Alex as the front man.

"I'm going to show Sonya the loft. I'll be back down in a few."

"All right then. Well, Miss Sonya, if you need anything, be sure to let me know. Any family of Brooks is a family of mine."

"Thank you, Alex. I will."

I followed Mr. Brooks through the aisles to the back of the shop where a staircase led up to a lone door.

"There's a back entrance as well, so you don't have to use the store if you don't want to."

Mr. Brooks opened the door, then felt around the wall for the light switch. When the lights clicked on, I thought I was going to faint. The spot looked like a penthouse. The spacious wall-less interior was decked out with modern everything. The only room that was enclosed was the bathroom. Everything else sat out in the open. The bed was sectioned off overlooking the Detroit River behind the shop. Six-foot crystal clear windows surrounded the loft providing the perfect view. It had a small kitchen, a fully stocked wet bar, and a corner of the loft was dedicated to media with a TV, video games, and stereo.

"So, umm, Sonya, what do you think?" Mr. Brooks was behind the bar mixing himself a drink.

"Oh my God, trust me. It's more than anything I ever expected. It's like a dream or something."

"I knew you'd like it. I haven't used this place in a while, so it's just been sitting idle."

"How much is it a month?" I could feel the money in my bag was going to be lighter behind staying in digs like this.

"Free to you."

"I really do appreciate that, Mr. Brooks. But I'd appreciate it even more if you allow me to pay rent."

"Aaah . . ." Mr. Brooks sighed after downing a glass of Crown Royal. He poured himself another round, then looked over at me.

"That's why I like you, Sonya. You remind me of myself growing up, hungry, but still not looking for any free rides. I respect that. And as long as you keep that mentality, you'll make it." He took a sip from his glass. "Okay, how does five hundred a month sound, utilities included?"

"Sounds like a deal. I can't thank you enough, Mr. Brooks. Just last week, I was dead broke, not knowing how I was going to make it. You seen what we were out there doing."

"Yeah, I saw it. But that's what it's all about in this world. Pulling each other up because them white folks damn sure ain't gonna do it. You hear Alex calling me 'Mister' and 'Sir'?"

I laughed out loud. "Yeah, I heard him."

"Well, I'm not going to have it no other way. The minute he shows any signs of disrespect, he's out on his ass."

"I understand. But, sir, I have one more thing I'd like to ask you."

"That's why I'm here. What's on your mind, Sonya?"

"I want you to hold half of my money. I really don't have anywhere else safe to keep it."

"Now, you're thinking. Sure, I'll do that. And as you need it, just tell me, and I'll have it ready."

"We can start right now," I pulled out my brown paper bag and counted out $12,500 and handed it to him.

"Smart move, Sonya. Well, listen, I'ma let you get settled in, and I'll see you in a few days. Do you need a ride back to your car?"

"Nope, I can catch a cab." I smiled. "Did I tell you, thank you?" I asked, walking him to the door.

"Yes, you did, and you're welcome. We'll speak soon. Have a good day."

I locked the door behind him, then leaned against it, still not believing that all this was temporarily mine. I had arrived. I had $12,500 in my pocket, all big faces, $12,500 put up with Mr. Brooks, a new ride, and a decked-out loft to lay my head at. I had to be dreaming. Now, the only thing that was missing was Devin. I was getting my little brother back—period.

I sank into the deep, plush pillows of the beige leather sectional sofa and stretched my arms around the back of the sofa, leaning my head back, eyes to the ceiling. "This is the life. I can see Auntie's wide face tightening if she only knew." At that moment, I had not a care in the world.

Chapter Thirteen

Melody

I couldn't believe Bags had her nose all up Mr. Brooks's ass after he pimped us like that. It was Mr. Brooks this, and Mr. Brooks that. I was so tired of hearing about his ass that I just wanted to get back to my roots. It had been a minute since I picked something, and I was beginning to feel like I was losing my touch. I swear if Bags said something else about his old ass again, I was going to slap all the shit out of her.

We were down in my basement, eating shrimp and catfish while counting our money. It had been weeks since I'd been to school. I said, fuck it. No more getting up in the morning to pretend that I was even going. Nope, I was straight-up done with that.

I'd given my mom a nice chunk of money and told her to get off my back. I was in the streets like a runaway, and there wasn't nothing she could do about it besides slap me. But even then, I'd still be out there doing what I felt I needed to do. I had embraced Detroit just as she hoped I would, but maybe not in the criminal fashion like I did. I told her that I promised I wouldn't do anything to get myself jammed up. Little did Mom know I had been on a full-blown deadly crime spree.

"So, okay, fam, what you gon' do with all that money you got sitting there?" I asked, eyeballing Bags's pile.

"You thought of any moves toward getting your little brother yet?"

"I'ma teach you how to stunt with this portion right here. I already gave—"

"Please don't say his motherfucking name. I swear to God, I'm tired of hearing his damn name."

"Anyway, I gave him half to hold for me."

"Half of what—your brain? Girl, is you stupid or dumb? Don't tell me you gonna trust his old, half-dead ass with your money. He already done jerked the shit outta us for real, for real," I snapped, genuinely believing this chick was really slow. I already knew she was confused, not knowing if she wanted to be a boy or a girl, but this was way too much for me.

"He's not about to beat me outta a li'l punk-ass twelve-five when we bringing him all that cake. Plus, he just put me in a decked-out loft. You think he'd be doing all that just to beat me? And besides, I asked him if he'd hold it. He didn't make no suggestions."

I just shook my head 'cause Bags had flipped her wig. This wasn't the same ballsy female across from me that I met at gunpoint awhile back. Sonya was on the verge of being brainwashed by an old gangsta.

"Trust me, dawg, he's good for it. I'm tryin'a show him that we're not just some petty stickup kids. I want to put some of that money we making into something legit, and he can help us. And he can help me get my little brother."

"Girl, you bugging if you think that dude 'bout to put us on like that. He's just using us right now."

"Nah, that old man just put me in a plushed out loft just because. He fucks with us the long way. Did you hear what he told the waitress and this guy named Alex, who is his business partner?"

"What is you talking about?"

"Mr. Brooks said we're his goddaughters." Bags was geeked like that was some badge of honor.

I grabbed my face and slowly rubbed down my cheeks. I was almost speechless that she was so fucked up in the head. "And hold up, you believe that shit, huh? You can't be serious. Please tell me you just bullshitting right now." My ears were burning. I had stopped even listening to her 'cause it was apparent to see that she had her mind set. I just wished she could see what I saw when looking at Mr. Brooks—which was a heartless old bastard out for self and who could care two shits less about anyone or anything that didn't get him money. I really didn't want us pulling capers anymore for him because I could see my homegirl changing for the worst. She was already lightweight crazy, but now I could see the insanity embedded deep in her eyes. I couldn't believe it when I read the newspaper article, and it said she shot those poor women execution style. Those women had kids . . . They were mothers. Bags shot them while their backs were turned. That meant that she didn't have to. This lunatic had given us letters if locked up—no chance of parole. As much as we called ourselves solid, it was time I rethought our alliance. I wasn't so sure I wanted to go down for a murder I didn't commit.

Chapter Fourteen

Sonya

"You ready?" Melody stood up.

"Yeah, but where we going?" I asked, tucking my ends, and Melody doing likewise.

"I think I'm losing my magic touch. I need to pick something before I lose my damn mind too." Melody wiggled her long, skinny fingers at me, which looked like tentacles like she always did when she was ready to get her pick on.

"It's calling yo' name, huh?" I laughed, not judging, even though we both had a bankroll.

"You don't feel me. That shits like my high. I don't even think I can stop pickin'."

"Yeah. You'll be fifty years old, filthy rich, and still pickin' pockets."

"Now, you feel me."

"Well, if it'll make you feel any damn better and get you off my back, I'll ride you around so you can get yo' shit off." Melody couldn't wait to dig somebody's pocket. I followed her up the steps and out of the door. "But after this, you needs to find another hobby. Start smoking weed or something. Anything that'll calm yo' ass down."

"I'm off a natural high."

"And that's what scares me."

I drove Melody from east to west so that she could do her thang. I sat in the car, laughing as I watched her work on all the "marks," as she called them. The shit was all one big game to Melody. But she was my peoples, so

I wasn't tripping about riding around back on the petty shit, just as long as she was ready to rock when Mr. Brooks gave us the next job. In the meantime, she could pick until her fingertips got sore.

I looked up, and Melody was high-stepping it back to the car. She was looking from left to right with that look in her eyes which said, "Yeah, I just did something."

I cranked up the car and held back a smile as she slid into the passenger seat, still scouring the lot for safety.

"What's up? You get what you came for?" I teased.

Melody was sweating bullets and breathing hard. "Pull off."

I pulled off from the strip mall. After we were in the clear, she dug in her pockets and emptied everything on the floor of the car. Excitedly, she rummaged through the large bankroll that she had just clipped from some random white man.

"Oh, hell naw. What in the entire fuck," she shouted in denial.

"Dang, what's wrong, what's wrong?" I was utterly confused. Melody had two fists full of money, looking at it in pure disgust.

"That hook nose beige bastard had a Jewish mint," she barked, throwing all the money on top of the dashboard.

"Had a what?" I puzzled, digging through the multitudes of bills.

"A motherfucking damn Jewish mint. You know, them bitch-ass Jews be so tight with their money. So that's what we call it when we catch somebody with a hundred singles or more. I outta go back there a sock him in that long nose for wasting my time."

I laughed so hard I was in tears. "Fuck it, girl. Chalk it up as just practice. I tell you what, let's use that shit to grab something to eat. Then you can try again. We got shit to discuss anyhow."

Chapter Fifteen

Sonya

My cell phone vibrated across the coffee table, breaking me from my moment of peace. As of late, my mind was all over the place. I don't know if it was the access to money that had me bugging or the fact that for once in my life, I was living somewhere that I could actually feel comfortable. "What up, doe?" I answered on the third ring.

"Where you at, Bags? I been blowing you up all morning."

"Oh yeah? Well, I'm at the crib," I yawned, trying to wake all the way up. "I been asleep. Why? What's up? What's the deal?"

"Shit, just calling to see what the business is. When you get up, come through and fuck with me."

"Okay, I'm 'bout to get up right now. I'ma see you in a minute or two. Let me just get myself together, and I'll be en route."

"Hey, Melody, yeah, I'm bending the block right now."

"Okay, cool. I'm on my way out."

I adjusted my clothes and took a deep breath as I pulled in front of Melody's crib. I was trying to figure out how I was going to get back on my grind. I don't know what it was all of a sudden. Everything was going good in my life . . . Then it dawned on me. It was Devin. Here I was getting all this cash and living the good life when I knew my little brother was back at Auntie's house suffering. Things for us were already bad enough at that dump. But now, I wasn't there to protect him when need be. Plus, after the last time I was there going off on that greedy bitch, I know she was taking it out on him. I had to get him out of there . . . maybe kidnap him or maybe kill Auntie. Shoot the bitch in the back of the head like I did them other two hoes. As I saw Melody come out the door, I got chills thinking about blowing Auntie's brains out.

"Hey, girl, it took you long enough. Where you been? What you been up to?"

"No shit, really, just in my head, that's all."

"Oh yeah?"

"I had to make a couple of stops before getting here, but what's the word?" I reached over and gave Melody a play. Right about now, outside of Devin, she'd become the only good, steady thing in my life. I can't lie, I was attracted to her at first, but she'd become more like family to me than my own flesh and blood. I could count on her, and she could count on me.

"Well, I kinda don't even wanna tell you, but you gonna get the word sooner or later anyhow."

"All right, now, you got a bitch on edge." I was on pause.

"Okay, well, I went to that restaurant to get a few of them meat and cheese omelets for my mom and 'em."

"And?"

"And, of course, your fake-ass godfather was in there, posted as always, talking to some young niggas about the NBA draft."

"Oh, word." I smiled, knowing that shit annoyed the hell outta my homegirl. "So, okay, then. What did 'our' godfather have to say? Did he ask about me?"

"Damn, slow your thirsty ass down. You acting like y'all two fucking or something. I mean, matter of fact, when I come to think about it, damn, let me find out."

"Don't get hit in your shit, Melody," I promise, knowing she was joking around. "But, naw, real talk. What did he say?"

"Here goes the part I hate telling you. The old man claims he got a hundred thousand-dollar lick for us."

"Say word?" I grew excited at just the mere mention and thought of that much cash.

"Yeah, some crazy-sounding, off-the-wall bullshit about an after-hours spot."

"Word! When? You already know a bitch like me down, especially with that kinda revenue involved."

"I knew you'd be extra geeked."

"And you not?" I quizzed her.

"Everything that glitters ain't always gold."

"Damn, Mel, get the fuck on with all of them old grand-ma, back-in-the-day sayings. Ease up some and live life."

"Whatever, girl. The fool wants us to meet him tomor-row morning so he can break the lick down."

"Cool."

"I don't know if that shit gonna be a go with me. We already dodged getting knocked on not only robbery but also them two murders."

"Okay, and?"

"Well, I say we don't fuck with it, fam."

"Are you serious right now? You must be nuts. Why not? We is talking about a hundred K to be made. I'm all over that shit like a mug. This shit is real."

"Sonya, so are our lives. They real too. Well, mine is," she fumed.

"I know what you saying, but, Melody—"

"But okay, Melody, what? Come on now, Sonya." She kept using my government name, so I know she was deep in her feelings. "You really think them guys is 'bout to let us run in some after-hours and take their shit? Hell naw. That don't even seem right—even in the movies."

"Well, Mr. Brooks ain't gonna—"

"Mr. Brooks ain't gonna *what?* His old ass ain't gonna take a bullet for either one of us or step up and do any time. You and me is on our own—period. What part of *that* don't you understand? The nigga is using us as pawns. We both expendable as fuck."

"I'm just saying he always has the inside score on whatever play is popping off."

"Look, fool, ain't no telling who all's going to be up in there, but I know whoever it is, they gon' have some heat. And they damn straight ain't gonna have no problem whatsoever in choosing between our black asses or keeping they money."

"Melody, I'm not stuntin' all of that you talking. I mean, it's real and all, but I'll lay all they ass down for a hundred racks. So, let's just chill and see what Mr. Brooks talking about. It can't hurt. Then we go from there."

Melody shook her head and sighed. "Fine. I'll listen, but that's all I'll guarantee."

Chapter Sixteen

Melody

I don't know how I kept letting Bags drag me along to meet up with Mr. Brooks. I didn't want nothing to do with his prehistoric disposition. I didn't trust him. I just kept having an eerie feeling something was going to happen . . . and it would not be positive. And when it did, I knew Mr. Brooks wouldn't be nowhere in sight to help us.

Walking through the restaurant door, there he was sitting in his favorite booth. I hated that I even saw him to get the word about this new gig. Nonetheless, he would've got at Bags anyway it went. After all, she was living in his private loft.

"So, hey, good morning, sir."

"Good morning, you two," Mr. Brooks replied to Bags while I shrugged my shoulders as if to say, "What-the-fuck-ever."

"Sonya told me a little bit, but you tell us about the new job on the floor." Bags was beyond all in. She was resting on her elbows, ready to do whatever Mr. Brooks said. He could have said jump off the Belle Isle Bridge to see if you make it across to Canada, and it would have been done. That's how brainwashed he had her dimwitted self.

"Here's the skinny. I have an interest in a private after-hours off Mack and Bewick. A lot of older guys make up the bulk of the membership; real movers and shakers in the city. Some white collar, some blue collar. But they all deep in their hustles."

"All right, okay, then." Bags's eyes grew, knowing the conversation part detailing the money that would be circulating that night was on the verge of being revealed.

Mr. Brooks knew at least he had Bags strong on his line. "Well, there's going to be a $100,000 lockout."

"Huh? What's that mean?"

"Simple. It means each player, member or not, has to have at least a $100,000 cash to get in the door."

"Wow, that's crazy," I finally interjected, thinking that this was going to be no more than a suicide mission. "So, how many players are you expecting?"

"Eighteen to possibly twenty guys. Depends on who's in town and who's not."

"And all we get is a $100K to split?" I shook my head, thinking aloud.

Mr. Brooks and Bags looked over at me as if I were out of line. But it was too late. I had said it, and that's exactly how I was feeling. In all honesty, we should get more money—especially if there was going to be nearly two million circulating in there. And besides, *we* were the ones putting our lives on the line to get it.

Mr. Brooks tried to clean it up, knowing I was wise to his game of underpaying us. "Oh no, Miss Melody. You must have misunderstood me yesterday. What I said was $100,000 *each*."

"I know what the hell you said, and I know what you meant." I glared at his greedy old ass. "I'm far from being deaf, Mr. Brooks."

Bags felt the increasing tension and cut in. "Hold up a minute. We're not concerned with the money."

"Fuck all that. If I'm doing any damn thing, I'm all the way concerned with the money and all I have coming."

"Well, like I was about to say, my only true concern is who do we have to kill to get that cash in hand, 'cause I'm down."

"Hopefully, no one." Mr. Brooks focused on Bags and only Bags. "But who knows what tomorrow may bring. As they say, shit happens."

"Wow, really?" I sat amazed at how in she was. She was straight sucker stroking and had been for weeks.

Mr. Brooks ignored me and kept talking to who he knew for a fact was a live wire trained to go. "Things are going to go easy peasy. My doorman is in on the take. He'll be the one to let you both in. So y'all gonna be good. We gonna be good."

"But what about the gamblers? Ain't they gonna be strapped?" Bags finally asked a sensible question that mattered.

"I'ma keep it real, as you young people like to say. For the most part, they're all my age, except for a few younger hustlers who are heavy hitters in the streets. They're all gonna be hand searched going in. Nevertheless, you both still need to be careful."

"Seriously, you think?" I snidely interjected, rolling my eyes.

"Well, you know us old men are stubborn when it comes to being robbed. We'd rather die than to let you take something from us. So, what's the deal, goddaughter? Can you handle it?" Mr. Brooks was pouring it on thick. "After this, you'll have enough money to get your little brother, and both be living on easy street. Maybe take him to Disney World or something. How does that sound to you?"

"It sounds like we can handle anything you got going." Bags sucked up the man's false admiration for her.

"Whoa. Whoa. How we gon' get those old niggas to stand still when we going in with the two old janky throwaways we got? If it's gonna be some real players in the spot, they gonna take one look at them pistols, coupled with the fact that we some females, and try us." I was giving it to Mr. Brooks in hopes he'd listen to reason and abandon the whole idea. Or at least find two more dummies to attempt to pull it off.

"Listen, stop by here later this evening before close. I'll have some hardware for you that not only looks the part but will also put a hole through a brick wall, if need be."

"Now, *that's* what I'm talking about. Oh yeah, I almost forgot. Where do you want the money taken to when we're done?" Bags smiled, ready to go to war for the old man.

"I'll pick it up from the loft." Mr. Brooks was smug, knowing once more he'd convinced his little weak-minded protégés to do his dirty work. "By the way, Sonya, how do you like the place? Are you good down there? Alex isn't bothering you, is he?"

"I love it. And I use the back entrance, so I haven't really even seen him."

"Wow, so maybe someday, I'll see this famous spot," Melody said.

"When we leave here, I'ma show you the crib, Melody. That shit is hot." Bags bragged as if it were truly hers and not on loan until Mr. Brooks grew tired of her . . . or she was locked up . . . or dead. "Sir, when can we invest some of our money into some business like the ones you have?"

"Listen up. No more 'sir' or 'Mr. Brooks.' You girls can call me 'Uncle Phillip,' okay?" he grinned. "And as far as that goes, first you have to have enough money to make an investment but still live comfortably. Just continue to save your money, and when the time is right, I'll be happy to help you girls make that transition. And after this next job, you two will be well on your way to living large."

I could tell his old bitch ass was lying. He didn't have no room for us in his plans outside of robbing people taking penitentiary chances and playing casket games. And no matter how much cheese I made dealing with him, I would never be as stupid as Bags. I wasn't putting a single coin in his greedy palms. Her foolish ass was sitting there buying everything Mr. Brooks, Uncle, or whoever he wanted to be, was selling. Sonya's sick-in-the-head ass just didn't get it. We were merely stickup pawns to this dude—and nothing more.

Just as mentioned, Sonya took me to her place. As much as I wanted to hate it because our "godfather/uncle" had blessed her with it, I couldn't find fault. Even though it was small, every square foot of it was plush.

We kicked back and watched the mild current of the Detroit River. It had me entranced. My mind kept playing through scenarios of the robbery he asked us to pull off. None of the options seemed good. Mr. Brooks made it sound so easy, but I knew it wasn't gonna be that way. Just like the previous jobs we'd pulled off, he swore this one would be just the same with a pot of gold at the end of the rainbow.

"Mel," Sonya said, breaking my meditation.

"What up?"

"You gonna do this, right? You know I need my homegirl by my side. It's 100K. I need this."

I sighed and continued to watch the river, her desperation obvious. I couldn't believe I was going to say it, but I did. "I'll do it. But this is the last time I do anything for that old-ass con man."

"I knew you were a down bitch."

I frowned. "Yeah, I'm a down bitch."

As planned, we slid by the restaurant near closing time. Like clockwork, Mr. Brooks was there anticipating our arrival. Waving us over to his favorite booth, he gave Sonya a duffle bag and told us to go into the bathroom and see what we thought about the contents. I unzipped it and could only shake my head. Leaning over to peek in, a gigantic smile graced Sonya's face. There were plastic gloves, two AK-47s, and two extra thirty-round clips each. At the bottom lay two bulletproof vests. I'm not going to lie. Holding up one of the vests had me a little shook. Taking a bullet was *not* on my list of things to do for the year.

Zipping the duffle back, we returned to the booth.

Mr. Brooks looked intensely at us. "When you get inside, by all means, pay attention. You're dealing with men who are and have been playing for keeps for decades. So, you gotta be extra careful we get all the money. In and out. You two girls got it?"

"We can handle it," reassured Bags, ready to kill again, if need be, all in the name of money.

I regretted getting deeper and deeper in with both Sonya and Mr. Brooks. I didn't like that feeling I was getting about going into an after-hours spot, guns practically blazing. Murder was never my hustle. I'd made up my mind for sure. This was my last lick with these two. Sonya had gone off the deep end and was following Mr. Brooks like some member of a cult. If I made it out alive after this, I would definitely never deal with Bags again . . . point-blank, period on *any* level.

Chapter Seventeen

Sonya

It took me twice as long to plot the lick on the after-hours joint. I was trying my best to concentrate and get in the zone, but I couldn't. Melody kept in my ear.

"I can't afford to get caught. We gotta be extra with the planning and execution of this lick," she told me.

"I know, let me think," I snapped back.

"I'm just sayin' I don't want to die for this old-ass man."

"We ain't gonna die. Mr. Brooks wouldn't put us in danger like that."

As always, Mr. Brooks had the inside plug to the late-night caper. He wanted the money just as badly as we did, or at least, I did. I was all the way invested in getting rich. We even had the doorman, Briscoe, on our side. Mr. Brooks had already paid him royally and promised him another nice chunk of change when it was all said and done.

Repeatedly, the high-adrenalin scenario ran through my brain, and each time, I saw us coming out on top. I visualized counting up my money. I mean, how hard could it be to run in the place unannounced and gangster all that cash from them old wannabe players? Even if we had to dust a few just to let them know we were serious, I ain't have no issues with doing so. As long as we got up out of there with them dollars, then it all made sense.

Earlier, I had got up with Briscoe, and he put me down on all the old gamblers that would be in the house. It was mostly regulars, he said. He gave me their names and let me know what they drove so that I'd know who's who when they pulled up to the club. Briscoe was thorough about earning his payout. He even blessed me with a two-way radio so I could listen in on the game. Since Briscoe was familiar with the flow of the night, we decided he should give us the signal to go.

He handed me the two-way radio. "There's always a point in the night when everyone lets their guard down a little, and then they are most vulnerable. When that point comes, I'll say 'pit bull' into the radio. That's when you come in a-blazin'."

I was convinced this would be like taking candy from a baby. Melody didn't feel that way. But I had enough courage and optimism for both of us.

Melody and I parked across the street, facing the main entrance of the small brown cobblestone building. To me, it looked like an old storage facility for bread or something. There were no windows, no signs—nothing. Just the simple brown paint, a lone camera pointed down at the entrance, and the club's name where the address should have been: *Xclusive Daze*.

"I don't know about this, Bags. That old motherfucker tryin'a get us killed this time around," Melody firmly insisted. "Something don't feel right. We need to fall back and go home."

"Shhh, chill with all that extra scary chatter in my ear." I was trying to listen to the two-way radio and what Briscoe was saying, but Melody was making that damn near impossible. "If you wanna bounce, go 'head. I'm all in on this." I wanted that 100K so badly that I'd risk going in solo, guns blazing.

We sat back in the stolen van, watching various club members pull up in Benzes, Caddys, Beamers, and Lexuses. Each carried in a bag or briefcase at their side. My heart was racing, knowing they all had at least a $100,000. I was looking at it like it was *my* money they were just borrowing. After tonight, it would be home with its "rightful owner."

Once inside, the men didn't waste any time cranking up the dice game. Briscoe was putting me on point to every move that was made over the two-way radio. When he said it was go time, Melody and I had to be ready to act. Mr. Brooks had already informed us we were working inside a small window of opportunity, so stay alert for Briscoe's signal.

My palm grew sweaty, holding the radio. It was as if I could feel my inner soul trembling in anticipation of what was to take place next.

"Hell yeah. Point fucking made," one of the players shouted loudly enough for me to pull the radio back some from my ear. Seconds later, Briscoe gave the signal: "pit bull."

I moved fast. I put the radio down and grabbed the door handle. "Come on, girl. You heard him say 'pit bull.' It's go time. Let's get 'em while they're celebrating."

Melody reluctantly got out of the van as I was already on the move with my weapon at the ready. She trailed me across the dark street. I could hear her mumbling something, but it didn't matter. As long as she was behind me ready to make this major money move, her comments mattered none.

"Girl, I'm telling you one last time. Mr. Brooks on some bullshit. He trying to get us killed," Melody whispered.

She kept protesting but still closely followed. Her yapping was pissing me off, and at the same time, making me feel grateful she had my back.

"Bitch, shut the fuck up and stop putting that bad Karma in the air." I pulled my mask down over my face preparing for battle.

"Sonya, will you look at all those Benzes and Beamers and other expensive-ass whips? Some serious niggas are in there. Probably killers."

"I don't give a shit. I'm a killer too. The only difference is I pee sitting down." I could see Melody's soul when I looked into her eyes. She was shaken, which concerned me. I was solid, ten toes to the ground. Nothing was going to deter me. Reassuringly, I placed my hand on her shoulder. "Just be cool. This is our come-up, so don't let nobody come in between it. If a dude looks like he's about to make a move . . . simple . . . blow his back the fuck out. You can do it. Just pull the damn trigger. Now, I need you right now. So, is you with me or not?"

"Yeah, I'm with you," Melody exhaled, still full of uncertainty.

"Good. Now, let's get this money and remember not to let nobody get up close to you. Stand back so you can control the room and everyone's movements." I waited for Melody to pull her mask down, and then we slid up underneath the camera. Briscoe was on point and waiting. As soon as he spotted us, he buzzed us inside the building.

He pointed to a hallway. "Yo, they all in the back, right around that corner," he whispered. "And ain't none of them strapped."

That was all I needed to know. I took the lead with my gun ready to bang. Melody was right on my heels. The voices of the men grew louder and clearer the closer we got. The room would soon be ground zero. Cautiously, I peeked in through the crack of the door and squinted through the smoke lingering high in the air. Taking a deep breath, I turned, nodding to Melody. Her eyes were bucked wide open, revealing her fear. It was too late for her to back out now, though. It was much too late to turn around or have second thoughts.

I was ready to get the party started and let our presence be known. And that I did. With attitude, I barged into the room, letting a single round off into the ceiling. I wanted complete silence and swiftly got my wish. All the slick talking instantly ceased, and they all snapped their heads in the direction of the gunshot. The shooter dropped the dice onto the table as his jaw dropped open.

Once I had everyone's attention, I tossed the duffel bag on the pool table. Melody did the same with hers. "Okay, y'all know what this is, so let's make this bullshit quick, fellas. I got things to do later on."

"Oh, hell naw. What the fuck is this shit?" one of the elder members dressed in a royal blue velour tracksuit yelled.

"Look, old man, you can either put all your money in that bag, or I can put yo' ass in it—dead. Your choice," I forcefully warned. "Matter of fact, strip down. All of y'all."

The members all looked at each other in disbelief. Two masked females were holding guns on them. I guess they waiting to see if somebody was going to grow a set of balls and buck the play.

"Whoa, slow down, you little bitches. I don't know who sent you or what in the fuck this about, but I ain't never been robbed a damn day in my life," a man fumed, not ready to give up his cash that freely.

"Okay, and good for you. That was then, and this is now. Today, you 'bout to lose yo' virginity. So, yeah, I'ma need that money."

"You hoes got the game fucked up. Do you know who we all are?" a drug dealer nicknamed Black Walt calmly asked with his chest stuck out.

Up to that point, Melody had yet to say a word. With her gun pointed at a cluster of members, she said, "Listen, all you hardheaded motherfuckers. You heard what was said. Fucking strip and live, or else you can die wearing them clothes. Your damn choice."

"I don't know about y'all niggas, but I'm not giving these once-a-month bleeding pussies jack shit." Black Walt made a move for the gun in his waistband. At the same time, his homeboy Zack did the same. Although they may have been quick in the streets, luck was not on their side tonight. They never made it to draw.

I split four shots between them, hitting them each in their upper chest area. I then spun around. With no effort at aiming, I caught the old man in the tracksuit in the back of his head as he attempted to get to the rear door. There'd be no run toward freedom tonight.

Some of the members turned directly to face us, hoping for mercy. Others stood frozen, staring at the dead bodies. Expressions of sheer panic, definite fear, and certain regret for past sins filled their troubled faces. There was no way out. Three of their comrades had already given their lives in defiance of giving up their coveted 100K. So it was clear they'd have to relinquish theirs or suffer the same fate.

"Okay, you two, calm the hell down and listen to reason," one man stuttered. He took a few aggressive steps toward the girls, which caused all hell to break loose.

"Start fucking shooting," I ordered Melody. I couldn't tell if she was letting them bullets fly or not because I was too busy dropping Negroes where they stood.

When the shots stopped, the only person alive in the building besides us was Briscoe. There was smoke in the air, blood flowing on the floor, and the only sounds were Melody and I breathing heavily. For the first time in weeks, I felt some sort of mixed emotions because of my actions. I looked around at all the carnage. I was shaken. I don't know what came over me. I can't lie. I was gone.

Suddenly, I heard a crunching sound behind me, and before I knew it, I had whipped around and shot Briscoe between the eyes.

Melody had to grab hold of my arm to break me out of my zombie-like trance. "Bags, Bags, hold the fuck up. Chill. That was Briscoe you just killed. You hear me? Briscoe."

"Fuck, I know." I was trembling with the gun in my hand. Briscoe was lying facedown in a pool of his own blood. "Damn, dude, my bad."

"Come on, Bags, we gotta go—now!" Melody insisted and pulled me toward the door. "I wish Mr. Brooks's old ass was lying here." She stepped over Briscoe's dead body.

"Okay, okay, you right. We gotta get ghost." I pulled away from her. "But not until we get what we came for. You get all the jewelry, while I get the money. If anyone else is still breathing, 'kill 'em. It's the only way if we don't wanna get knocked for murder. Don't leave any witnesses alive able to tell the tale."

We finished loading the duffle bags with money, jewelry, car keys, and cell phones to smash and toss later. Then we zipped the bags shut and threw them over our shoulders.

"So, you got everything, right?" I inquired, looking over at Melody, who looked stunned and dumbfounded.

"Yeah, girl, but what about all these damn bodies?"

"What about them? Not our problem. Is any of them still living?"

"Nah, I don't think so." Melody shook her head at the dead men sprawled across the floor.

"Cool, then we out. We finished our job. We got the cash, and the rest don't mean shit," I said, returning to the old Sonya . . . confident, with no remorse, and ready to get hers.

Chapter Eighteen

Mr. Brooks

Mr. Brooks was sitting in a leather club chair in the study eagerly waiting for news from Briscoe. The stickup should have been in progress at that moment. He tapped his right hand on the arm of the chair, and with his left, he sipped Cognac. Once he got the money from this lick, he'd be set. He planned to pay off all his gambling debts and loan sharks, then buy as much coke and pussy as he wanted. The phone rang, snapping him out of the fantasy playing in his head. He eagerly picked up the receiver.

"What's good?"

"It's Herb. We need to talk."

Mr. Brooks slumped into the chair, disappointed that it was his attorney calling and not Briscoe. "I don't really have time right now. Let me get back to you tomorrow."

"No, we have to speak now. I just got off the phone with the Feds," Herb stated.

"The Feds? For what?" Mr. Brooks's spine stiffened.

"They were asking questions about you. Letting me know that they were looking into you. I tried to get more out of them, but they were evasive and vague."

"Come on now, Herb, are you serious?" Mr. Brooks chuckled.

"Yes, as serious as two heart attacks. They on to you."

"I have no idea what they'd want with me."

Herb sighed. "Look, Phil, me and you go way, way back."

"Yeah, I know."

"And we've been through some really tough times and came out on top, in most cases."

"Herb, I know all of that."

"Then you know how this thing works between us. If you want me to do my best, then you have to give me something to work with."

"I know, I know."

"Okay, then start with the truth. And don't leave shit out. Because trust me when I tell you, this ain't no regular state investigation bullshit going down. This the damn Feds. And if they come knocking, nine outta ten times, they already have an airtight case to convict."

"This is so fucked-up. I've got plans."

"Plans? You've got plans? No. What's so fucked up is you being so desperate for money. In between gambling, women, and snorting, you've been spiraling out of control. I tried to warn you."

Brooks knew his attorney was right. He did warn him, but Brooks ignored it, hoping he could somehow keep up with his lifestyle.

"You're right, you did warn me. But believe me, I have no idea what they want with me. I've got some things in the works that will solve everything. Just hold them off for as long as you can." Brooks didn't want to say any more than that. His plans had suddenly changed. He would get the money and leave the country. Fuck the gambling debts and bookies. He was officially on the run. Beads of sweat dripped from his forehead. "Come on now, Herb, things can't be all that bad." He tried to sound relaxed.

"Brooks, just sit down, and I'ma tell you completely what I've heard they know thus far. It would be better if we get a jump on some sort of defense. But to be brutally honest, my old friend, you about done for."

Not ready to give up, Mr. Brooks drove around a good hour or so playing back in his head what his lawyer just told him. For years, he'd dodged the bullet, so to speak. He lived life on the edge, moving and shaking. He'd been broke, then rich, then broke again. This time around, the various businesses he had his hand in weren't paying off as he felt they should. In his eyes, if money wasn't making more money, then what was the point? Those business alliances were no longer beneficial and became expendable. Although he felt that he was smooth in the crimes he'd put into motion, his business partners saw through the plots and schemes.

When some of the stolen cars and parts showed up at a local chop shop that had got raided, the FBI was called in. Upon investigation and threat of serious jail time to everyone involved, they all quickly gave up Mr. Brooks's involvement as the mastermind. And if that wasn't enough to bring down his house of cards, when they came sniffing around the check-cashing business, Sal was already nervous and folded without much pressure. These, along with several other petty crimes and the murders at the check-cashing shop, pretty much guaranteed Mr. Brooks a long life in prison. He had to come up with a plan . . . quick.

Chapter Nineteen

Melody

"I can't believe things had to go down like they did. I swear I feel sick to my stomach. I feel like I can't breathe." I paced the floor of the loft. There was no settling down. There was already a strong sense that things were doomed before we even drove to the club. Why didn't I listen to my gut?

Sonya may have drunk the Kool-Aid, but not me. Now, we here with not just the two bodies from the check-cashing place but a vicious, all-out massacre to avoid getting charged with. It was only a matter of time before the crime scene was discovered, and they'd have the entire police force looking for the people responsible. No amount of money was worth that. I'd allowed Sonya and Mr. Brooks jointly to ruin my life. And now, it was what it was.

Damn, my mother is going to be so disappointed in me. Why did we ever move here from Chicago? Shit been fucked-up ever since.

Sonya

"Oh my God, I can't believe we made it. We did it. We pulled it off. Look at all this fucking money. Not to mention this damn jewelry." I tossed a huge handful of bills up into the air and walked over to the mirror, where I slipped one of the stolen gold rope necklaces around my neck. As far as I was concerned, I was about to be living like a hood rock star. "You need to stop being so damn sad around this motherfucker, Melody. We rich. Did you see all that shit in both duffels? I'ma buy me a new car. Maybe a motorcycle or some shit like that." I checked myself in the mirror. I liked what I saw—a playa who gets shit done and takes no shit.

I walked out onto the balcony and stared at the Detroit River. All my dreams had come true. I'd never had this much money or even seen this much money in person. The only place I'd seen it was on TV or in movies. But the most important thing to me was that I'd come through for Mr. Brooks, and I knew he'd be proud. We were going to make a great team and own this city.

At night when I was alone, I'd lie awake knowing I'd eventually meet the devil for all the wrong I'd done. There was no reason whatsoever to make those two women at the check-cashing place get down on their knees. It was true. They had complied, and I did have the money. But something felt empowering to hear them plea for their lives to be spared. I knew that any other time our paths crossed, the two women would have looked down on me. But that day, they had to respect me. I finally felt like I had control. For now, I was living my best life. My day of reckoning would come when it came.

Chapter Twenty

Mr. Brooks

It didn't matter what time it was. I'd thought long and hard about what my next move would be. Herb had me shook. He said the Feds were more than likely watching the dealership, the check-cashing spot, my house, and the restaurant. I kept looking in my rearview to see if anyone was tailing me. I didn't feel comfortable going anywhere, at least not now.

I drove to see if anyone was watching the loft. I hoped since my name wasn't on the lease, they didn't know to surveil it.

I pulled up to the empty parking lot and shined my headlights around the perimeter. It looked deserted. I didn't see anything unusual. The cops must've not known about the loft. I parked in a dark corner of the lot, then opened the glove compartment, removed a pistol, and put it in the inside pocket of my sports coat.

Silently, I approached the front door of the loft and heard talking on the other side. It was Melody and Sonya. My heart sped up. I rushed through the door. "You get it?" I blurted out.

Melody was standing at the kitchen counter. "Yeah, we got it."

"Where is it?"

She nodded toward the bed.

I rushed to the duffel bags and spread them open. Greedily, I reached in to feel the bills between my fingers. My smile was uncontrollable.

"Where's Briscoe?" I asked.

Sonya walked in from the balcony. "Briscoe didn't make it."

"What do you mean?"

"I mean, everything didn't go as planned, and Briscoe didn't make it."

"Goddamn. What did you do?"

"Whatever we needed to get out of there alive and with the loot."

My jaws tightened. I rolled my head in a circle to loosen my tense neck muscles and sighed.

"One less witness," I said.

As long as they had my money, I was content.

"Do you realized how many husbands, fathers, brothers, uncles, cousins, and friends ain't going home tonight because of what we did?" Melody said.

"Melody, please, just shut the fuck up with all that complaining. I mean, shit. Mr. Brooks ain't did nothing but make us up our game, and here you acting straight ungrateful. Look at all this money. We just got paid."

Melody stood to her feet. "You know what? You two can have all this bullshit. I don't want no part of this blood money. Shit done went too far."

I addressed Melody. "It may have been too far, but there's no turning back the hands of time. If there were, I might have done things differently in my youth. But I didn't."

"Well, I'm still young. And the way you and Sonya wanna live ain't for me. I'm not gonna live my life foul anymore, for no amount of money. If we don't end up getting knocked for all the shit we've done, I'm turning over a new leaf." Melody marched past us. She'd made it a few feet when I pulled the trigger. No words of anguish managed to come out of her mouth. She slumped to the floor, and a small stream of blood leaked from her head. The bullet had found its mark in the rear of Melody's skull, most certainly shattering the bone.

"What in the fuck! Oh, hell naw. Why did you do that—why?" Sonya grew hysterical.

"Sonya, calm down. I didn't have any choice." I calmly put my gun away.

She sobbed over Melody's lifeless body. "You didn't have to do this."

"You were just standing hear listening to what she was saying like I was," I replied. "She was going to the police. She was going to tell on us both."

Wiping her eyes, Sonya looked her mentor in his face. "You really think so?"

"Of course, I do. Be smart, goddaughter. You could read between the lines. Besides, she was not cut like you and me. We are born hustlers. She was holding you back from being great. Now, it's unfortunate that she had to go, but it was you and me. . . or her. I chose us."

"I guess she was bugging out. She has been tripping for days."

Just as I thought, Sonya bit into my poison apple of deception. "Look, I've been thinking about this, and now is as good a time as ever. I want you to pack up all of your stuff and stay with my family and me. I mean, you're a part of it now, right?"

Sonya's face lit up. "Wow, do you mean it?"

"Of course, I do. So, I tell you what. I have to run out to my car to grab something. You gather up all the money and jewelry and put it all back into the duffle bags. Then pack your stuff up so we can both go home. I'll have some of my people come and make sure Melody gets a proper burial. No expenses spared."

"Home," Sonya smiled.

"Yeah, home, so hurry up, and I'll be right back."

Chapter Twenty-one

Mr. Brooks

I ran to my car to move it in front of the back stairs. I left it running with the trunk open after I took a look around the parking lot. Thankfully, no one was around or heard the gunshot. Once again, I was going to win.

"You got everything together, goddaughter?" I yelled from the bottom of the stairs.

"Yeah, both the duffle bags and the rest of my stuff are packed. I just have to get my sneakers together and a few personal items out of the bathroom," Sonya gleefully belted out.

I ascended the stairs with my gun drawn and waited at the door for Sonya. She came rushing out of the bathroom—and stopped dead in her tracks when she saw me standing there with a gun pointed at her.

"Yeah, Sonya, about these duffle bags. I'ma need both these before I leave. I got some moves to make. Come drop the bags over here."

Sonya complied with my command. "Now, step back," I ordered. She obeyed.

I used one hand to toss both bags down the flight of stairs while the other hand stayed aimed at Sonya. "So, yeah, let's make this trade-off easy."

"Yoooou—have you lost your fucking mind?" Her disposition changed quickly, realizing that he had played her. There was a hint of confidence in her tone that I didn't like. She tried to sneak a peek to locate her gun across the room.

"Don't even think about it," I warned. "Moving forward, you little stupid bitch, never let the next man know your weakness."

"You don't need to do this. I'm all the way down with you. Just ask, and I'll do it."

"Sonya, I'm not a man that asks; I take. And your usefulness has run out, so I'ma take this here. See, I've got two other young protégés that are just as eager to please like you. Matter of fact, Melody saw them at the restaurant with me." I laughed. "See, you and your homegirl aren't the only youngins on my payroll. I recruit you dumb asses from all over the fucking city."

"Look, you have the money, just go," she begged for mercy.

"Yeah, I do have the money, but I can't have any loose ends. Remember the streets' golden rule . . . leave no witness alive." I pointed the gun at Sonya. Without an inch of hesitation, I pulled the trigger. Like her hustle partner, Sonya instantly fell to the ground dead.

I took one quick look around to make sure all the loot was packed. There was no way I was leaving without every last dollar. Sonya had done good and packed it all. I bounced down the stairs full of energy. It wouldn't be long before I was on a private jet out of the country.

I stopped dead when I didn't see the duffle bags at the bottom of the stairs. "What the hell?" I said. I stepped out of the doorway.

"FBI. Put your damn hands up," a man screamed from the other side of the blinding light shining in my eyes. About a dozen vehicles surrounded me with their headlights on high. Standing next to each car were several agents aiming guns at me.

I was old school . . . gangster to the end. I reached for my pocket with a smirk on my face. "Satan, welcome me home." Before my hand reached my gun, bullets riddled my body.

While the crime scene was being roped off, the FBI's supervisor commended Alex for calling in the tip that Mr. Brooks had shown up at the business. Alex didn't mind that there was no reward for the arrest. He'd known Mr. Brooks had been skimming off his business for a while, so this was his payback.

At home, after Alex had closed his garage door, he opened his trunk. Sitting there were the two duffle bags he'd taken from the bottom of the stairs before the FBI showed up. He smiled and promised he'd make a toast from the yacht he was going to rent . . . to everyone who had lost their lives over his newfound blessing . . . RIP.

Escaping a Thug's Love

Ms. Michel Moore

Prologue

Once Upon My Life . . .

Without question, my childhood growing up in Detroit absolutely sucked. I know multitudes of people have painfully staked that dramatic claim, but mine was certifiably horrendous. The borderline of Dexter, Linwood, and Davison areas was brutal. Abandoned houses, vacant lots, drugs, crime, and practically a zero employment rate . . . The days of absolute poverty as a kid were long and grueling. And the nights mirrored the days, seeming to drag on forever. With a life filled with turmoil, thanks to my mother and her sometimes live-in boyfriend, I didn't know if I were coming or going. I was an emotional wreck most times. Others, I was just plain numb. She, Gayle, my mother, was an alcoholic, while her man favored sticking a needle in his arm. A Wild Irish Rose and heroin combination made for a toxic household, to say the least.

When the first of the month came around, we were blessed to get at least one, if not two, decent meals. That was *before* my mother got thirsty for a taste. When that urge came into play, our first-of-the-month holiday was over. She'd sell all of our food stamps to the highest bidder. Then it was countless trips to the free food pantry with my head lowered in shame. Gayle had no guilt doing as she did. If there was any, she kept that emotion well hidden.

In the dead of winter, my humiliation was worse. In a donated coat and a pair of boots two sizes bigger than what I wore, religiously, I would hit the streets. My friend Mike Mike and I would post up at the gas station, begging for spare change just to make it through the day. See, as luck would have it, sadly, I wasn't the only kid in the neighborhood suffering. Mike Mike lived on the other side of my block, three houses down. His mother and mine were occasional drinking buddies. That fun fact was what bonded him and me over time. In the long run, that connection would be what made us a power couple throughout the hood and a force to be reckoned with.

A year younger than he, initially, I never looked at Mike Mike as anything more than my homeboy, a cool friend. The older we got, even though I could see the way he'd sneak-lusted at me, I was far from interested. At 14, I should not have had a "type" or even been thinking about that quality in a man. All I wanted to do was go to sleep in a safe environment and without an empty, growling stomach. Sadly, with Gayle and her wild, unpredictable antics, that feat was close to impossible.

Mike Mike would always let me know that one day he was going to hit the lottery and get rich. And when that far-fetched pipe dream would pop off, I would want for nothing. Just shy of my sixteenth birthday, Mike Mike did hit a lick. But it wasn't by playing a number. The local drug dealer had blessed my neighbor with a bag. And each time Mike Mike made something shake, he made sure I was straight. After he came through so much when needed, I started to see him in a different light. Not just because of the money he was throwing in my direction, but also his loyalty and overly protective actions where I was concerned. Mike Mike loved him some Sable Turner, and when it was all said and done, the feeling was mutual. He was my man. Our devoted love and gangster lifestyle were picture-perfect . . . that was until it was not. Mike Mike was not the same man-child I'd grown to love and respect. He'd rapidly become an animal; a savage and a thug, all rolled into one.

"Look, Sable, just chill. I need to take care of a few things." Visibly intoxicated, Mike Mike slurred, fighting hard to stand still and focus.

Jeans sagging, my once beloved needed a shower. He'd been running the streets for well over forty-eight hours and counting. His eyes were bloodshot red, which I easily recognized as looking just as Gayle's were almost daily while I was growing up. Each word Mike Mike spoke took on added syllables, and his attitude was stank. Checking the time on my cell, I grew increasingly agitated. Here it was nine in the morning, and my supposed man had just dragged in the house two hours before, locking himself in the basement. Without as much as a simple apology or even offer an excuse about his whereabouts, he dared me—his woman—to bat an eye. Here, this drug dealer felt that since he went out in the street, risking his life and freedom all in the name of hustling, I had no right to question him. With pride and chest stuck out, Mike Mike made it clear that he was a grown-ass man. He boasted that he was the head of our household. Repeatedly, the pill-popping creep urged me to get the fuck out and go back to my skid row mother if I didn't like or didn't want to abide by his anything-goes rules.

"Baby, slow down. You about to be out again? Where you headed? Ya ass just got back home a little while ago," Sable said, twisting her face to show her annoyance. Mike Mike's lips poked out. He ignored her. Mike Mike shrugged his shoulders before slamming the door shut.

I swear his time is running out with me. All of that drinking lean and popping them pills is getting real old. This year has been driving me crazy. I'm not cut like that anything-goes madness that our childhood detailed. If his ass wanna be out in the streets getting fucked up and giving them random sloppy females the dick, then so be it. I just gotta think about it a li'l more. I'ma find a way out of this bullshit. Then he'll be fucking sorry he lost a bad bitch like me. Until then, I'ma let him play himself.

Chapter One

Sable

"What up, doe? You know what it is. Leave that message, and I'll holla back. One," Mike Mike's thugged-out voicemail recording played into my ear. Low-keyed annoyed, I slammed the house phone down onto the receiver. Sucking my teeth, I swopped my long weave up into a ponytail, allowing a few loose strands to sculpt the sides of my jawline. This nigga got on my last nerve, not answering the phone when I already knew he was out here dead-ass wrong. What dude wasn't? Knowing Mike Mike, my supposed man, he was probably posted up somewhere with another young girl getting his fat, black, uncircumcised dick slobbered on. Nevertheless, my pretty ass wasn't about to lose no sleep on it, though. Good for the next bitch getting her knees dirty and a complimentary throat full of thick come. The more she swallowed, the less I'd have to.

"Oh well, guess I'm free a little while longer," I spoke out into the empty house, shaking my head repeatedly. I paced back and forth on the hardwood floors, and betrayal was staring me head-on. He was starting to stay out, constantly claiming to be with his boys. But I wasn't no fool—far from it. After all the years we'd known each other, I knew the tricks he was playing.

After checking the chipped red polish of a three-week-old manicure, I lit the flame to my last cherry-wrapped cigarillo. Hitting it a few times, I let a stream of smoke fill the air. I laughed again at how dumb of a girl Mike Mike took me for. Little did he know his bullshit had run its course, and it was now *my* time to shine. I'm definitely not in denial of who and what Mike Mike really was. He's a hound dog for pussy, with an assembly line of simple-minded tricks willing to do handstands, belly crawls, and whatever else he demanded for milk shakes. He could continue to run wild. I was not about to squander my life babysitting and handcuffing him down to keep his dick in his pants.

Unlike most kept chicks with a street sponsor headlining their grind, I didn't run up behind Mike Mike's sour ass. I never checked text messages or call logs. And as for monitoring his time lines on social media, miss me with all that nonsense. I knew what was up with Mike Mike from jump street since our youth, but I got caught up in the hype. And like most females at some point, I thought my fine-wine pussy was gonna be good enough to keep him tied down. But, nope. Not in this world or any other planet you want to explore. Ain't no keeping a man that don't wanna be kept. That's the first rule you learn in Bad Bitch Training 101.

Yeah, I know you're wondering how I could go around, not giving two sweet fucks about his cheating ways. Or also him getting down on me with every hot heffa walking, willing to drop it low and spread it wide for him. But that nigga Mike Mike made heavy moves in the city of Detroit, making his pockets even deeper when shit was good. I was in love with the cash and wasn't leaving the door open for another bitch to sneak in on my come-up, even if my man fell on hard times now and then.

First, him and all of that excessive drinking. That bull-shit reminded me of my mother and made me sick to my stomach. With the combination of that, smoking weed, and them damn pills, our once-comfortable environment was the pits. Mike Mike had stopped paying the bills. We had shutoff notices left and right. And most humiliating, my prized custom-painted BMW had been repossessed one day when I was at the grocery store. I came outside, buggy full, and *bam!* My shit was getting placed on a flatbed. Thankfully, I had some cash of my own to get it back. But that was beyond the point. Mike Mike was supposed to pay the note and lied about doing so.

Then some of my jewelry had come up missing. He blamed it on one of my girls, but deep down inside, I knew it was him. Now, over the past few months, he'd come back up on the rise, moneywise, but was still getting high. I'd taken a lot from that man over the years, and he owed me big time.

I'd damn near tired myself out attempting to figure out Mike Mike. He was a puzzle, one I didn't want to figure out. I'd lain back, stood up, and had lain back down once more. I was going insane. Getting up from our king-sized cherry oak bed, I stood in front of the floor-length mirror, sipping on my personal-sized chilled Sutter Home Moscato. The original six-pack was down to three, and I was planning on taking another one out shortly. Our flight was set to leave in a few hours, and I wanted my buzz to be just right for what needed to be pulled off. Getting over on Mike Mike wasn't a small feat by far. The one-inch bruise on my cheek was proof enough that he'd pop off with no restraints.

Come on, bitch, Get your nerves right. I stared into my eye's reflection, trying to find some courage. This wasn't a rip-off I could do in my sleep. Walking into the closet we shared, I reached on the shelf. Putting both calf muscles to work, I pulled down Mike Mike's safe deposit box full of cash. There were only two people in this world, him and me, trusted enough to know the combination.

Unlocking it quickly, I gasped at how much cash laid neatly stacked and rubber banded. Besides him cheating and getting high as of late, there was never a reason for me to dip 'cause Mike Mike kept my pockets on full now, and all other needs met. This money was set aside for emergencies only, but since he'd personally sent me traveling in an ambulance more than once, my case was definitely considered a crisis. Transferring one stack at a time from the box to my book bag, I left nothing to spare for Mike Mike to flip into. He deserved nothing, but I wanted him to have even less.

Roxanne, a.k.a. Roxy

"Oooh, girl, that's right. Tilt your head back and take that dick," Mike Mike grunted as I kneeled in front of him at his mercy. I closed my eyes and allowed him to pump himself in and out of my eager mouth as tears gathered in the corner of my eyes. He was face fucking me at full force. I dared not move as he grabbed the back of my head, holding me firmly in place, introducing the tip of his dick to my tonsils.

"Yup, hold it . . . right there." Not being able to drill any farther, his eyes rolled into the back of his head, and his body began to jerk.

Moving my long, blond weave to the side with my right hand holding it in place, I allowed my tongue to slide up and down his nut sac. Imitating what I'd seen in pornos, I sucked and slurped hard, praying I was better than Holy Sable. The struggle was real for me, and swallowing her man's thick cream would put me one step closer to knocking her unworthy ass off the throne.

"Damn, ma, all right then, do that shit."

A smile spread across Roxy's face, and even though she didn't get the type of explosion he'd got to experience, him just being in bed with her was satisfaction enough. Relationships weren't Roxy's strong suit, always having a dude run her into the ground. But Mike Mike had promised her the world once Sable's time expired, and that day wasn't coming soon enough for Roxanne. Dumb and naive, she really thought he was gonna save her ass from the pole he'd found her on. To him, this was just some late-night, after-the-club sex—nothing more, but everything less.

Roxy couldn't resist the good loving she was getting from Mike Mike. He was giving her hard dick and bubble gum, fucking her raw and rough, and she was eating it up. The last thing on his mind was the fact she was best friends with his girl. The pills and liquor he was off of had his mind spent. "I'm about to get in the shower, but I'll bring you a rag to wipe up with," I winked, dragging myself up from my earlier stance.

"Cool, that's what's up, baby. Gon' and get that body together. I might smash that in the shower. Give you an extra taste of daddy dick before I go."

"Um, yeah, I'd like that a lot, but you don't have to go," I whined, wishing he'd stay the night. Feeling a thump between my legs, I badly needed his caress and touch. Nothing in this world was a lower feeling than being the second-runner-up in a two-man race. Who wants to be the girl in the background?

"Come on, now, Roxy. You know Sable's been blowing up this phone, and I've gotta get back to the crib." He deflated my optimism, waving his iPhone in my face.

"I don't give a fuck about that pampered princess." I rolled my eyes, throwing shade his way. "She can call that mug until the battery dies, for all I care. Just stay here."

Annoyed and ready to throw an all-out tantrum, I stood my ground and refused to budge.

"Aww, that's cute. You're jealous of your best friend," he laughed, mocking me as he made fun of our situation. "You're already fucking her dude, babe, so I think it's safe to say you've already got one up on her. You ain't gotta go get all territorial on a nigga," he jokingly replied, reaching for the washcloth on the nightstand. Wiping the pussy juice and slob from his still-thick, throbbing penis, he eyed me and flexed it my way, hinting for some more attention.

"Fuck you, nigga. I'm serious. You keep acting like you're going to leave Sable but ain't making no moves. Keeping me on a leash ain't gonna work no more, Mike Mike. It's time to make a decision." Even though I was madly in love with my best friend's man, I still got jealous every time he dissed me for her and couldn't take no more.

"Damn, Roxy, you're tripping," he yelled, reaching for his boxers and jeans. It was apparent Mike Mike was about to run back to Sable, leaving me high and dry, plus lonely.

"Oh naw, nigga, I'm not the one tripping. *You're* the one running your ass over here every chance you get," I honestly pointed out, refusing to look like the thirsty go-getter I was. We both knew the truth, and I'd checked for him nonstop since my girl first brought him around. Mike Mike slipped on his jeans, his hoodie, and grey Foam Nikes. His swag couldn't be copied or imitated, one of the many things that attracted me to Mike Mike initially.

"You pumped your own head up, thinking I was about to leave her. I know I ain't told you no shit like that. Me and her go way back ever to be talking about parting ways. That part is a wrap—period." By this time, he was standing firm to walk out the door, and my animosity had grown. How dare he just finish a fuck-fest marathon with me only to shoot me down on something more intimate and tangible. Even though I was holding back tears of regret and self-pity, it was a must for me to hold on to the last drop of self-esteem left. Mike Mike had made me feel low. The few dollars he'd leave on the nightstand and shut-off notices he'd saved me from was nothing compared to this humiliation or broken friendship rules committed.

"You ain't shit, Mike Mike. Gon' and get your dog ass up out of here. The door is that-a-way, but you've been through that bitch enough," I sarcastically got grim, pointing him in the direction out.

"Girl, you ain't nothing but a bootleg version of my girl, so save that guilt trip you trying to run. Don't be dumb, Roxy. You knew what this was about when I first hit that," he laughed again, grabbing at his nuts. As much as I daydreamed and fantasized about cooking and swallowing his babies every night, he was making my feelings turn sour with every word. "And truth be told, if I did—it wouldn't be for you," he continuously belittled me, driving the knife deeper into my heart.

"Get the fuck out of my house, Mike Mike," I screamed at the top of my lungs as the tears forced their way through the thin barricade. I let them flow down my puffy cheeks freely as realization set in. What we had going was just a jump-off type thing, and he never had any real intentions of leaving Sable for me. My run-down, subsidized apartment, snot-nosed kids, and needy-ass ways kept me from truly having him, and for that alone—spite ran through my veins. "You ain't moving fast enough, nigga." I stood my ground, now letting my anger overpower the weakness he had me feeling.

"Oh, you can trust I'm about to be up out of here." He turned to bounce, not even caring about the tears and snot freely running down my face. "You can hit a nigga up once you get yourself together." He turned to eye me up and down. Going into his pocket, he tossed a few bills onto the dresser as usual and made good on his word about leaving. My momma didn't raise no fool, and I hadn't swallowed his nut for nothing, so the money wasn't a factor in this conversation.

"The only person I'll be calling is Sable—to apologize for my part and rat on your trifling ass." For some reason, I had to test Mike Mike by having the last word. It had been rumored he'd beat a female's ass, but my girl had never shared a firsthand account of having gotten swung on, so I took the tales as fiction.

Turning around, he grabbed my throat and rushed me toward the wall. Holding me with purpose and an ice-cold stare in his eyes, I regretted running my mouth so recklessly. "I'll kill your trick ass, Roxy, and you can trust that. The day Sable or anyone brings your snake ass up to me is the one your funeral planning will start." Mike Mike's threat seemed real, and at that moment, I was scared straight.

"O-o-k-ay," I was able to mutter through his tightly clenched fingers around my fragile throat. With no choice but to agree, I had to deal with the reality of being nothing to a nigga once again.

Mike Mike let me go and left, not caring about my sobs and begging for him to rethink the possibility of us. I felt like such a fool and looked even more pathetic. Hearing his ignition start and his tires burn rubber up the street away from my life, a full meltdown erupted. Kids in the back room or not, I couldn't control the shame, guilt, and disgrace I felt.

Having to get my mind right and craft a plan, I sat down on the edge of the bed with a Kush blunt. Since Mike Mike was out of the picture, having him help with the next month's rent was a no-go, so I didn't have time to spare for recovery. Putting my weave into flexi rods and securing it tightly into a bonnet, I lit my blunt and let the smoke intoxicate my lungs and cloud my mind.

A new day was coming because I was getting tired of having men disrespect me and treat me like yesterday's trash. Me having gone through this with the opposite sex my whole life, the entire dynamic of being a sidechick was, without doubt, played out. I had kids to worry about, but instead, my time had been devoted to Mike Mike's trifling ass, hope-seller who did nothing but leave me alone to explain to my kids why another one bit the dust. From now on, it was about to be strictly my babies and me. No men and their dog-ass ways were allowed. There was no one to blame but myself. Stupid, dumb, naive-minded Roxy.

A short time later, the phone rang. Jumping up, I sprang across the room to answer it, desperately hoping it was Mike Mike calling to talk it out. No such luck, though.

"Hey, what's up, girl?"

"Ugh, you don't sound so excited to hear my voice." Jazz annoyed me instantly. I didn't want to take it out on her but now wasn't the right time.

"It ain't that, Jazz. The dude I've been telling you about just pissed me off and stormed out of here on some bad-boy shit," I only half-confessed.

"Well, I hope you got your bread up for the trip 'cause the time has come." She brought the conversation back to her once again since we were going for her birthday.

"Yeah yeah yeah. I've got my cash. You already know that's a must. Anyway, let me get my gatherings straight, and I'll be on my way."

"All right, boo, I'll see you in a few. Don't fret. We're going to paradise." She was on ten about this vacation and had been for months. I tried not to be a hater and pop her bubble about the hype up she was giving Miami.

Don't get me wrong; I loved my girls and was once loyal to the so-called team. But I'd outgrown that childhood "best friend" bullshit and was only out for me now.

Chapter Two

Sable

My bags were packed, my boarding pass, ticket, and identification card were secured, and I'd smoked all of the paraphernalia left in my stash. The only thing left to do was to lock up on my way out. As I looked around the bedroom we've shared many nights together, part of me wanted to unpack and give love another try. Before Mike Mike, my life had been living by a hustle, talking to this nigga and the next. I never saw him as being my man. I guess all we'd been through as kids made it one way. But thank God he saw it another and had rescued me from myself. Now, because of his weight and clout in the streets, I was living lavishly by hood standards. Looking around at the plasma television, showroom Art Van cherrywood furniture, and the photographs capturing our once-happy moments, it was evident, I had to admit, that I'd miss my man.

Damn, here the fuck he comes. The disruptive, half-raised Negro was rocking the neighborhood with his sounds blasting, headed to my doorstep. I got to the window in just enough time to see Mike Mike's cocaine-white Infiniti truck burn rubber up the street and jump the curb, skidding across our front lawn. This man was crazy, no doubt. I stood frozen, staring discreetly out the blinds, careful not to rattle them and blow my cover.

When he opened the door to climb out, I flew toward my bags. Heart racing, I dragged them quickly into the second bedroom. My timing couldn't have been much worse, and playing the reminiscing game had me caught up, once again, with this alcoholic pill head.

Hearing his keys rattling at the doorway, I could almost smell the liquor in his system creep through the keyhole. Tossing my cell in my purse, I darted back up the hallway like a track star going for gold. Even though I couldn't stop him from coming inside, no matter how hard I prayed, I still wasn't going to meet Mike Mike and his guaranteed bullshit at the front door like some devoted puppy dog. From experience, I ran into the bathroom, locked the door, and turned the shower water on full blast. With my luck, he'd come in frisky, seeing me wet and naked. With my back planted against the flimsy white door, I slid my body down toward the floor as hot steam filled the air. My heart raced, and my adrenalin pumped as I waited for what was gonna happen after what came next. Hopefully, he wouldn't find my luggage or his missing stash, because if so, my demise was inevitable.

Every time Mike Mike drank and popped pills, he'd become belligerent, turned up, and ready to beat my ass. He would argue with me over petty shit and start drama for no reason. I can't count the number of times I've been yoked up, smacked down, and talked about by his ass. Either the dishes weren't washed clean enough, dinner wasn't seasoned as good as his punk-ass momma would've seasoned it, or he couldn't see his reflection in the toilet bowl water while he stood to take a piss. I had been a fool for getting caught up loving the good times with Mike Mike when I should have been focusing on the more consistent moments like this.

"Yo, Sable, where you at, girl?" he shouted into the otherwise quiet house as if he had no home training.

As the hot water started to steam the room, I downed the last of my Moscato, setting the wineglass on the sink. Undressing, I eased my body under the hot flow of the water. Instantly, it felt so good, so relaxing, and it temporarily took control of my anxiety. I tried hard to drown out Mike Mike's voice, but he was yelling . . . screaming at the top of his lungs. I was hoping the neighbors had called the police. Matter-of-fact, I wanted to call them myself. At least that would guarantee me a night free from him laying hands on me.

"Sable, get your scary ass out here. Hey, I need some face time, girl. I know you better be here. Where the hell you be's at?"

Damn, did he know about the getaway? Have I been busted? Through the sounds of the pounding water, I could hear glass shattering across the marble floors. I assumed it was the vase and flowers he'd just given me as an apology for last week's one-sided battle royal.

"Sable, don't make me find you," he bellowed, sending chills down my spine.

This is the drama you only see in movies. *Why me?* was all I could think as I put my head underneath the water, whispering a prayer for safety. I knew the routine. I knew things were about to get way worse before they got better. I wish it could go back to the old Sable and Mike Mike—when the gifts flowed in, no strings attached, and he'd flaunt me around town like a trophy. He was selling me a dream, getting me joked up, thinking I was "the one."

"Hey, bitch, come out here and stop playing. I need you, girl, right damn now."

My momma barely raised me, but what I did pick up on was not to run to trouble. If he wanted it with me, he was going to have to go through it to get me. I wasn't about to run downstairs and meet his fist in the process.

"Are you in here?" *Damn, my time has run out.* "Sable," he shook at the doorknob, causing it to rattle. "Why is a door locked in my house?—I told you about that bullshit. Now, open this motherfucker. Bring your ass out here," Mike Mike shouted like he meant every word.

"Calm down before the neighbors call the police, Mike Mike. You see how you swerved up on the front yard and shit." I stuck my head out of the shower, trying to reason with him.

"Okay, bitch, I'm done playing."

"Mike Mike, wait. What the fuck?"

This lunatic was kicking the bathroom door in. I snatched back the shower curtain in just enough time to see the wooden frame splitting. My jaw dropped as splinters flew, scattering onto the damp floor. "I don't care about no neighbors, you nothing-ass bitch. I'm about my respect."

"Mike Mike, please, stop. Oh my God, stop!" Naked and wet, I grabbed a towel running toward the door. Desperately trying to open it and prevent him from fully kicking it down, I was too late. The frame was cracked, and the bottom hinge was bent. I had made matters worse by staying here. I couldn't wait to get the fuck out of his life forever.

"Awe, now, look what you made me do," he taunted, pushing the door, or what was left of it, open, walking inside the still-steamy bathroom. "Now, again, why is a door locked in my house?" Giving me fever, he stood breathing heavily with big beads of sweat dripping down his forehead.

"To keep from fighting with you," I sarcastically mumbled loud enough for him to hear. "But I guess that shit didn't work, did it?" I reached over, turning the shower water off, hesitant to turn my back—and for a good reason. With malice, he yanked my hair from the rear, twisted it around his hand, and slung me down onto the cold, wet, and slippery porcelain floor.

"Aaah, shit," I let out a high-pitched scream at the top of my lungs. It felt like he tore my scalp from my head. As I reached my hands up in an attempt to hold on to what little bit of hair I thought I had left, he forced my body to arch up automatically. My back was in excruciating pain as the splinters that littered the floor pricked my skin. I couldn't breathe, I couldn't think, I couldn't speak. The small room was spinning.

"Again, I ask you, why is your sneaky ass up in my house with the doors locked? I warned you, now, didn't I?" His breath reeked with a cross between weed and liquor. "You make me do this shit to you, ho. I can't trust you. Who else up in here—up in my fucking house? Who, trick? Who?—And don't lie."

I opened my mouth to beg him to stop, but no words came out. While he cruelly slammed my head against the side of the vanity, there was nothing else I could do but cry and take it. I knew not to fight back. It'd only make matters worse. The slight buzz I was feeling from the wine had left my body and was replaced by feelings of hatred, anger, and fear. There was no way I could shield myself from whatever was coming next. I never could. I just braced myself for what was sure to follow. By this time, he was standing over my naked, shivering-in-fear body, rubbing at the bulge in his pants.

"I'm sorry. Please, Mike Mike," I pleaded with him through sobs. "I won't do it again. I'm sorry," I cried, finally finding the courage to speak.

"You think I'm stupid, huh?" His response was quick and direct. "Is *that* what in the fuck you think?"

"No," I fired back just as quickly. "I was only taking a shower. I swear that was it."

"Shut up, Sable. I ain't stupid. You sneaky just like that bottle-guzzling mother of yours." His insults cut like a knife. "Now, what was you doing while I was gone that you needed to take a shower? Who you done fucked up in my damn house, you tramp?" His anger increased with each passing slurred word. "I'm about to go kill them right before I off you."

"Whoa, wait, Mike Mike. Stop. I've been here talking to Jazz, drinking wine. Stop tripping, please," I begged, holding both hands up, trying to slow down his attack. I started to scoot back, looking up at him with tears covering my face. "I'm sorry. Please let me up."

He didn't say anything. He was silent, giving me a strange look. Amazingly with the Almighty Spirit taking over me, I was able to slide up the wall and stand. My body was shaking from fear and excruciating pain as he stared me up and down while still nursing a hard-on. I wept harder, hoping he'd have compassion on me. I prayed he'd let me go, but, of course, my prayers went unanswered. My agonizing grief seemed to have the opposite effect on Mike Mike. He was getting turned on by me being at his mercy.

"That crying and whining don't mean nothing to me, Sable. If I catch your punk ass cheating, I'm gonna kill you, no questions asked. You can believe that."

The way we rocked in and around his house, those words were bond to me. Once I got to Miami, he could trust or swear on his life that I'd never be back.

"I don't like no sneaky shit, Sable. You already know how I get down."

"I know," I whispered, wiping my face, smearing tears and snot.

"Spread your legs," he suddenly commanded, grabbing himself again.

I knew this was coming. He walked over toward me with an evil expression plastered on his face. With deliberate force, he plunged two fingers deep inside my dryness. I wasn't sexually turned on at all. "Stop." I pulled back as the tears welled up again. I was far from being turned on from his strong-arm tactics, his harsh words of criticism and accusations, not to mention, I had no idea where his filthy fingers had been earlier that night.

"Oh, was you wet for him before I got home?"

"There wasn't a 'him,' Mike Mike. Stop . . ."

He backed up from me, unbuckling his pants. It was time to get boogie, and I wanted to scream out. His dick fell out of his pants hard, thick, and ready for attention. "The thought of getting this pipe don't get that pussy wet?" he asked, rubbing it longer. He was definitely off a pill. My mind couldn't make my coochie react. Relentless to get his rocks off, he barked out more demands. "Okay, then, you useless slut, get on your knees."

Terrified to say no, I dropped down. Opening wide, I allowed him to glide in and out of my mouth. Strangely, my body automatically reacted as I started to get wet finally. As he picked up on my willingness, he began to drill harder, holding my head still by my now-matted hair. "This mouth is mine too, you dirty come dumpster, ain't it?" He eased his manhood out, staring at me for confirmation.

Wasting no time, in one motion, he grabbed me by my throat, lifting me off the ground. I was shocked and stunned and brought back to the reality of him being a drunken monster. My feet dangled from the ground as his ashy-worked hands choked my throat. I wasn't no fool, so I played along with him, but my eyes bulged with fear. Pulling at his braids and tugging his ears, which always turned him on, I prayed for it to begin so that it could be over.

Chapter Three

Sable

The love-hate relationship we'd grown to revel in since childhood had ended. The beatings had gone too far. My life was in constant turmoil, trying to love this man. I had to get the fuck out of Dodge—and fast. Mike Mike moved lightly in his sleep, cuddled up close with his arm draped over my stiff body. Nothing had gone as planned thus far, and I knew Jazz was waiting impatiently for my vehicle to pull up. The digital red numbers on the clock read 5:22 a.m., and the sun was slowly trying to creep up.

"Baby," I whispered to him, nudging his side. "I've gotta go pee." I tried coming up with anything so that I could get ghost. But in the long run, this lie was the best excuse for me to attempt to get out from underneath him. If he'd thought I was bullshitting with him, things would get worse. "Babe—"

Opening his eyes, he grimaced with pain. "Bring me one of those strong painkillers, ma. My head is thumping." Closing his eyes, Mike Mike rolled over, rubbing his temples, trying to relieve pressure.

Hurrying to the medicine cabinet which resembled a well-stocked narcotic pharmacy, I scanned the shelves for a Motrin or Tramadol. Every time he sent me to the emergency room for some trauma or blunt force to the head, the doctors prescribed these. Stopping on the Valium, I snatched the orange bottle off the shelf and read the warning label. "May cause drowsiness, alcohol intensifies the effect, may cause blurred vision and dizziness." Perfect.

Unscrewing the cap, I took three out and filled a glass of water for him to wash them down. It wasn't the best plan laid by a genius, but the only way I saw to buy me enough time to get out. If Mike Mike noticed his money had been tampered with, he'd beat me dead for sure. Hopefully, the pills would make him sicker than a dog or too delirious to react to me disappearing. Either way, I needed time to get out of Detroit.

"Here, baby," I handed him three small pills and the water. "These will help with the headache and nausea soon to come," I lied.

"Yeah, my girl be having all the shit. We ought to start slanging these in the streets." He popped them down his throat before taking a large gulp of water.

"I've made a few friends, some nurses from being down there so much who can probably hook me up with a few scripts for some side cash." Even though he heard the truth, I knew there'd be no chance of my sold pipe dream to play out for him.

"Cool, that's what's up," he groggily replied, making me wonder if the Valium had kicked in already. "Start putting that shit together, ma." Mike Mike rested his head on the pillow as I moved toward the dresser to pull out some clothes and underwear.

"Oh, for sure. Let me get her number out and put it on the nightstand, so I'll make sure to remember," I played it off. Hearing him grunting, I turned around to see him grabbing his stomach, twisting his face in agony.

"Mike Mike," I screamed, seemingly concerned but knowing what was up. "Are you okay?" I knew he had been drinking and popping pills with some hothead whore. So, of course, taking the Valium could only cause him distress, be uncomfortable, nauseated and sick, or overdosed. Whatever the case, I was about to be a witness to it.

"Bitch, you know I ain't . . ." he huffed, grabbing at his stomach. I slipped on my panties and bra right before he leaned over the bed and threw up. "Urg, Urg," he violently hurled all over our shiny hardwood floor.

"Oh no, Mike Mike, you seem sick," I taunted him, knowing he wasn't coming back from the three-pill dosage any time soon. Finished putting on my clothes and my sneakers, I left him to dehydrate himself and got my luggage and come-up money out of the spare bedroom.

Dragging it out and fiddling with the keypad to pop the trunk and unlock the doors was taking forever. My nerves had me shaken. "God, please, help me get it together," I quietly whispered, looking into the dusk sky. Feeling my phone vibrating, I jumped. With everything going on around me, every bump was bound to have me shaken and stepping cautiously. Knowing it was Jazz, I quickly answered to let her know what was up.

"Girl, I know you're over there, calling me all types of bitches. But it's been crazy this way, and to make a long story short, I gave Mike Mike a Valium off his liquor and probably Molly." Finally, tossing my luggage into the car, I awaited her stalled reaction.

"Oh, hell naw. Get in that damn car and bust up. What are you waiting for?" Jazz screamed.

"I've gotta get one more bag, and then I'll be straight to you."

Running back in the house, Jazz warned me to be careful, and I took that as true friend love. Mike Mike was loud and sounded like he was regurgitating his internal organs. "He sounds bad, Jazz. I'm about to peek in on him."

"You're crazy—"

Ignoring her, I chose to look. Peeking in the room, I saw Mike Mike covered in sweat and some of his vomit. He looked weak, and something deep down inside made me feel powerful and wanting to cause him more harm.

"So, how does it feel, nigga? You over there in pain, and I don't give a fuck. Payback is a bitch, huh?" I continued to mock him, getting tough and feeling myself.

"Fuck you. I'm gonna get your raggedy ass," he managed to spit through his teeth.

"Naw, fuck *you*. This is for my damn jewelry I know you took and tried to blame on my girls, with your leaned-out ass." I stood up on the bed and stomped him in the midsection. As he threw up in his mouth and began to choke, I could hear Jazz shout, asking what I had done. Mike Mike was busy sobbing and curled up in the fetal position. "All these years, you've been kicking my ass." I smacked him upside the head a few times. It felt good to swing on him and have him too weak to fight back. I took my rage out on him like never before, kicking, punching, and trying to claw his skin away. Every battle his cowardly behind whipped my ass in . . . This brawl was to get back at him. "Yeah, boy, it's payback time."

He tried to shield himself from my vicious, brutal attack but was much too weak. "So, after all we been through, it's like this?" He had tears in his eyes as if he thought this day of me being fed up with his bullshit antics and disrespect would never come.

I peered at him with contempt. Before leaving him forever, I left him with these words . . . "Nigga, I'd rather be dead than deal with you again on *any* fucking level."

Once done with the second revengeful act—the first being robbing his stash and then my violent words and actions—I turned to walk out of the room and out of our tiny house full of beatings and lockdowns. Mike Mike was left facedown to suffocate. It was on him to roll over. At this point, I was washing my hands. I could care less about his well-being.

"Sable, are you okay?" Jazz questioned with much sincerity, shouting into the phone. "Please, tell me you're out of there on your way here."

"Yeah, I am, so be on the curb. We've gotta get up out of Detroit and fast. That tough asshole won't die, I'm sure." Running to the car, I had every intention of breaking every traffic law put into place.

"I've been looking out the window since we got off the phone last night. You can trust I'm more than ready, babes." I could hear her grabbing keys in the background. Jazz meant business. "I'm about to call Roxy so she can cab it over to the airport. And, Sable, don't worry about ole boy. Just get here so that we can fly up out of here on time."

"Oh, I'm good. Just please, don't tell Roxy what happened or what's up. You know she's got a habit of talking way too damn much. I don't need the world to know about my whereabouts." Jazz was always good with not running her mouth, but I needed extra reassurance.

"Oh, fa'sho. No doubt, my baby." Jazz's words were one hundred, and I knew my girl was real. In life, you don't run across true loyal friends, so having Jazz was a blessing. "Loyalty is a must. I'm all about protecting you and my fam, so no worries, homegirl."

"Real talk, I love you. And thanks for keeping it real about leaving Mike Mike and getting on."

Even though life was dramatic right about now, I was grateful for her friendship and trusted she'd always be reliable. Hanging up, I tossed my phone into the cup holder and pushed my foot onto the gas pedal and coasted up Seven Mile toward the Lodge Freeway. Jazz had just moved into a refurbished apartment building in the Midtown area. Good thing it was right off I-94, a straight shot to Metro Airport. Panting and fighting to keep my sanity, my body shook from the adrenaline rush and fear from what just went down with Mike Mike. Even though I told Jazz I was cool, *nothing* inside of me was level. I'd just ripped off my only provider and left the only place I could call home. If burning bridges are wrong, I'd blazed them bitches to no repair with Mike Mike. Never in my wildest dreams did I think I'd have enough gall and courage to fight back or leave his black ass. We'd been down the majority of our life.

Rolling the windows down in an attempt to let the cool April breeze relax my nerves, I said a prayer to God for his protection and guidance. In a few short hours, I'd be landing on the sunny beaches of South Beach, and Mike Mike's ass wouldn't have the slightest clue. I was on edge and couldn't wait to get to my girl.

Chapter Four

Sable

This thing I called life kept going from bad to worse. Airport security had been a total nightmare, and, of course, it probably hadn't been a fluke as to why *I'd* been flagged, detained, and searched. Mike Mike had probably got up and phoned the goons. With life constantly throwing curve balls my way, it was easy for me to think the devil rode shotgun as my right-hand man. Clutching the empty black Nike duffel bag handle until my knuckles ached, I stared at the rubber-banded presidents scattered across the table. My beginning was someone else's ending, and this white man had the power to determine my fate.

"What are you, a prostitute, stripper, or dope man's girl?" the muscular, square-jawed officer questioned me. At every turn, some punk-ass man with a point to prove was holding me hostage.

"A stripper," I lied, feeding into the simple tale. I had over fifty grand in one hundred-dollar bills trying to break out of Detroit and hadn't planned a feasible explanation as to why. His improvised tale would have to do, 'cause I, for damn sure, wasn't about to admit the bills had been washed clean.

"Is that so?" Rubbing his chin, nodding in my direction, I continued with my make-believe story, searching for a glint of sympathy.

"That money is my life savings, sir. I don't have a family or anyone trustworthy to leave it with." Even though I was putting on my best innocent-girl act, it would be foolish to think he'd have empathy for me and let me walk out of here with no repercussions. My right leg shook uncontrollably underneath the table, waiting for him to respond.

"Okay, well, we didn't find a dancing license in your wallet, Sable, so you're either illegally taking your clothes off for men, or you're being untruthful to me. In either case, I must frown upon that."

I cut my eyes at him and kept quiet. What more could I say that wouldn't get me caught up? There was no way this Cracker-Jack fool was about to hold me back from having a chance at starting over or send me back to Mike Mike's killer grip. The oversized circle wall clock mounted above the doorway ticked loudly as my mind raced, searching for a solution out of here. Something had to be done; a move had to be made.

"Look, man, what do you want from me? I ain't did shit, and I don't plan on being a threat to you or none of your passengers, so please, don't make me miss my flight. What can I do? I know with you being such an esteemed law enforcement officer, you'd be willing to work with such a hardworking young lady like me," I pleaded with the officer, laying it on thick. My words were nothing but made up bullshit, but with so much at stake, what other choice did I have?

"Well, as a matter-of-fact, there *is* a way we can work through this unfortunate situation." Not only did sex sell, but it also would get you out of tough hold situations. Every man on earth was weak to what a woman possessed between her legs, and from the hunger in his eyes, this white man with a badge was no different. Running his finger across my cheek while leaning down into the nape of my neck, I jerked from his hot breath and the feel of his clammy, wet lips.

"Show me some of those moves that made you all of that cash." His nasty, perverted ass was trying to get frisky, making me believe I was never a threat all along.

I was never the regulator in my life. If there wasn't one controlling dude putting my back against the wall, there was another. Black or white, fuck both types. I was tired of being misused by men for their own selfish needs. Not seeing another way but to cooperate, I stood up and swayed my hips, covering my face in shame and guilt. My tits jiggled and flopped around as the thin material of his security uniform pants rose to full attention. I prayed he wouldn't force himself in me as he grabbed at his black leather belt, unfastening it. Refusing to let him see me sweat, I swallowed my nerves and continued to dance for him.

"Let me check you one more time, ma'am, just to make sure you're clean and clear to fly per regulations of our airways." Officer Taylor spoke up loudly so that anyone listening would think the search was official.

"I am—" making one last attempt to change his mind, he cut me off prematurely, not giving a fuck about my state of mind or pleads for him to stop.

"Keep it moving, trick. Hurry up and undress." He lowered his voice, whispering, walking toward me with his pink prick hanging out. The sickening grin plastered from ear to ear on his face made my stomach bubble with repulsion.

It only took him two minutes, and then my clothes were back on. He couldn't hang as long as I thought, with semen spilling over onto his hands and drawers. Boy, was I grateful for not having to taste or feel his sick-looking dick. I couldn't help but wonder how many young girls he'd felt up while jacking his little palmful of a ding-a-ling empty and limp.

"Hopefully, you'll be clean flying back from Miami." Handing back my boarding pass and holding the door open for my exit, I knew he was referring to the sticky goo Mike Mike had left behind busting his nut in me earlier. But I simply had no time to get the coochie back right, trying to jump ship from Mike Mike. What nerve of this officer thinking his rapist ass deserved an Irish Spring fresh smell? Dudes were straight tripping, and that's my word.

Snatching my belongings, I quick-stepped out of the room, running through the busy airport to the gate. No one said anything to me as they knew I'd just cleared security. For them to have their eyes and ears open to foul behavior going on in their airport, how did this officer's perverted ass just intrude upon me so easily? Jazz and Roxanne had already boarded the plane and were buckled in once I finally handed the flight attendant my ticket.

"Oh, you made it." Roxy cut her eyes at me peculiarly, not knowing what I'd just gone through. This wasn't the time to fuck with me—even if you were my ace boon coon.

"It was just a monkey wrench thrown in the game, but they had no reason to snatch me back in the first place." I gave Jazz a play, trying to make myself believe the pep talk. Truth was, after what had just popped off, my ego had taken a dump into the gutter. Putting my bag overhead in plain sight and squeezing past them to my window seat, a rush of relief took over my body.

Chapter Five

Mike Mike

I knew one day Karma would bite me in the ass, but it had come sooner than expected. The pills Sable served me hadn't made their way down my throat before I knew something was terribly wrong. Seeing the room start to spin, and my vision get blurry was a clear sign she was starting to get me back for all the years of abuse and probably the months of neglect I've dished to her. Deep down inside, I couldn't blame my wifey for poisoning me. I'd beat her ass on any given day for random petty reasons, sending her to the emergency room on numerous occasions. If it weren't for my kicks and punches to her stomach and back, I wouldn't be lying in my own vomit, blacking in and out.

Last night, I remembered fucking Roxy raw, something I should've never done. Knowing she was Sable's friend, I'd crossed the limits by banging her and even breaking her off my usual trick's salary. See, I kept a line of bitches willing to suck me off on schedule, and in return, I kept them and treated them to gifts or small-time shopping sprees. When Roxy approached me in her housing projects on some "off the record shit," I knew she wanted to take a ride on my dick, just like every other project chick I rammed my meat into. What made Roxy a threat and a groupie I had to watch was because she caught feelings for a guy and was directly linked to my home life. In the back of my mind, I wondered if she'd snitched to Sable and was the cause of my suffering. It was official. I wasn't sticking my dick back up in her never again—she was trouble waiting to happen. What type of girl fucks with their ace's man anyway? Even though I couldn't shift all the blame on Roxy, a man was gonna be a man, and if nothing else, I could always play the dog card.

Roxy had amped me up and got my blood boiling over, threatening to snitch on me. She'd taken me to the limits and almost got her head snatched straight off her neck, snapping like a turtle by the mouth. Having a record full of warrants and suspicions I was guilty of, I couldn't have her sneaky rat ass call the cops on a nigga and have me locked up. Bouncing on her ass, I came home and took my anger out on the wrong person. Being able to admit that in this fucked-up position only, I dreaded making the wrong decision over and over again. Sable had become my punching bag over the years when shit didn't go right on the streets with a sideline bitch or drug transaction, sending my fist straight into her face.

Don't get me wrong. I truly loved Sable. She kept it one hundred with a nigga and held me down even though I was kicking off into her ass. The same insecurities that made me run in the streets with all these low-budget hoes were the same lack of confidence that made me go upside her head a million times. None of these chicks could compare to my sweet love in my eyes, but I never treated her with the gentle touch she deserved. Once this shit moves through my system, I'd get my shit together and show my baby girl how much I really loved her.

Mike Mike blanked in and out from the overdose of Valium Sable intentionally gave him. Naively, he assumed his girl was still in the house and temporarily punishing him. He had no clue she'd stolen his stash and fled the city of Detroit. The joke was finally on him.

"Baby, I'm sorry," I barely could murmur as the drug had taken full control of my entire body. Trying to roll over out of my vomit was damn near impossible as my mind could hardly tell my limbs what to do. *Fuck, please, don't let me die like this.* My heart rate was slow as I feared the worst was coming. If she would just come in the room and save me, everything would be all good. Trying to grab my chest, I couldn't. My lungs could barely take in the reeking, foul-smelling air around me. I felt myself gasping, then wheezing. I was struggling to hold on and not lose consciousness. I was done. No matter how hard I resisted, I was not able to win over the narcotic. Once again, I blacked out.

Chapter Six

Sable

"Good morning, ladies and gentlemen. I'd like to welcome you aboard United Airways. Today, we will be flying directly from Metro-Detroit to Miami International and will arrive at approximately 11:25 a.m. The weather is projected to be clear for our route, but please adhere to all following safety regulations. I'd like to thank you all for flying the skies with us. Flight attendants, please," the pilot greeted us passengers who entrusted our lives in his hands. Fastening my seat belt tightly and clutching the armrests with fear, my stomach fizzed with nervousness, feeling the Boeing 747 pull off toward the tarmac. This would be one hell of a time to have Karma catch up to my ass, but it was too late for fear, and definitely too late for being a wimp.

As the plane began to accelerate in speed, we gradually started to rise into the skies. My heart was racing as I closed my eyes and held my breath, scared out of my damn mind.

"Come on now, Sable, you are gonna have to quit tripping and relax." Jazz grabbed my hand, noticing the troubled expression on my face.

"I'm really trying. Please believe I am. But what if his ass finds me?" I asked, staring at my friend. I searched for comfort and a sign my fate wasn't looking bleak. Jazz was cool, calm, and collected, having devised the plan for me to meet up with her cousin in Miami. Having been my best friend, confidante, and ride or die since childhood, she knew my real woes with Mike Mike and gave me the initial idea to escape.

"Now ain't the time for regrets. It ain't like you can redo the shit and get brownie points for telling the truth and coming clean." She gave me the side-eye, knowing I wouldn't reject her truth. "You can't be on that soft-girl shit now, boo. This is a new life, and it requires a new game plan. My cuz keeps it real and is gonna set you up tight," she whispered, even though Roxanne's headphones were on blast. "Be easy. You've got enough Benjamins to work with, babes," she winked, glancing up toward the Nike bag. There was nothing I could do but trust her every word.

"Yeah, you're right," I nodded, trying to find a sign or some type of reassurance things were going to work out in my favor finally. The rubber banded stacks were compliments of Mike Mike's savings from cleaning his drug money, and I'd hit a lick in robbing him blind. He was probably tearing the city up by now looking for my fine, brown behind. But I was on my way to paradise, hoping to be free from his living hell finally.

"Don't be stingy when you get down there either, bitch. It's my birthday weekend, and I'm trying to party," Jazz openly admitted putting her earbuds back in.

"Whatever, girl," I rolled my eyes. "You already know I've got my girls." I was just glad that we were on our way. Secretly, I said a prayer thanking God as the plane took off and elevated. When the seat belt lights finally flashed safe for us to remove, I hurriedly rushed in the bathroom to wipe away the scent of Officer Taylor. The bathroom was constricted and cramped, barely allowing me to move around in there. With every twist, turn, and air bubble we hit, I could still smell his funky body odor lingering on my skin.

Taking my jogging pants and panties off, I wrapped the red silk thong in a paper towel, tossing it into the trash. Pulling the Summer's Eve wipes from my purse, I began to wipe away the trace of sex from both Mike Mike and the officer. My vagina was screaming for soap and water—even a douche to flush out more of the damage they'd done, but for now, these wipes would have to do.

Rubbing the thin, white, disposable cloths all over my body till emptying the container, I smelled a little fresher but still felt tainted and damaged by both men. *I bet another man won't put his hands on you, kitty.* I pulled my pants up and fixed my clothes just right. It was time to drop the weight I'd been carrying on my shoulders and move on to a new life. Having flown over a thousand miles to get away from Mike Mike's abusive ways, this would be my vacation before living my remaining years, basically, on the run.

My girls and I had been the best of friends for some time now. Somewhere down the line when Roxy and I got off into puberty, hormones, and boys, Jazz stayed behind and joined the "tomboy movement," never growing into the phase of running behind no-good, dick-slanging boys. Only having experienced a boy's touch because we forced her in high school, Jazz was only attracted to females. A beast in her own right, she had run through plenty. We were flying to Miami to celebrate her birthday, which happened to be the weekend of them wrapping up their gay pride festivities. Because Mike Mike kept me under lock and key, preventing much spare time to run and floss with my girls, I'd never been to a gig with Jazz before, and I couldn't even lie about being excited.

I'm sure with being in Miami, my experience would be double the fun.

Well off into the flight, my clique and I chopped it up about how we were about to tear Miami up. This wasn't our first time on a girls' trip, but none of us had been to the hot beaches everyone raved about. The flight attendants started to roll their carts up the cramped aisle with drinks, chips, and pretzels. Our row kept the drinks flowing since our whole mission was to turn up and get the party started. This had been the break I was waiting for, and from the looks of it all, three of us were ready to live it up.

"I can't believe y'all heffas actually came." Jazz's shock was written all over her high-yellow face. "With it being a gay event and all, I thought there might be some fakeness involved."

"Girl, stop it. That's your business if you get down like that. I'm not about to miss no trip to South Beach 'cause a bunch of chicks running around." I dug into my purse, searching for my headphones.

"Yeah . . . what she said," Roxanne cut in. "But they better not come for me, friend-friend. Or you know we've got an instant problem."

"Oh my God, girl, don't nobody want your dried-up ass." Jazz laughed out loud as a few passengers turned to look our way. We returned the evil glares, not ever trained to back down or take necessary precautions to stay cool.

"Okay, think I'm playing?" she nodded matter-of-factly, and with a serious look in her eye, Jazz's best bet was to believe her. "If I can't find one nigga to spend some attention on in this whole city, then I'm whack as hell with no story to tell. As Sable said, I ain't missing no Miami vacation." I had to giggle at my girl. She was setting the record straight and wasn't to be misunderstood. Out of us three, Roxy was most vociferous and unflinching.

"Well, I didn't make an itinerary for us. Since we'll be getting there in enough time to hit the parade and festival, we can figure out what venue to party at tonight."

"That's cool. I'm just ready to hit the beaches in this tiny two-piece I got from the sale at the mall last week. My ass looks phat in it," Roxy nodded, powering off her phone.

"I'm just ready to relax and release. I'm down to party hard, drink heavy, and hit the beaches too. Hell, I don't want to sleep none of the time we're here." I put more than my two cents in on the wish list. "Let's make a pact like on *The Hangover*. Whatever happens in Miami stays in Miami." I needed extra reassurance that Mike Mike wouldn't find out any details from our "get it in" weekend.

"I'm so glad you feel like that." Jazz threw her hand in for the handshake first. Roxy and I joined in unison what I thought was a shatterproof bond that had been formed between best friends.

Plugging the headphones into my loaded-up Android of music, I made myself as comfortable as possible in my coach-class seat. In a few short hours, my girls and I were about to make our mark in the party city, and I was sure it was about to be epic.

Chapter Seven

Carla—Welcome to South Beach

My body had been stuck in the same position all morning, and here it was, after one o'clock in the afternoon. This weekend's festivities were planned to wrap up a blocked-off week dedicated to Miami Beach Gay Pride, but I was only looking forward to the one including my team and me. I'd been tearing the city up nightly, living it up and promoting the party I was throwing on my *Sunrise* Party Boat. Every year, my party sold out, so I was pleased and looking forward to the payout.

"I think the heat has arrived," the disc jockey hummed through my radio speakers. *"Maybe the rainbow world brought in the heat when they came to invade South Beach. It's gonna top 82 degrees to start the weekend. Wake up and party with Power 96."* Her stale joke was actually close to on point 'cause we knew how to party and were doing so in big numbers. Back in the day, people hid their sexuality and got down behind closed doors. But in today's time, not only were we living in the light and out of the closet, but also same-sex marriages were allowed, and our rights were increasing. Rolling back over, I tried to get comfortable under the covers, but business kept calling. It was obvious tonight was bound to a banger as the guest list kept growing.

"Money damn sure ain't gonna make itself in this bed," I spoke out loudly, yawning and stretching from the deep slumber I'd drunk and smoked myself into. Taking in my surroundings, I was more than pleased with my lifestyle and the road taken to get here. As a lesbian party boat owner in Miami, Florida, my pockets never saw a sad day. To say the least, my team and I were eating hella good and enjoying life while doing so. I was like Hugh Hefner but gay. It was no secret. I loved the ladies, and they love me back.

It was time to get my day started and make sure my employees had it together for tonight's show. Not only was *Sunrise* hosting the after-party for the Gay Pride Festival and Parade, but also our annual show was planned to go down as well. We allowed hosts and entertainers from all over the states to sign up to perform at our venue this one and only night of the year. It was bound to be a night of amazement with drag queens and celebrity impressions, and I, amongst others, was ready to rock. I wasn't into flaming and standing out in the crowd. Everyone knew me by my swag and undying style. I kept it low key, but one hundred at all times. To me, it wasn't necessary to run around with red hair and a matching thong, but to each is his or her own. I was all-gay, all the time, and motherfucking loving it. I dare you to judge me. 'Cause by the end of it, you'll be trying to check for me too. Climbing out of bed still hungover, I lit the prerolled blunt on my nightstand, hoping it would heal the nausea.

"Hey, now, it's about time you woke up." Gianna stumbled in the room, obviously still hungover as well. "Let's go get some brunch at Wet Willie's," she whined, leaning all over me.

"Come on now, back up." I rudely lifted my shoulder to block her trails of begging or affection. She was fucking up the flow of my blunt, and real talk, I thought she'd already gone home.

"Damn, it's like that?" She stepped back, letting me know off the top she was coming with much attitude. I wasn't in the mood for her bullshit, but you can trust—I'd pop back if she chose to pop off.

"I'm just saying, ma, I'm trying to get one in and get my day started." I held up my cigarillo and pointed to my still halfway nude body. I was naked other than the silk boxers she'd bought me for my birthday. "You've had time to make plans for my money and shit, so give me the privilege of waking up," I continued to brush her off. Gianna and I just weren't working out, and I wasn't waiting on her to get the memo. I wasn't down for commitment or relationships. Everything about me was a free spirit and an abuser. Gianna was just another notch on my belt, and it was time for her to be gone.

"Oh, it's like that? You were all in my ear last night on some . . . *I miss you, Gianna,* shit, and now, you're telling me to back down? I just can't with you." She threw her hands up, raising her already squeaky voice.

"Chill out with all that yelling, girl," I warned her, taking a few more puffs of the loud before handing it in her direction. "Hit this fire and settle your nerves. You're doing way too much for me right now." I started to survey my closet for something to wear for our brunch. Even though she nagged a lot, and it appeared she was forcing the outing down my throat, my stomach grumbled from hunger pains, and I needed something to coat it fast. Not to mention I could slurp down a Bob Marley to get my buzz started. She wasted no time taking the burning fire from my hands and inhaling the calm-me-down we both needed her to feel.

"So, you're performing tonight?" she questioned, eying the clothes I'd draped across the ottoman.

"As a matter-of-fact, I am. It's a tradition that won't be broken." Already having one up on Gianna, I was ready for the blowup before the first word left her lips. Baby girl couldn't stand the thought of sharing me and would fight to let the world know. With me being up on stage with girls giving me their undivided attention, it was too much for her to think or endure.

"I can't stand that fucking boat," she hissed underneath her breath.

"Bitch, what? There's no way I could afford your high-priced ass without it, so back down with all that." There was no secret about her love-hate relationship with the *Sunrise,* but when it came to how I survived, no one—even her—could compare.

"See, you always getting so sensitive about that damn boat. That's how I know it's more than just your love for the money." Snatching the tail end of the joint, I abruptly ended the conversation. She must've been snorting coke to think I'd walk away from the best moneymaker since hot butter popcorn.

"Kill that noise, ma. You already know I love the taste of your pussy and your pussy only," I lied, hoping she'd bought it. "Please don't ruin my day—it just started." I reached into my nightstand and pulled a small, sealed, Ziploc bag of treats. "Come on, let's have a do over and get off to the right start." I dangled the goodies in front of her face.

Gianna had just turned 19 and was a party girl gone wild. She ran away from home at the tender age of 15 and had been hustling on the streets and stripping in exotic clubs under the radar for years. Unfortunately, her uninhibited lifestyle left the door open for many demons to travel through.

Since meeting Carla cleaning cabins on the *Sunrise*, she'd been led down a twisting path of jealousy, lies, and deceit. Having gotten down with girls regularly, Gianna didn't think that getting into a relationship with Carla would be so complicated. She was accustomed to being the young, sought-after girl who everyone adored and desired to be like. This junkie Carla had created within her was a stranger she was growing to hate and despise. Spending the last few months devoting every moment in her life trying to please her girlfriend, she was lost and caught up. She'd done everything Carla had commanded of her—and still came up empty. Any time the topic of a monogamous relationship was on the table, drugs suddenly appeared too. All she truly wanted was to be loved, but unfortunately for her, she couldn't differentiate between the bullshit and drugs Carla kept her full of. Whoever said temptation was an easy thing to fight couldn't have been more wrong.

"Why do you act like you don't want me sometimes?" Gianna asked, snatching the bag of ecstasy pills. As I watched her pop the pill, washing it down with bathroom sink water, a small smile perched my lips. She was so beautiful, yet so dumb and easily manipulated.

"I always want you, Gianna. You're my little baby," I smiled devilishly, knowing I wanted only the package between her thighs.

"Don't play with me, Carla. You know I can't take another blow to the heart." Gianna's mouth told the truth. As the ecstasy pill worked its way through her system, the buildup of negative emotion started to sink into the pit of her stomach. Many days it was hard for her to live with the decisions she'd made and the life she'd chosen.

"I'm not playing. Come over here, girl, and let me show you," I seductively responded to her, glad she'd started to feel the drug. I loved it when she was space-time high and couldn't function. She'd really get wild off coke in her system, so I kept a stash of both for play.

She modeled her long, loving legs across toward me, submissive to my every desire. Smoking on the blunt, I was feeling my high getting more intense. It was safe to say we were both ready to fuck. Her eyes were red and low, slanted like Chinese eyes from the drug taking over. Now, more relaxed and mellow, I moved over to her and kissed her neck softly three times.

"Umph, don't get me worked up—seriously," she whispered as I backed up, taking another puff. Her eyes were closed, allowing me to take her in as I ran my fingers through hair. Her chocolate skin was smooth and silky, and I couldn't take my hands off her.

"So, tell me, sweet Gianna, why would you be here with me if I wasn't feeling you?" I was laying it on thick.

"You can show me better than you can tell me," she whispered with lust. After that, it was on.

Chapter Eight

Sable

"I want to thank you for flying United Airways. We'll be landing in sunny Miami, Florida, in approximately fifteen minutes. I'm going to ask you to secure your seat belts . . ." The flight had been fairly unexciting, one you'd hope for, so no complaints here. I'd slept most of the flight, getting my energy up for the good time ahead of us.

Miami was everything I'd seen on Instagram . . . and more. The palm trees, clear blue water, and even the *Miami-Vice* video game layout made me forget about the home Mike Mike and I shared. It didn't take much for me to get caught up in the flash, flare, and hype the city portrayed. As the taxi drove us through the overcrowded streets to our hotel on Ocean Drive, I regretted even thinking about Mike Mike, because even the mere mention of his name could ruin my mood.

"Y'all go grab a drink. I'll go check us in." Jazz hurriedly jumped out of the cab as the non-English taxicab driver swerved up to the curb. With my face glued to the window like a true tourist, I was floored by the abundance of gay pride flags that waved up and down the strip. It's like we drove into the Crayola color explosion. As the bellhop of the Clevelander met us on the curb to help with our luggage, we slid out of the cab in awe at what we'd been sucked into.

"What the fuck? It's raining rainbows." Roxy's expression was one of pure repulsion and disappointment. "Yeah, Jazz really got me good. This ain't even cool."

By this time, Jazz had disappeared through the revolving doors of the brightly lit, busy hotel. Even though Roxy was complaining and finding every excuse possible to hate on how turned up the gay, lesbian, bisexual, and transgender (GLBT) community were, I had to admit they were representing for their belief and had my vote for support.

"Oh, you can leave my bag in the trunk of that taxi, sir." She stomped over to the confused-looking bellhop, who followed her orders and released her bag's strap. "This right here ain't even for me."

"Oh, so, you didn't know about it being Gay Pride Week? This weekend wraps it." He chuckled as if she weren't the first foolish girl of the day to be discouraged about what the city had to offer with the GLBT's being out, but when Roxy cut her eyes at him with brashness, he quickly swallowed his laughter.

"That's a dumb-ass question to ask. Does it look like it?" Giving him the "dumb look" face and starting to raise her voice, I could tell the bellhop was only backing down because he was dressed in a uniform with a badge, on the clock, and working. Even I could see she was testing her limits, but with Roxy, she was always set on go.

"Whoa, baby girl, you can chill coming on me like that. It's cool. I'll leave your bags right where they sit. Hey, ma," he waved for me as I stood to the side, watching and waiting on their explosion, "point out your bags so I can do my job." His nerves had worn thin with Roxy, and I couldn't blame him. He didn't owe her shit and was only out here trying to make his cash.

"It's the purple bags," I called out. "And you can bring hers too, even though she's acting all grumpy and shit. Roxy, get your stubborn acting ass over here now." Even though she was grown and entitled to her right to an opinion and clown session, I couldn't let the bellhop get caught up in her fury.

"Why you tell him to get my bags?" She stomped back over to me with folded arms acting real childish.

"Because we're on vacation with a room reserved here at the Clevelander. You might as well live it up and not let a little gay pride ruin your plans to party."

"Okay, maybe I'm crazy." Roxy looked around dumbfounded like she could've been seeing something more than what I was taking in. "It's men posing as chicks, women loving every minute of the impersonations, and a kaleidoscope of colors. My motherfucking head is hurting, just having my eyes opened out here." Sliding her knockoff Tom Ford sunglasses down over her eyes, Roxy was overly dramatic, and I couldn't wait for Jazz to come out here and give her what she had coming. Up to this point, my girl was out here stunting and performing for everyone out here willing to watch.

"Well, that would be one way to describe it." I scanned the streets full of rainbow flags, posters, banners, and couples wearing their gayness with pride. It was true we weren't expecting the event to be so grand and spectacular, but at this point, all I could say was . . . It is what it is.

"Okay, then . . . So he can leave my bags be, and the fare can keep running."

I couldn't take it anymore. The tantrum was too much. Having to be checked and brought back down to earth, I immediately took charge of the awkward situation. "Quit all of that, Roxy. That nigga don't know you no different from the next bitch in the street. Don't make his day all bad 'cause you've got a problem with Jazz." Being truthful with my girl, I didn't really want to see her making a fool of herself to this innocent brother, who looked good, by the way. "And if you looking for a big dick to ride while we're down here, you might want to play it cool and not further embarrass yourself. He could be the perfect fuck buddy candidate while we're down here," I nudged and winked at her, trying to cool the situation.

"Here's your bag, sweetheart." He set my luggage down on my side. "I don't want no problems, so just say the word, and I'm on it." He looked at Roxy, and she followed my advice and took it easy on him.

"Fuck it. I'm too far locked into this vacation and away from home. Go on and bring the bags." When he returned, she apologized, not wanting to look like a common fool. But deep down inside, I knew Roxy was boiling and regretted her decision to come. "My bad. It ain't nothing personal, playa. I shouldn't have cut into you like that," she humbled herself, apologizing for her out-of-line outburst. Proud that she had taken a cop, I patted her on the back for encouragement and reassurance.

"It's cool. I'm not even tripping." His tight lips said one thing, but his mean mug told another. With Roxy being so caught up in her emotions, she didn't peep his look of disdain for her presence and continued with her rant.

"Shiiiit, this is some motherfucking bullshit, Sable. Tell Jazz's behind I'm at the bar," Roxy screamed, turning away from the bellhop, even though he hadn't walked away. "I was trying to get boo'ed up on this vacation. But it looks like that won't be happening. Wait until she brings her sneaky ass back out here." Snatching her rollaway luggage, huffing and puffing her way toward the crowded bar, I was left speechless with the taxi driver and bellhop standing in my face.

"Oh shit, here." I dug in my purse for two twenties and waited for my change. Offering him three dollars for a tip, he snatched it angrily like that wasn't enough.

"Hey, yo, wait up." It was my turn to act a Detroit fool to show him to be a little more appreciative. "Do you need me to give you more of a tip?" I asked honestly and wanting an honorable response in return.

"Ah, yes. This cheap. I drive you all the way from airport and lug you bags in and out. You girls chitchat and laugh too loud. Yes, I need more tip." The Indian driver must've had his head wrapped too tight.

"Give me back my money." I snatched my three singles from his hand. "That's your *job* to tote bags and drive bad bitches all day, you greedy, salmonella-infested, chicken-smelling fool. You signed up to do this shit."

"Rude b—" Taking one look at the bellhop swell up, he backed down in his words and stance. Wanting to call me a bitch or worse than that, I'm sure a black bitch, me and the bellhop were going to have to take turns stomping this sandal-wearing sucker into the ground. Making a better judgment call, he turned and walked back toward his cab, not uttering a single solitary word.

"Good looking," I acknowledged his strong backing and continued to stare until the rude prick drove away.

"Oh, it's nothing. But you and your girls have brought some ra-ra to the city. Where y'all from?"

Detroit," I blushed, realizing he'd seen nothing but going ham since the cab pulled up a few minutes ago. I couldn't take a cop, 'cause, real talk, this probably wouldn't be our first, second, or last confrontation while down here.

"Yeah, I should've known. Every time I run into some chicks from the D, they be cutting up and clowning."

"Is that so? You could be right." If not, I sure wasn't in the place to be defensive. He just witnessed me being petty and rowdy over three measly dollars. But my point was the principle, so whatever. Let's move on.

"Oh, I know I am." His confidence was shining through, reminding me of Mike Mike.

"Hey, babe, what's your name?"

"Tyrell." Turning toward the hotel, peeping his head over an oversized statue, I could only assume he was checking to see if his managers were watching. "I'm on duty till five."

"Nice meeting you, Tyrell. I'm Sable, and that's Roxy. Ole girl who ran inside is Jazz, and we're the disorderly bad girls staying at your hotel this weekend." I stuck out my hand for him to shake. He smiled, taking it pleasantly, and kissing it gently. If Mike Mike could see another man touching me right now, he'd kill us both on sight—no questions asked, and no remorse felt afterward.

"Anything I can do for you, sweetheart, just let me know." He was debonair and courteous, very handsome with what seemed to be a laid-back personality. If things weren't so complicated in my life right now, I'd be checking for him. Being just my type, well-groomed and hardworking, if nothing more, he could've been a one-night stand while here.

Glad he brought it up. I couldn't wait to use his generosity as a crutch. "Well, I'm sorry to ask so soon and excuse me if I'm being too up front, but where can we get some Kush from?" Not wanting to get caught up with airport security, I was forced to smoke up all my stash at home and take this trip with the possibility of not having any marijuana to start, proceed, continue, and end my day. My nerves were already in a funk, and I was itching to get my lips wrapped around a blunt. I felt relaxed as he smiled the All-American, "Oh, you smoke" expression or another, "Yeah, you're a Detroit girl" grin.

"That's not too up front for a dealer to hear," he chuckled, turning to walk toward where Jazz was now coming from. "I've gotta get back to work, but trust, I've got you." Even though his words were like music to my ears, I didn't know why a dealer would be working as a bellhop, but whatever. As long as he came through with his promise on the weed, it wasn't any of my business. I was a true fiend to the weed, and even though admitting it was the first step to recovery, I wasn't searching for the strength to quit. It was a problem I desired and happily welcomed into my life.

With that, I joined Roxy at the bar as she nursed her anger with a Long Island. I could feel her pain but not enough for it to ruin my vacation. Jazz had stopped Tyrell in his tracks, walking back from talking with me. Only exchanging a few words before continuing on, I'd summed the situation up as irrelevant and moved on trying to flag the waitress down. This would be my first drink in South Beach, and with the small drama that had occurred so far, it was safe to assume I'd be living with a bottle the next seventy-two hours.

"Hey, boos." Jazz walked up with a bright smile on her face, and Mardi Gras beads flowing around her neck.

"Don't 'Hey, boo' me, bitch. You set us up," Roxy yelled, bringing attention our way. "I'm strictly dickly around all this gay bullshit."

"Lower your voice and quit being so disrespectful. I know you don't get down like that, but I do . . . so be cool." Jazz waved for the bartender before looking at me for assistance. But what could I say? "Why are you acting like you didn't know about gay pride?" she quizzed Roxy.

"I knew, but damn, this right here is way more than I could've been paid to imagine." Roxy was honest and sounded sincere.

"Okay, well—I wasn't about to have an introductory seminar on being around gay people or pride events," she taunted Roxy. "If it were something you felt unsure about or whatever the case might be . . ." Jazz waved her hand in the air with the most *"sister, girl, please, you better say it"* attitude Sable had ever witnessed her girl imitate. "You should've asked or looked it up online. Everybody has Google." Not wanting to seem foolish like Roxy, I kept quiet about not expecting what was on display either and played the role of an agreeable, caught-in-the-middle friend. However, I was caught off guard just as much as Roxy, if not more.

"Whatever, Jazz. Clue a bitch in, like I said. You know me and Sable don't get down like that and ain't about to be researching no rituals or traditions," she truthfully spoke, even though now my eyes were wide open. A change was coming or had arrived, so I was ready to live in it.

"Okay, maybe I should've, could've, would've, but I fucked up and didn't. Let it go while we're here, and let's just enjoy our vacation as planned," she pleaded as the waitress returned with our drinks. I could tell Jazz wasn't backing down because she genuinely felt some guilt. She didn't want her birthday weekend ruined over something petty and preventable.

"Fuck it. I'll chill out and try to have a decent time." She still looked exasperated but was trying to be a good sport. I'd seen my girl in rare form, so I knew Jazz was getting off tremendously easy.

"Thank you. I appreciate it and owe you both one," she cheered to us both, but I didn't need none of the reassurance like Roxy. This vacation wasn't long enough to be giving all this energy and time to not wanting to be here. Downing my drink, ready to experience what everyone around me seemed to be captivated in, the warm kickback of the rum, tequila, vodka, and gin in the Long Island had me twisted up already. "Let's hurry up and finish these drinks so we can hit the streets and get thick in this festival."

"Hold up now. Can we get dressed first? This might not be my type of crowd, but you know I must keep it fly, regardless." Roxy was right. Most importantly, I had to get my Nike bag to a safe place.

The Clevelander was on point. Of course, I'd been in more luxurious hotels, but never one solely dedicated to partying. With it being in the center of everything, the nightclub scene appeared to be twenty-four hours a day. We could live in paradise and never step foot out of the hotel. They had a pool and patio on the ground floor, plus a rooftop terrace, deck, lounge, and sports bar. But for damn near three hundred a night, it was expected to be a deluxe stay with supreme amenities.

"Wow, this hotel is slamming." Roxy's attitude appeared to be improving. Even though this week and its end were dedicated to the gay and lesbian community, there were a few cute guys and couples that weren't into the life either.

Even though we wanted to chill and take in the vibe of our hotel, Jazz was busy rushing us toward the double queen suite for us to get dressed and back to the festival. "Girl, you should've booked us a room at a Quality Inn or some low-budget shit like that. Why pay all this money to have the party scene at our doorsteps not to enjoy it?" I secretly wanted to kick back and chill in the lobby. It seemed like all the straight folks reserved their deluxe stay here.

"Because it's my birthday, and I want to be with my people in the streets, celebrating our freedom to live out in the open. And they'll have the hot tickets to tonight's shows, I'm sure." Keeping up with her quick steps, we bypassed the sports bar of loud music and the clanking of beer glasses and went into our oceanfront double suite.

I wouldn't describe the room as being overly elegant or designed to the extreme. It was simple and chic, with its layout of fresh white linen and breathtaking views of the Atlantic Ocean. I was expecting a little more flash to the room since everything else around here was gaudy and meant to grandstand. But with the flat-screen, high-definition television and the rain showerhead, which I was dying to experiment with, I guess it would do, especially since Jazz intended to drag us all over this city, starting right now. I loved my girl. She was the most fun out of all of us.

Jazz, having been in tune with standing out in a crowd and not being sensitive about judgment, was always willing to try new things. Roxy was the feistiest of us three but could always be counted on to have our backs in a fight or disagreement. Many times we've ridden down on a group of supposed "tough-tone chicks" with bats or broken bottles in hand. My contribution was to be the laid-back one of the group, and with the two strong personalities Jazz and Roxy interjected into our clique, they needed me to mediate inner beefs and keep us all working on one accord.

"Hurry up, Sable. Let's not keep the birthday girl waiting." Jazz came from the quick two-minute ho bath she was taking in the bathroom. I'm sure she was getting ready to squeeze her plump behind into some skimpy type of material that was too revealing and too small for her thick curves.

"Mike Mike ain't here, so it won't be no slow-dragging bullshitting going on fa'sho." I shot a quick move behind her for the shower, ready to relax and zone out for a few. My clothes were laid out across the 300-thread count bedding that I couldn't wait to drown in after our first drunken night.

"You better not be. I'll be twenty-two at midnight, and I'm not wasting any time on either one of you two slowpokes." Jazz stepped into one of the many mirrors and slid into a pair of too short booty shorts with rips and studs.

Slamming the door and turning the water on full blast at a cool temperature, I slid my clothes off, leaving them in a pile on the granite-like tiled floor. The rainfall relaxed every nerve and muscle in my worked-up body. Stepping underneath the massaging flow, I allowed the water to run through my thirty-inch, deep-wave Brazilian weave. I loved the curls when they were wet and wavy, and since I was in Miami, what better way to rock my hair? After rubbing my body over with the Jergens cherry-almond soap, I made sure to take my time on each nook and cranny. Fuck what ya heard . . . wasn't nothing fly about a thick girl with a body odor. I was on a strict schedule. I finished up and hurried out to dry off and get dressed. Checking my phone again, I saw that Mike Mike hadn't called. I was thankful 'cause I'm pretty sure he'd be throwing some salt in my game otherwise.

Chapter Nine

Sable

The streets were lined with colorful floats from the parade, decorated vehicles, walking groups, and vendors all down for the cause of celebrating and advocating for gay pride and unity. I'd never seen anything like it. If strength is in numbers, Jazz and her people were holding it down. Between the live bands, potent drinks, and all-around hippie vibe, I hadn't regretted being tricked down here one bit. We walked the block, stopping and collecting trinkets from the interesting organizations. They were giving out free passes to clubs, coupons, and discounts at local restaurants, and you already know we loaded up.

"Hey, pretty ladies, come let me talk to you over by this table," a Jamaican guy with Ray-Bans approached us out of the crowd. He didn't look to be a part of the GLBT community, but nevertheless, here we were.

"Off rip, y'all looking lovely today," he eyed us three, taking our hands each individually and kissing them.

"What do you want, dude? Whatever you're selling, we ain't buying," Roxy rudely responded. My girl definitely needed a downer. Her being uptight made me wonder what was up with that bellhop's hookup and why we hadn't seen him since.

"I can bet you do, pretty lady." Turning his attention from her toward Jazz and me, we were all into whatever presentation he had planned. "Where are y'all partying tonight?"

"Probably one of these free joints we got passes to," Jazz spoke up. Jazz was still looking salty as I was still caught up in the hype of everything going on around us. The public display of same-sex affection still had me tripping out.

"Oh, no no no, pretty ladies. Here." He handed us each a sexy flyer for a party boat called *Sunrise*. "This is the place you three should be in tonight. I can guarantee it." As we scanned the flyer for details, he went to what I called fast-talking us in circles. "For one hundred dollars each, you'll ride the party bus with unlimited liquor and get on board the *Sunrise* boat to swim and really have fun. For an extra hundred each, you'll get a cabin on the boat, fully stocked."

"Whoa, playa. I knew you were on some straight bull-shit. Gon' on with that." Roxy got tough, straight D girl all the time.

"Chill me, lady. Hey, ma, tell ya girl to relax." He looked at me for support and sympathy. I tried to ignore him and continue reading the flyer. The boat seemed to go all night from 8:00 p.m. to 8:00 a.m.

"She ain't gotta tell me nothing." Roxy's hand flew up to stop any words I possibly had coming for her. "Explain why we should pay your ratchet ass off the streets and not know if we'll ever see you again? Who knows if what you're saying is true?" She had a point, and Jazz verbally agreed. None of us had been to Miami to know if this was even customary. In the Motor City, that shit would be a no-brainer Hell No!

"I'll give you my phone number." He waved his late-model refurbished cell.

"Burn out," Roxy rolled her eyes, continuing to go hard, not giving the dude an opportunity to get his second wind.

"Okay, look, can we pay you when the party bus picks us up?" We tried to negotiate, not wanting to be scammed out of our cash.

"No no no." He threw his hands up, backing away from the table. "I'm telling you right now, *Sunrise* is the spot to be at, even when these motherfuckers ain't here," he waved to the parade. "No disrespect 'cause with them coming for the after-party, it's a guaranteed sellout. But it ain't a girl club like it." He stood back over us, pressing for an on-the-spot decision.

By now, Jazz had done a Google search on the *Sunrise* boat and was moments away from pulling her share out of her purse. Thoroughly impressed with the photos and reviews, she passed the phone to me for a second approval. I was down to make my girl happy as an added bonus for keeping my secret.

"But, Jazz, how do you know this dude ain't gonna rip us off still? That club can be nice and all, but we can just go on our own," Roxy relentlessly shot down giving this hustler any play whatsoever.

"Look, ma, I ain't no thief, and it ain't no way you're gonna get a deal like this nowhere else. Take it or leave it, but real talk, this is what I do. I'm a party promoter—one of the best, you better believe." Standing back with his hands crossed, I felt he meant business, but just like Roxy, I had my reservations.

"All right, I'm in," I finally broke the ice. Jazz was staring at us both, waiting on one of us to give in. Going into my purse, I could feel Roxy watching me with cold eyes. I was the monkey stuck in the middle.

"Roxy, you can fall back. We're getting a party bus, boat ride, pool party, a cabin, and bar time, not to mention unlimited liquor—we really can't beat it," I finally pitched his calling card for him. Pulling eight crisp one hundred-dollar bills out of my backpack and sliding it across the table, I'd sealed the deal for us to party all night long. The glare in Roxy's eyes was nothing but hate.

"Well, if Mike Mike gave you that money to floss boss down here, then fuck it. I'm gonna ride that bus with you." She hunched her shoulders, giving me more attitude.

"What hotel are you pretty ladies at?" the promoter asked, now more upbeat and sliding my cash into his pocket with dancing eyes.

"The Clevelander."

"Cool. The party bus will be arriving tere around six thirty or seven. Be in the lobby and ready. Call when you're down tere." He was strict with his directions. "This part is serious, pretty ladies. If you're not on time, we *will* leave." Roxy rolled her eyes at his words, but Jazz and I understood and vowed to be on time.

We decided to slide by the infamous Wet Willie's before heading back to the hotel. With only a few hours before the planned boat cruise, there was only a little time to kill mingling with others on the strip. Even though the gay and lesbian crowd was in the spot, there were still groups like us hanging around looking for trouble. Grabbing a table and ordering a Call-A-Cab, I checked my phone for the first time, seeing Mike Mike had just called. With only one missed call and no messages, I guessed that he hadn't realized he was now broke as a joke.

Jazz nudged me. "Sis, everything good?"

"Yeah, I was just seeing if Mike Mike called." I played it off, noticing Roxy checking her phone but listening with all ears. I wasn't ready for her to be in what Jazz and I privately shared, especially with her attitude still being so up and down.

"You might want to call and check for that nigga. If he were my man, I wouldn't be letting him dangle. Chicks around my area always spitting game his way. Mike Mike stock always high as hell," Roxy spoke up, letting me know for certain she was all ears.

"Oh, straight-up? Well, I ain't worried about them home-wrecking hoes. I got that comeback, so it's nothing. But I hope you cut into them thirsty McMuffin-eating broads you call neighbors."

"That's on you. He ain't my man or cashing out so I can pop tags, so, hell naw. I ain't about to start no beef where I lay my head. Like I said, you better check for your man."

"I got it, boo, and I've got shit with Mike Mike under control too. What's been really eating me up, however, is your funky-ass disposition. Why do you keep cutting into Jazz and me with that grim attitude like you've got a problem with us?"

Roxy looked stunned, caught off guard, or either surprised I'd called her out on her stank behavior. Enough was enough, though, and I didn't want our trip ruined any longer.

"Fuck y'all and that tag-team shit. I'm straight and been that way the whole time." Shrugging her shoulders and sipping her drink in an attempt to play me like a fool, I shook my head, done with the conversation.

"Girl, bye. I've gotta go pee some of this liquor out. Be real by the time I get back." Leaving Jazz to fill her in on the obvious, I dipped out to the bathroom to handle my business.

Chapter Ten

Carla

"What in the entire hell. Your fucking cell is ringing again," I could hear Gianna calling from the front room. Getting my bag of clothes for the boat ride, I must've been tripping to leave my phone unattended around her. What was I thinking? And why wasn't it silenced in the first place? Snatching up the suitcase and the Ziploc bag of pills, I ran up the small hallway, trying to get to both and my incriminating phone.

"Hello." Turning toward me with a devilish grin, I watched her answer my phone to whoever was about to determine how our afternoon would play out. If it were some jump-off, she'd be ready to fight and rip a mud hole in my ass. With her already buzzing off ecstasy and Kush, the repercussions would most certainly be severe.

"Why are you always cutting in on our personal time, bro? It's not enough that you'll be cruising with my girl all night? You've gotta be calling all day too?" Gianna's disposition was nothing to be fucked with, snapping at any given moment. When it came to me, she had no limits. Realizing it wasn't another girl on the line, I backed down and chilled, letting her go hard on my business partner.

"Here," she tossed the phone toward me, grabbing her Gucci purse. Standing near the door, tapping her foot, being impatient, she waited on me to make one false move before going crazy. "Your business is always ruining our quality time," she huffed as I answered the phone to see what was up.

"Aye, Madame Ma, I filled up your reserved seats," my Jamaican promoter started babbling before I had a chance to turn down the volume.

"That's good," I nodded, thinking of how well he worked. On any given day, he could find the baddest broads for my eye-viewing pleasure. "I knew I could count on you and your street crew to make it happen."

"No doubt, that's fa'sho. I'm going to do my job 100 percent of the time. Me loves the cash."

"Fa'sho, playa. We all do, and a filled-to-capacity boat is like the dessert topping on a cake." He laughed, knowing I couldn't wait to fuck around with a few of the sweets partying on the *Sunrise* tonight. He knew my style and what flavor I preferred and would seek out honeys I'd like. Not only was I into making money hand over fist, but also doing a few taste tests didn't hurt. Most people couldn't handle having their cake and eating it too. I just didn't fit in that category.

"Hey, Boss, me not want no trouble from the ladies you don't think fit status quo. The last time you turned a girl away, her whole posse went straight hella ham on me." I grinned, remembering the isolated event. With me, it didn't happen on many occasions, but across South Beach, Miami, if you weren't a diva or paper-thin with a pretty face—you were denied entry into clubs or the most happening scenes.

"They oughta have their shit tight right then. You already know how I get down, but since you have the knack for picking the cream of the crop, everything should be a straight go." I kept it real with him knowing I'd deny a bold bitch entry or amenities in a minute. Fuck being nice. In my world, people would cut me with a knife and stab me in the back without thinking twice or second-guessing. So every man on their own—fuck a hurt feeling.

Pissed, Gianna watched me. It was written all over her face. But business was business, and if I said it once, I'd said a million times—ain't no ho slowing my go. Part of the reason I was gay is that I didn't like the control, muscle-throwing cockiness a man presented or brought to the table. With women, I floated the boat and would drown a bitch for jumping ship or making it rock. Once I claimed you, I owned you. You can call me Stevie J. pimping hoes, but whatever the case, Gianna was the exception to my rule.

"Sheesh, girl, it's harder working for you than a man." I could believe this to be true. "I'll catch up with you on the boat in a few, lady."

"Yup, in a few." Hanging up, I silenced the sound on my phone before stuffing it into my white cargo shorts pocket. "Open the door and bring that ass." I waved at Gianna to push on with the attitude so we could catch lunch.

Traffic was triple thick in South Beach, with it being a Friday, lunchtime, and a gay pride event. Gianna was riding shotgun for me. I kept cool in the bumper-to-bumper traffic with the windows up and air conditioner on bang. I was intrigued and impressed with this year's layout, and if luck served me right, *Sunrise* would be a sellout. Once Gianna was fed and full, I'd drop her off immediately so I could get to the boat.

"Carla, can the girls and I get a free cabin tonight?" She reached over to rub my thigh, but I'd smashed that earlier. Right now, it was played. "We trying to party right for pride too," she devilishly smiled. The look on her face was serious, but her stupidity was priceless. Her partying with me was a definite no-go.

"Hell naw, Gianna, you know that shit ain't happening." I laughed, not caring if my words hurt her feelings. "But them cabins better had been cleaned right." Ignoring anything else in regards to doing favors and running charity cases, I jumped out of my Lexus and tossed the attendant my keys. She climbed out heated—ready to cause a scene. If she didn't slow her roll quickly, Gianna only had cab fare coming. I didn't play that public embarrassment shit, and she knew that. Throwing my hand up to silence her, I pulled out some flyers to give the doorman and valet attendants.

"Ugh. I hate that boat with a passion, I swear." Gianna smacked her lips while twisting up her adorable face. As I watched her long legs and firm ass stomp up the stairs, even her body couldn't mask her ghetto-girl attitude. "Come on. Damn." She turned back, watching with disdain.

"Look, Gianna, you better chill on that fucking mouth, ma. You know good and damn well I ain't for that ra-ra girl shit. Me and you eat off that boat, and if you don't like it, quit." Catching up with her, I smacked her on the behind with aggression in an attempt to get her in line.

"Whatever, Carla, I ain't scared. We can't smoke or pop pills here, baby, so you ain't doing shit." She switched off to the bar, leaving me steaming, ready to snatch her sew-in out. It was taking everything in me not to leave her smart-talking ass here.

Finding us a seat near the balcony, I scoped out the girls next to me, suddenly wishing I'd hit this venue alone. They looked to be out of towners, having the eager eye to catch all of what's going on. Gianna had that same look of excitement when I first picked her up too. The light-skinned, jazz-haired chick caught my eye first. Meant to be the one who stands out in her two live crew, she was the loudest, boldest, and happiest—dancing around the table ordering rounds of drinks. She wasn't my type but was fun to watch.

Gianna

Carla was starting to get on my last fucking nerve. Always promoting that damn party boat and checking for new pussy like I was stupid. No fool here—just a girl that loves the high of drugs. How dare she not look out for my crew and me? For me to be her girl, that was mad foul and disrespectful. Out of anybody, I should've been the one partying lavishly, getting the royal treatment.

Ordering a Bob Marley, I watched Carla lose focus on me and start scanning the room. I'd already peeped a bar full of women and regretted whining to come here. With it being Gay Pride Weekend, she could have her choice of any swimsuit-wearing female in here. When she found herself entertaining a table of two uninteresting broads, I fought back the urge to remind her of my presence. But when some brown-skinned wannabe Barbie doll ho walked up commanding her attention full throttle, my jealousy couldn't be contained.

Getting our drinks from the waitress, I tossed my twenty onto the counter and stormed toward Carla. I noticed the stack of passes in her hand, and my anger smoldered. How dare she be treating these skeezers but putting me and mine on the back burner?

Carla

"You and your homegirl should come dance on the party boat tonight," I interrupted their girl talk to pass them both a flyer. Light Skin took it with no problem, but her friend wasn't so pleasant, turning her face up, rejecting my advertisement. I got too much pussy to give a fuck about her shade, so I ignored baby girl, as requested.

"Oh my God, Roxy." She shook her head in disbelief at her friend. "Don't mind her. For some reason, that ass has been tripping." Snapping her neck toward her friend while talking to me, I could tell ole girl was upset about Light Skin, putting her on blast.

"Oh, you can trust I ain't." Making it perfectly clear that her friend meant nothing to my game plan or how I ran business, I continued. "Look, I can throw y'all down to get a bottle at the party. All the VIP spots are sold out." They were both cute, but ole girl's pissy attitude almost made them irrelevant. I didn't want to dis them, and Light Skin was a party girl, so I kept with my original intentions on inviting them.

"Do VIP guests get bottles at the party too?" she eagerly quizzed, continuing to flip it over.

"Yeah, they get everything our boat has to offer, ma. So you want me to list you down for that bottle or what?" Trying to move along, I didn't know why they were wasting my time checking for sold-out seats. I didn't refund money to those who already cashed out, and for the evil one, I most definitely wasn't breaking any rules.

"Oh well, then we're tight right, and you can go. My girl got us VIP tickets earlier," this Roxy chick bossed up again, begging me to acknowledge her. My luck with mouthy hoes had been going way west today. "Speaking of my girl, here she comes."

Pleasantly pleased, I turned to see another friend joining them who was stunning and sexy. As she brushed past me to sit down, her Beyoncé Heat perfume lingered underneath my nose. My eyes danced all over her body, turning at every curve.

"Y'all ready to go, or what? Quit nursing that fucking slush, and let's dip." Plopping her phat ass down into the cheap plastic lawn chair, she looked up at me and smiled politely. "Hey, now, I'm Sable."

Reaching over to take her hand, I rubbed it gently, loving how smooth her skin felt. "Carla." My radar didn't go off, but she seemed to be utterly comfortable with me holding and kissing her hand.

"Carla was just about to go back to her table and business. She was trying to pitch a free bottle when we've already bought the boat." Roxy threw her arm over Sable's shoulder, glaring at me.

"Roxy was actually rude as fuck, but that's only my opinion," Light Skin jumped in to defend me.

"Naw . . . What's rude is this bitch making googly eyes over here with you hoes." Gianna was now standing beside me, sipping her drink and passing me mine. From the tone in her voice, I knew she was about to set trip.

"Yeah, so, Carla, so what the fuck? What's good? You done with these rats, or what?" Looking them over closely, I wasn't impressed, which ticked me off even more. I was a redbone with hazel-brown eyes. This clown crew didn't compare. They looked around at each other to question if I'd just cut into them like that—and, yup, the truth was real.

Chapter Eleven

Sable

"Damn, what did I miss?" I looked around the table and saw that all three of us were caught off guard.

"Well, let me catch y'all crazy asses up to speed." She got grim and began yakking off at the mouth. I didn't care what ole girl was talking about. I was about to be gunning for her head. "This right here is all me," she pointed at Carla. "So y'all thirsty ass can be gone."

"Hey, Carla," Roxy shouted out. "I told you to get gone. Now, you've got your broad's feelings hurt." Knowing my girl and that hysterical laughter she was filling the bar with—crunch time was near. Roxy and I were the firecrackers, and Jazz was the cheerleader.

"Stop it. I ain't for the games, so just check the bullshit and stay away from this one." The girl was going hard, proving to be a head-to-head matchup for Roxy.

"Quit with all that talking and do something." I stood up now eye to eye with this skinny chick, ready to go toe for blow. "Either pop off or get the fuck on. You ain't fucking with us. I'm telling ya ass now—you don't want none."

"Whoa, chill out, baby girl." Carla threw her hands up, trying to pull her girl back from her initiated conversation. The girl kept getting tough, talking shit behind her girlfriend barricade. I hadn't come all the way to palm trees and sunny skies to beat a bitch down, but I wasn't backing up either.

"Let me go, babe. I'm about to claw up that floozy's face. I'm ready to pop you, crispy bitch." As Carla pulled her back, I kept walking up on her. With Jazz and Roxy bringing up the tail end, we were a force to be reckoned with. Crowds were no longer fighting for the bartender's attention but circling us, waiting on a fight.

At first, I kept taunting her, laughing while she juiced her ego up, going ham on me. Mike Mike had assured I could take a beat-down, and compared to him, she was nothing. Her bony ass wasn't in my weight class, but her mouth was running a marathon. When the time was right, I was gonna pounce on this tramp and make her regret the day she ever stepped foot to a pedigree of my nature. "Gon' keep talking," I nodded, taking off my earrings, tossing them back to Jazz. "By the time I slow walk you through here, they're gonna be naming a drink after my pretty ass." Spectators giggled, but I'd come to the end of my jokes.

Carla kept trying to calm ole girl down, but once a dog is off its leash, it's hard to tame it back. She was going, and I couldn't blame her. Carla was flirting, and I was accepting. But I wasn't the one to confront, and besides, she'd caught me on a bad day.

"Back up, Carla. I've got this." Shoving her girlfriend out of the way was the second-to-worse mistake she'd made after approaching us.

"Bitch, you ain't tough. Let's get boogie." With full force and strength, I rushed Carla's girl, taking my forearm to her throat as we collided against a table, knocking it over. People jumped up, drinks toppled over, and fists flew. Instantly, I went in on beating her face in like Mike Mike had done me so many times before. Seeing red, I popped her upside the head a few more times before catching two sneak shots to the stomach.

"Roxy, snatch that ho," Jazz screamed as I grabbed my stomach, taking another blow to the chest. She was trying to fight back, but with my weight more than hers, it was too much.

"One on one. Nobody touch nobody." I'm assuming that was Carla who shouted out, but there wasn't time to figure it out. Ole girl was starting to swing and swim crazily, things chicks do when they're frantically clawing for a win. Grabbing my hair, pulling my sew-in slightly loose, I turned and punched her square in the mouth twice. Now, using both hands to cover her bloody mouth, my opportunity to finish her off was near. Using all of my strength, I pushed her forehead backward, making her head grind into the cement.

"Get this slut off me," she spat out blood as I snuck her in the eye before using my knee to prop myself up on her titty.

"Fuck, you scared now, huh?" Provoking her, I stood up and looked down at my now-ruined sundress. Jazz was helping me regain my composure, but Roxy wanted to be tagged in. The girl was too busy getting paper towels to aid her wounds to notice my girl sneak her from behind, pouring the rest of her slush all over her. I burst out laughing loudest as the purple, cold, icy liquor slid down her white bikini top and low-waist shorts. Ole girl threw her hands up and screamed in disgust. Roxy dared her to jump twice or even look like she wanted to jump tough.

Carla stood to the side, staring at me with a look I couldn't place. If she wanted some for me whopping her girl down, hell, she could get some too. Posing like a stud or not, I've been battling a street nigga for the crown nightly. Remembering my purse, I shot to our table immediately with my heart pounding, nearly dropping to the floor. That girl wasn't nearly as important as the weight in my bag. Snatching it up, vowing to never part from it again, I turned to see Carla behind me on my heels.

"So ya girl told me y'all was VIP on the *Sunrise* tonight. I'll check for your sexy ass there later." She crossed the line again. With her steaming girlfriend across the room still staring like she wanted some, I leaned in and hugged Carla like we had been acquainted for years. Pressing my breasts into her body and leaning my face into her neck, my intentions were to mock ole girl, but it actually sparked a flame in me.

"Oh, please do. I wasn't gay till now." I winked at her girl as Jazz giggled, grabbing her purse. Roxy was still standing by ole girl waiting on a response, and as she waved at us to go, you could tell she'd become bored with the nonsense. Dismissing everyone in Wet Willie's but my girls, I walked toward the exit. Carla was following me with her eyes, and I was enjoying the feel of her stare. Once Jazz and I were alone, I'd have to question her about this.

"You know if I want, I'll fuck yo' girl," I shouted out as we finally got to the top of the stairs. Carla laughed and shifted all the heat to herself, where it should have been in the first place. My girls and I darted out of the infamous bar without a buzz but had a lot of adrenaline to burn.

"Blaze that blunt up, Sable. I'm out here with some whatever they are getting fronted off and shit. No disrespect 'cause y'all all my girls, but, damn. First, Jazz, and now you. It fa'damn sure won't be me."

Even though she had a funky way of putting it, Roxy had a point. Miami was off to a rocky start, and I needed it to get better for me—fast.

Carla

"Gianna, bring your motherfucking ass on." I twisted her arm, yanking her toward the stairs so we could haul ass out of here. Getting my name or image caught up in the middle of a bar brawl wasn't a good look for the reputation I'd created for myself in the streets.

"Fuck you, Carla. I'm not going anywhere with you," she shouted, making the crowd that had started to dissipate redirect their attention toward us.

"Look, if you don't calm down and bring your jealous ass on down these stairs, you're going to regret it." I spoke without a doubt, already moving down a few steps to give my ticket to the valet. If I could get her alone, I'd dope her up with some of the more potent shit in my suitcase. Planning to experiment with it later, she could be my tester right now. It was supposed to get the erotic side of a person aroused. There was open and willing pussy floating around this time of year, but I needed to boost them up for extra fun. If the dope could put her in more of a tranquil state, we'd be back to normal.

"I ain't going nowhere with your disrespectful ass. You don't think I deserve better than some used up, old-head lesbian tearing me down?" Gianna was huffing and screaming. And this point was my cue to break camp completely, making good on my word to leave her young ass in here. "And I quit."

Without tossing a tip or a few bucks Gianna's way to guarantee she made it home by cab, bus, jitney, or gas fare to a kind friend for the short notice ride, I left her with a room of nosy outsiders. “Later. I warned, youngster.”

Jazz

My birthday weekend had to be recovered. Roxy was dead-on about it being off to a horrible start. But part of the problem was her whack-ass arrogance with everyone and her salty approach toward being down here during a Gay Pride Weekend. Yeah, I’d invited my crew and probably withheld how outright and downright flaring my group of people could be. They had never been exposed to my side of the rainbow, so this trip might’ve been a little too much, particularly for my girl, Roxy. But my girls were all I had. They never judged me and never came with no bullshit about not being a fiend over the dick like them.

Men have never been my cup of tea, and I didn’t give a fuck what a spectator had to say. Having disowned my parents for not accepting my lifestyle, anyone else on the street had even less value and meant nothing when it came to kicking them to the curb. Neither Roxanne nor Sable made me feel less than human for loving girls and sometimes taking on the stud role.

Sable had played with fire, and I was partially responsible for that. Mike Mike had been whipping off into her ass, sending my girl into a spiral of negative thoughts and depression. I had grown tired of keeping her company in the hospital ’cause he’d come home from fucking “our girl” on the low. He was a monster, and for months, his secret had been safe with me. Lucky for him, I didn’t want to ruin the friendship between my girls and me. They were all I had, so if they broke up, my family would be totally dismantled.

Roxy was giving herself away, though. Not wanting to be in the middle of the drama or present myself to Sable as betraying her by withholding information, I kept my mouth closed and slowly watched the drama unfold. Since I knew about Mike Mike being a low-down, dirty dog who happened to have a slightly loaded stash, I put a bug in my girl's ear to get ghost with him for my birthday, robbing him blind in the process. Talking her out of being too terrified to reclaim her life, I persuaded my comrade to get her life and leave Mike Mike clueless. I'd promised her that my cousin would set her up straight once we got down here, but I'd been dodging her on the hookup and the mention of it since we got in town.

The truth was, Sable had already met my cousin, and he was feeling her up, trying to see if he could even fuck with her on that level. The reason for me immediately running in the hotel, leaving them outside so suddenly was to greet him inside and let him get a first impression without my persuasion. It was no thang. He was doing me a favor, so I had to play by his rules. Tyrell was fresh out of jail on probation and had to secure a job for parole purposes. Working at the Clevelander kept him in the loop and still able to make significant moves and profit. From our previous conversations, he could get Sable a new identity—Social Security number, identification, the whole works, plus set her up with some connects to keep her safe for a small fee. The only thing I hadn't worked out yet was what Plan B would be if he didn't think my friend could be trusted to withhold his name if she were tracked down. Already having three strikes, another case could send him up for a longtime bid—if not life.

On my way back to the hotel, I shot him a text to see what was up. Dreading the reply, I still tried to keep a cool attitude and enjoy the one day of the year reserved for me. With Sable treating me to outfits, accessories, shoes, and a slamming great time around so many beautiful girls, there was much to smile and live it up for.

Chapter Twelve

Sable

The bellhop had looked out. Leaving me a quarter of Loud-cough Kush and a pack of cigarillos underneath my pillow, it took me no time to fill the room with steam and have the blunt in rotation. Roxy had her iPhone in the dock on blast. With him watching our back for haters in the hotel, we blazed up and got our minds right. No matter what the situation, weed could bond us together and get our tempers back down from flare. We'd had a great time at the festival, even more so than expected, and it was time to hit the bar. Jazz and I were excited about going on the bus ride and even more so about the *Sunrise*. Roxy was still in rare form, hating every chance she got. Already promising her today would be the last of gay pride festivities, she still couldn't be a team player.

Sliding on my romper, I stepped in front of the floor-length mirror to check how it complimented my curves. It hugged every proportion just right. Over the years, my body had really filled out. The peek-a-boo cut down the center exposed a pleasant amount of cleavage, a perky rack I was very proud of. My breasts were a calling card I exposed on the regular. Even though I had a slight pouch, it was nothing 'cause I'd just suck it in for the photographs. Turning around to make sure the bottom of my cheeks weren't hanging out, I jiggled my junk and smiled at how far I'd come. I ain't gonna front, I used to be a broken-down, black, crusty-looking scallywag, but now you'd consider me to be a bad-girl-type bitch . . . long weave, expensive clothing, breasts and booty for days. Mike Mike had money and made sure my appearance was top of the line. Thanks to him, I could stunt right in Miami the way a female was supposed to.

Since hitting his pockets, leaving him for dry, I'd tried to question Jazz several times on this alleged cousin who could help me get right. She'd bragged on this dude about having top-notch plugs, a boss attitude, and enough clout in the city to make money matter. If I could get connected to him, I'd for sure be set and not have to worry about Mike Mike's wrath if he caught up to me. Jazz, however, was making me suspicious and question just how real she had been with me. If my girl came out to be a liar on the other end of this rainbow, things were bound to get ugly. Over fifty grand was on the table attached to my life.

"All right now, Sable, you look hot." Jazz looked up from her phone momentarily to compliment me. "I don't know who they're gonna be checking for more tonight, me or you," she buttered it up more. You can always count on true friends to boost you up. Now, knowing the situation with Officer Taylor from the airport, she was probably making sure my ego wasn't still in the dumps. But I was straight and had moved on, for sure.

"I was thinking about getting a romper just like that the other day," Roxy had to comment and front, always jocking my style. My girl was always doing the most—but you couldn't help who you loved. She was my girl, fake or not.

"Oh, for real, Roxy, that's what's up," I sarcastically replied. Slipping on my Red Bottom heels, I struck a bad-girl pose for the camera. Jazz was making sure I was truly feeling myself.

"Carla won't be able to take her eyes off you." Jazz brought the attention back to our conversation, already knowing how Roxy could be cut.

"Quit playing, girl. I'm not thinking about getting down with that stud Carla like that—or any girl, for that matter." Even though ole girl had crossed my thoughts a few times, something in the back of my mind was blocking the unnatural, unusual feeling.

"Girl, ain't nobody dumb. You took all that time getting ready and look good enough for me to make love to, going on a boat with a bunch of gay bitches—and you think I don't know you want to try the life? Yeah, the fuck right," she replied, pulling on the blunt again before passing it. "All I'm saying is that you could've asked me to spread your legs and break you in. You didn't have to come to Miami and find a stranger."

"First of all, freeze on that 'Sable is bisexual crap.' I just like to keep my appearance A1 and going to a lesbo party don't change that. And you know I'd let you hit any day, baby momma." I blew her a kiss, now taking my turn on the marijuana.

Jazz always joked with her girls, but we never took it seriously. She was just comfortable with her sexuality and didn't mind who knew about it.

"Naw, but for real, it's 'cause your eyes light up when you see a bad bitch like Carla," she snickered. "But it's okay to explore your other personality. Be free."

"Oh, little, innocent, sweet Sable ain't hardly gonna be checking for no girls. Not with Mike Mike on that ass," Roxy slyly smirked. "He's been blowing that phone up since Wet Willie's. Why aren't you answering, huh?"

She was too nosy and sarcastic, and I was ready to cold check her once again. I was still upset about not being able to get the problem resolved earlier. "Girl, stop it with Mike Mike. You've been bringing his ass up more than me," I said, putting her on front street. I raised my brow to let her know I'd peeped her reoccurring concern. "You checking for him or something?" I was waiting for an answer. The room went quiet as Jazz stopped taking pictures. With the phone in her lap staring at Roxy too, we both were ready to react.

"Bitch, quit playing. Y'all are like my sisters, and I don't get down like that. How could you even cut into me with some bullshit on that magnitude, Sable?" Roxy was going ham, yelling and damn near in tears. "Oh, and you can quit looking all innocent and shit, Jazz, over there cosigning, acting like you don't know me better than that too. Y'all are both foul."

"Chill out, drama queen." I kinda felt bad for drawing all of these emotions out of her. If she wasn't getting down with Mike Mike, then I've just slammed some over-the-top accusations down on my friend. However, let it be known I had my eye on her and had just made it perfectly clear my man was now a dead subject.

"Fuck a drama queen, Sable. I love y'all. Apologize," Roxy demanded with tears now coming down her cheeks. Jazz was the first to get up and hug our girl, and I hesitantly followed. Something just didn't seem right about this overly emotional behavior. She was too extra for me.

Small taps interrupted my girls and me from joking about bringing the D to the Dirty South earlier. Having only a few minor cuts and bruises, nothing about ole girl's tough-guy act was impressive. Since we weren't on ten any longer with each other or Carla and her girl, everything was back to normal and on chill mode. Looking out the peephole, I saw Tyrell, the bellhop, standing on the other side with a bottle of Moët and four glasses. Swinging the door open, he walked in greeting us all, paying extra close attention to Roxy. She smiled and greeted him back.

"Thanks, honey. I'm glad to see you're feeling better from earlier." Pouring her the first glass, he handed it over and then followed by giving Jazz and me ours. "Let's toast to you guys' first night in South Beach. What's the plan?"

"We're going on the *Sunrise* boat ride," Jazz answered him as she stood in the mirror applying makeup. "I hope it's all my manz hyped it up to be."

"Oh, snap. That bitch be rocking. Y'all got the whole party bus hookup too?"

"Oh, okay, I'm glad you heard of it. Roxy was nervous about being ripped off. We're from the Dirty D—and you just don't give your money to a wannabe promoter walking the streets."

"That's right. I feel you on that. A lot of these promoters be out here faking like they've got serious connects, but don't be having a pot to piss in. Real talk, you're lucky not to have gotten scammed. *Sunrise* promoters usually are on the up and up, though. Carla don't be for cats mixing her boat up with bad business."

"Damn, Tyrell, you know Carla too?" My eyes perked up in curiosity. I couldn't front her Gucci Guilty cologne was melted into my sundress earlier, and I loved the scent and reminder.

"Oh, baby doll, you can trust the whole city knows Carla. She's a moneymaker and fucks with only bad bitches." He downed his glass, pouring another like he wasn't wearing a uniform and badge. "It's supposed to be a drag queen show or some type of anniversary blowout tonight too. So, y'all came on the right weekend, for sure."

Tyrell and I could be cool. His swag was on top. I could hear Roxy sucking her teeth in the background, probably hating on the drag queen show idea. "Damn, too bad for you, Sable. Looks like you weren't that special. She dykes with everyone." Roxy laughed out loud.

"Hey, watch your mouth, heffa." Jazz tossed her pillow across the room, half-jokingly and half-serious. Even though she wasn't a true advocate and rally-er for the GLTB community, she was still a girl fucking a girl and didn't want the disrespect.

"I didn't know you got down like that, Sable." Tyrell looked at me, hoping I'd correct the insinuations.

"I was just having fun after scrapping it out with her girl. It wasn't nothing like that." I pranced over to my purse to pack it for the boat ride. He kept watching me with suspicion, but I couldn't match his glare. It was weird to admit to a nigga so fine I was possibly attracted to a female. Jazz had no problems with the bullshit, and I'd wondered if she ever had.

"Damn, Detroit. Y'all ain't been here less than twenty-four hours and already scrapping. I told you earlier that firecracker shit was gonna have you in trouble. Fuck that. I won't be keeping in touch and visiting you, thugs." He lay back on the bed, laughing. "Just gangsta."

Continuing to chop it up and finish the bottle of wine Tyrell had treated us with, it was close to seven and time for us to meet ole dude in the lobby. I was glad the hotel had called themselves sticking us with the only black bellhop they employed. He kept it one hundred, looking out, helping us have a good time. He'd even volunteered to pick us up from the dock in the morning, no charge, since it was on his way to work. Every lobby in each hotel on the strip doubled as a bar, restaurant, and hangout scene. The Clevelander had one of the hippest happening venues with lights, waterfalls, and a parade of people dancing to the live pop rock band. People had been partying all day, and the moonlight only brought out more drugs, more alcohol, and more intent to get into trouble. We all looked tasty and were serving it up, ready for the party bus to arrive. Even though my buzz was already on point, I'd be drinking eight-hundred worth of liquor, so it was time for the unlimited flow to start.

"Come on, y'all, let's take some more pictures." Roxy handed her phone to Tyrell. We all got up with our drinks and modeled for the camera. Losing our minds and loving our looks, we even let a few people walking by take pictures with us too. We loved to be the life of the party and the center of attention at all times.

"Tyrell, you're needed in room 101 for a checkout." His manager crept up on us, standing short and compact with his arms folded. Caught up in all our hype, we hadn't noticed him sneak up and ain't no telling how long he'd been there.

"Okay, I got that, Boss. Here," he handed Roxy's phone to him, "take this picture first, though." Not thinking twice or hesitating as if his manager had a choice but to say yes or not, he leaned in, hugging us all close to him, letting ole dude know he was ready. The expression on his face matched the thoughts on our minds. Had Tyrell the bellhop just macked his boss? He was more nut heavy than I thought.

Chapter Thirteen

Roxy

Being broke should've never been my reality. With the acting skills of a professional, I had squirmed my way out of having my cover blown up. Sable had fronted me off about sexing Mike Mike, but turning on the waterworks and laying the guilt trip on thickly left her and Jazz apologizing for their fucked-up but very true accusations. Trying to blend back in and not show my true colors, I swallowed my pride and attitude and started to take pictures with my girls, playing it off like everything was peachy cream.

Low-key though, I was burning with anger each time Sable pulled a hundred-dollar bill out, flaunting like she was a real baller. Why had Mike Mike put her on a pedestal she didn't deserve to be on? This rat was ranked first when she was no better than me—if not worse. I'd never even play around or leave it open for anyone out here breathing to think I was gay. Strictly dickly to the day I die. Mike Mike was going to regret seeing his precious gem had flown down here and forgotten she was in a relationship. Creating a mini-collage on Pic Stitch of our gay pride girls' vacation, I sent him a text of the picture and posted a few of the ones we'd just taken in the lobby on social media for my fans. I made sure to update my location and tag South Beach to make all my friends green with envy.

***

There was barely room for the girls and me to squeeze in on the jam-packed party bus. From outside, you could hear the music blasting and see shadows of people through the windows having a good time. But being in the thick of things was proving to be a totally different experience. Flat-screen televisions were mounted, three stripper poles were lined up in the center aisle, and the small bar was stacked with bottles of Cîroc, Grey Goose, Remy VSOP, and Everfresh cranberry juice. Passing me a red cup filled to the top, I didn't even question what it was before tipping it back, drinking half down.

"That's what the fuck I'm talking about. Party over here," one of the male promoters, I assumed, raised his hands dancing behind me. Not having many men to choose from on this flamboyant weekend, I backed my ass up on him to see what he was working with.

"*There's* the Roxy I know," Sable high-fived me, taking the drink from my hand as ole boy and I started to get down and dirty. Little did she know I was working out some of the aggression I'd built up from her so-called man pissing me off.

From the hard poke in my behind, I could tell ole boy was well-endowed, and a hung nigga was exactly the cure for a broken heart. The thought of a one-night stand never crossed my mind until now. With one hand firmly around my waist, keeping my prize behind close up on the imprint in his pants, he didn't have to worry about me moving anyway. Each time the driver hit a bump or pothole, his dick bounced up and down on my backside, confirming he was hung like a horse. *Fuck Mike Mike and his be-drunk-pilled-out ass*. Ole boy was on me like white on rice, so a bitch must still got it. He wasn't checking nor sweating for a played-out-think-she's-the-shit Sable.

Chapter Fourteen

Mike Mike

My phone had been ringing off the hook, but my head felt much too heavy to lift off of the pillow. The pungent smell of vomit had started to reek, making my eyes burn and water. I'd watched the sun rise and set in this same spot, having no choice but to piss and shit on myself. Calling out to Sable was useless since it was apparent she'd left me here to rot. Feeling like this was a sick skit of *Diary of a Mad Black Woman,* I vowed to get her sneaky snake ass back in the worst way. You can call me what you want and judge me whichever way, truth is, I beat her down to her face, and she snuck me with some loopy pills. Whatever the fuck I swallowed had done my body in.

In agonizing pain, I mustered up enough strength to crawl out of bed through the stinking, fly-infested vomit to my phone. I had no choice. Sick to my stomach, fighting the gagging sensation and urge to regurgitate again, I wasn't accustomed to being the weak nigga on set. I caused dudes this type of discomfort—never being dealt the hand to live it. Pebbles of sweat covered my face, and my body was starting to overheat. This dirty-minded bitch had gotten me good.

Finally, pulling the phone from my pants pocket, I focused my eyes, realizing it was just my notifications going off. Secretly following all the tricks I fucked with on social media as an alias, I kept a tab on the life they lived on the low. You could never let a female know your every move or that you were concerned about theirs. Real talk, I was just watching the company I kept. Seeing it was an update from Roxy, I didn't even feel like reading what sneak dis innuendo status she'd put up about me this time. Hitting Sable's icon, I tried calling her over and over, wishing she'd answer at least once. Baby girl was playing hardball, and my patience had worn thin.

Suddenly, my text message notification popped up on my screen as an image from Roxy. Hesitating to press the *open* button, a picture of her, Jazz, and Sable popped up. *What the fuck?* They were laced in rainbow attire with drinks in hand. As I studied Sable's face, she didn't seem the least bit worried or concerned about me. The smile plastered across her face while I lay here in my piss made me want to slice her fucking head off. Any love and chance of an apology I thought I had for this slick bitch faded the longer I studied the picture.

Damn, if Roxy sent me this—then what the fuck did she put on social media? Was the world seeing my girl hugged up, representing that gay pride bullshit? Or worse yet, had Roxy snitched on me anyway, and this was the real *reason Sable had flipped out? And they both together laughing about me being fucked up?*

Hurriedly sliding down my notifications to Roxy's post, my eyes bugged wide open. Her album was flooded with pictures of her, Jazz, and the slut bucket I called my precious Sable. They were living it up with a bunch of he-shes, fems, and studs. Each one of them was dressed looking good, even the gay one, Jazz, who I despised for hating on the whole existence of dick.

Miami? What in the entire fuck is this bitch doing way down there? How long have I been out of my shit? Naw, I gotta be tripping.

All men and women have a love for money, the root of all evil, to the inner depths of their soul. Mike Mike felt he'd been crossed, betrayed, and deceived by Sable on the worst level. He knew she couldn't have gotten all the way down there on the small budget he rationed to her weekly. Mustering up enough strength to crawl into the closet, he didn't need to devise a plan to get enough power to reach on the shelf. The safe he and Sable shared with part of his savings had been emptied and left upside down in the middle of the floor.

"That conniving, two-legged, dick-sucking snake. I'ma kill that rotten ass," he shouted, banging his fist on the floor. Mike Mike couldn't believe she'd gotten down on him and had flown the coop for Miami. But as far as he was concerned, she couldn't run and hide from him, and he was about to make sure she understood the definitions of limitations and revenge. *Besides, after all I've done for Sable since we were kids, that tramp and her miserable life belong to me.*

"Look, girl, what you need to do is stop messing around with all of these lames. They don't care about you like I do."

"Yeah, but—" Sable tried interrupting but was swiftly shut down.

"Yeah, but nothing. You already know ain't none of these assholes getting money like me," Mike Mike boasted with pride. "You see me out in these streets making moves. I done came a long way from me and you begging motherfuckers for spare change. That bullshit ain't my life no more, and shouldn't be yours."

"Me and you go way back. And you know how I feel."

"Girl, fuck however you feeling, and let's link up and get this bread. You smart as a motherfucker. And me

and you together can make some real noise on they ass here in Detroit. So what up, doe? What you wanna do?"

"But, Mike Mike, I don't love you like that," she whined, wanting to keep shit as real as possible. "I want us always to be cool."

The thug took a small rubber banded knot out of his front pocket. He grinned, tossing it to Sable. "Who gives a fuck if you love me? As long as you love that right there, then we gonna be on top of the world. Now, I gotta be out in a minute or two. And I swear to you this gonna be the last time I'ma be checking for you like this."

"Huh, what?" Sable was thrown off, never hearing Mike Mike claim he was going to be done chasing behind her. He'd done so for years, being her protector. Now, she'd be cut off from being safely tucked underneath his protective wing.

Glancing at his ringing cell, Mike Mike grinned, knowing time was money. "All right, girl, you ready to be my girl all the way and make hood history? You gonna be on Queen Status to these random birds out here. You gonna want for nothing. Just tell me you gonna be mine forever and five days after that . . . and the world is yours."

Sable sat back on the top stairs of her house. As she looked back at the screen door barely on the hinges and the cardboard duct taped up to one of the broken front windows, all she could do was shake her head. She knew her friend was right in what he was saying. Her current situation was dismal. Unemployed, no leads on at least a part-time job and a mother that nursed Wild Irish Rose as if it were a baby's bottle, the young girl was on the verge of tears. Fighting them back, not one part of her being had any physical desire to link with Mike Mike, but what choice did she have? Although she was cute and had a decent shape, that meant much of nothing. A pretty girl came a dime a dozen. Not wanting to continue to struggle, Sable chose wisely. She gave in to the man that was blessing her with cash from time to time. Now, she could have access to Mike Mike's money on the regular. Licking her lips, she spoke while standing up. "So, okay, boy, I'm in. I'ma rock out with you."

"Forever and fucking five days after that shit?" Mike Mike asked with a huge smile plastered across his face. "'Cause when you mines, you mines for life."

"Forever and five fucking days," Sable reaffirmed before going into her house to pack her bags and gather whatever other belongings she was going to take into her new existence.

Suffering both physically and financially, Mike Mike had bloody murder on his mind. The woman he'd cherished so much had played him for a total fool. He knew he'd been outta pocket from time to time with them ass kickings and getting high. But so fucking what? When Sable signed on to be on his team, she understood it was until death do they part. Now she was trying to violate the rules. And for that, she would have to pay. Having to throw up once more, Mike Mike collapsed, forced to lie in his own vomit while plotting revenge.

Chapter Fifteen

Carla

I watched from the second-floor deck as piles of beautiful ladies raced to line up to board the *Sunrise*. The palms of my hands were itching, which could only mean money was about to be made once again in large quantities. Our team of promoters had done good by fetching the female bitches on the beach, and I was ready to show myself, as well as them, a good time. After Gianna's explosion at Wet Willie's, once on ole girl and once with me, that relationship and connection had been seriously burned. A reckless chick could sneak into my camp now and then, but Gianna had crazy mapped out to a different level. Calling a few times to check what type of mood she was in, she shot me straight to voicemail, letting me know negotiations for an apology or make up weren't a possibility anyway.

She should've kept it cool, not fronting tough on me knowing, real talk, how I got down. Something deep down inside told me her sneaky ass was closely lurking, but business had to go on. Keeping a keen eye on my surroundings and watching over my shoulder, I had to stop fucking with chicks from the gutter. Being on the boat ever since leaving the strip, I made sure to get everything together and prepared for the clientele expected to arrive. Since all tickets were presold, I'm sure they'd buy all the liquor available too. My main focus was to have the entertainers make tips during their performances. Not wanting my name and reputation tarnished, I worked hard to make sure things were perfectly set up, and our special guests had their needs accommodated.

"Carla, your ass is a genius. We saved hella big buying that bottom-grade, cheap liquor," my partner walked up, giving me a high-five. "This time around, I mixed and matched them so that the heavy drinkers wouldn't peep our front game."

"Look at the crowd, though." I waved my hand upon even those stumbling up to the line dancing and getting the parking lot party started. "They're already turned up and tipsy. So by now, they ain't going for the taste." I was schooled on this trick by another club owner who's been scamming people for years. If you drink in Miami, it's best to pop your own seal. Down here, we'll sneak some shit in your drink and have you loose as a goose.

"Yo' sneaky ass trying to smash something tonight, ain't you?" He leaned over, letting his dreads dangle. "Like that little shorty from Wet Willie's," he grinned, already knowing what was up.

"Oh yeah, I was gonna holla at shorty, at least to apologize for Gianna making a scene." I shook my head, not wanting to relive the incident. "I didn't even know you were there."

"Excuse me ahead of time for saying this, Carla, but that chick is a straight firecracker. If she went straight nutty over the phone, I can only imagine how she'd clown on me in public. She can miss me with all that."

"You ain't never lied, my dude, and I don't blame you for staying in the shadows with Gianna in the perimeter. She's the craziest pussy I've ever ran a dildo up in. I'm working on cutting her off, though. Especially if new booty gets at me," I honestly admitted, knowing my prowl started on ole girl when I first kissed her soft hand.

"Aaah, I feel that. I should try to holla at that evil-looking bitch. She could use some dick in her life," he joked, giving me another play. "On second thought, she probably needs to be licked, so I'll leave that to you. A nigga probably fucked her scorned ass."

"That pussy has got to be tainted as mean as she's acting. Who in the hell comes to Miami with a pissy attitude?" We ran the joke into the ground as we both chilled back and waited for the official party to start. On cue, we'd welcome the guests aboard, then join them for a pool party they'd never forget.

"Hey, check for new booty right there," he pointed toward ole girl from earlier. With all the dumb shit and hollering Gianna was doing, I could barely catch her name, but I think it was Sable.

"Aww, yeah, she showed up despite Gianna's threats. I'm tapping that tonight, for sure," I cockily nodded, watching my soon-to-be conquest with intensity.

"Yeah, playa, you be having females out here thinking you all about girl power shit since you are one. But real talk, you're worse than most males." To me, he was hating 'cause I was touching more coochies than him on the regular. Most guys don't want to be schooled by a chick, but I'm the queen of getting pussy, so take a lesson from me.

I left his opinionated self with his thoughts, moving quickly to my cabin with a well-rolled blunt of some Kush and a little white lady. Surely, this fine, powdery substance would tame any spunk pretty li'l Sable had inside of her. I dipped some across the top of the weed before rolling it up. Feeling my tongue numb as I licked to seal it closed, I placed it behind my ear only to smoke later with my unsuspecting girl.

Chapter Sixteen

Sable

Walking up to the roped-off wooden dock to load on the *Sunrise*, Mike Mike was the last thing swirling around on my mind. He had been calling nonstop and sending threatening text messages requesting my whereabouts, but his fists couldn't pound my face for ignoring him this time, so to the voicemail his calls kept going. Mike Mike deserved to be feeling like a broken-down piece of shit. I had no regrets finally being the woman to get over on him. The parking lot was already filled to the max with party buses, cars, and trucks of men and women ready to party on the boat known to rock the seas. And you could see at least a mile-long line of people still trying to pile in.

"Welcome to the *Sunrise,* pretty ladies," the greeter welcomed us as we handed over our boarding passes. "Let me guide you to your private cabins in preparation for the adventure we provide," she grinned genuinely.

"Oh, fa'sho, we picked the right promoter to trust," Jazz blurted out, starting to skip up ahead of us. Walking to our private VIP cabin, she was eager to start her official birthday celebration. I was too, but Roxy was killing my vibe. Something about the way she was moving giving me fake grins still seemed suspect like earlier, but with having other problems, her snags were insignificant. She did get turned up and was back to herself on the bus—so maybe I was overreacting.

Our jaws dropped in awe at how massively big and busy this ship was. The jazz waters were illuminating, and our room was directly off the main deck pool. With double queen-sized, pillow-top beds, couches, a flat-screen television, stacked bar, and Jacuzzi—the $800 was well worth it. We were stunting hard on the other partyers who only had access to low-level rooms or straggle privileges around common areas.

"Ladies, there's an activity list on the coffee table. We'll be pulling away from shore at 8:00 p.m. sharp and pulling back at 8:00 a.m. sharp. Your personal emergency needs cannot be met unless you are in need of medical help. Other rules can be found next to the list. Please adhere to them for your safety and full enjoyment. Trust me, *Sunrise* is an experience none of you will *ever* forget. Your VIP status grants you all access at no additional charge, but please keep your wristbands on. The party starts now. Enjoy." She waited momentarily for questions and concerns by us being first-time passengers and then exited immediately afterward.

"Oh, it's turnup time, bitches. Light that bizzle, Roxy." Jazz danced around before doing a big belly flop onto the bed. "It's my birthday, and we're set up right. Thank you, Sable. You've made my day so special, honey."

Jazz was truly grateful for her friend 'cause under normal circumstances, taking this party boat right might not have happened. Besides all that, she didn't want her girl to be sweating bullets worrying over Mike Mike.

Roxy's face frowned up at the continued praise of her once-best friend. She was tired of everyone acting like little Miss Sable's shit didn't stink like hers. First, Mike Mike, and now, Jazz. Roxy was feeling left out and like the dispensable friend. Lighting the blunt, not fearing repercussions, the girls sat back to absorb all of what

Sunrise had to offer. Tyrell hadn't exaggerated. As a matter-of-fact, he'd done the amenities no justice.

We were allowed only one carry-on bag since the Captain's Party was the last event of the night, and a change of clothes was a must. Besides the custom-made romper and Louboutin heels folded and placed neatly in the bag, the cash I'd swooped from Mike Mike was nestled in the zipped side compartment. I'd been tearing a hole into his profits, living the life and spoiling my girls. Taking my outfit out, shaking it for any possible wrinkles, I slid it onto an empty hanger and into the tiny closet. Then I saw the safe inconspicuously built into the wall, and my eyes lit up, knowing my small pot of gold would be secure now. Stuffing it inside and slamming it shut, I set the code to unlock it to the same one Mike Mike and I shared. Having it already embedded into my head, even under the drunkest circumstances, I would remember it. Not once did Mike Mike catching up to me cross my mind.

"To my homegirl, Jazz . . . I could get all mushy like I love you, and we ride or die till the end, but fuck all that. Drink this shot and turn up . . . It's your birthday, bitch," Roxy shouted as we all cheered and toasted. The Kush smoke had her at ease. If only she could keep the stick from up her ass.

"Well, we ain't here to relax and bond. Let's hit the pool." Jazz slipped her clothes off, revealing a banging golden-toned body. She wore a tiny turquoise bikini that glistened with stones and barely covered her petite frame. With a firm thumper-shaped bottom and a big grip handful of breasts, as her friend, I could admit she was sexy. We followed suit and got undressed, not wanting to slow the party down. Roxy and I were thicker and considered brown girls. It was no thang our duo was often called Oreo 'cause no one denied any of our beauty. She wore a black one-piece with slits, and I let every piece of ass and titty meat hang out in my winter-white, high-cut, asymmetrical, one-piece.

"Oh, that swimsuit is gonna have Carla's eyes twisted and turned inside out. Her girl better not be on here," Jazz joked as I modeled once again for Roxy snapping shots.

"I'm not worried about Carla or her whack-ass girlfriend. Come on, let's hit this party." Grabbing our drinks, we stepped out the door directly onto the deck of the pool.

Chapter Seventeen

Carla

"*Clap for a nigga with his rapping ass. Blow a stack for your niggas with your trapping ass. I don't pop molly, I rock Tom Ford,*" Jay-Z's *Holy Grail* album was being remixed, and the whole boat was rocking their heads to his lyrical flows. By nature, we also joined in, quickly getting caught up in the upbeat vibe.

People were partying and talking in groups around the main pool. Others swam, sunbathed, or drank. Not wanting to stay glued to our room, we set out to mix and mingle and have a good time. We were living the life, and I loved the feeling. No longer worrying about Mike Mike or if Jazz was going to come through on the hookup, I tossed all my apprehension out the window and partied like a rock star. Drinks aboard the ship were free, for VIP anyway. We weren't concerned or paying attention to the crowd missing wristbands. From the looks of surveying the venue, there wasn't a body in attendance that wasn't enjoying themselves, even ole Roxy.

Even though there were bad bodies everywhere, my crew and I turned heads. There's something about Detroit girls that stood out amongst any crowd, and why we, as a city, always felt it was us versus everybody. We chilled sipping on our drinks as we took in the scene. We were lucky enough to get three lounge chairs in a row where we lay back to take in the drunken scene of naked bodies. Rap videos were playing on the theater-sized screen over the pool. We continued to lap dance on each other and those that stopped by to show us love.

"So, are you still gay or what?" Carla's soft hands were on my waist from behind. I smiled, caught by Jazz, who spit out some of her drink.

"Hey, I was wondering where you were." Before I knew it, the words had eased out of my mouth. Jazz and Roxy's eyes widened, not believing my slip of the tongue either.

"Well, I'm here now." Carla was looking good, just like earlier, in a simple pair of pink trunks, white wife beater, and pink Nike flip-flops. For a girl, she dressed like a cute boy, a total opposite from Mike Mike's all-man, sagging pants and Aviator boots rocking style. I couldn't knock it, though, 'cause she had me wide open. Blushing as her grip around my waist got firmer, she continued to embrace me, and I didn't want her to stop. "So, what did you want with me?"

"First things first, where's your little girlfriend? I'm not trying to get thrown over the railings and into the water 'cause she's on that tip." I pulled away from her, looking around for the tall, light-skinned chick. For some reason, the bitch popped into mind bringing me back up on my square. If she came for round two, I planned on knocking her head off.

"Be cool." Carla choked on her drink, backing away to scope the scene too. She didn't think I'd noticed the worry wrinkles on her face from the mention of ole girl, but no such luck. "She was invited, but with the ass kicking you put on her earlier, I'm sure she doesn't want to be in the company of you three anyway."

"Well, she's probably somewhere chasing some of your other groupies off. We heard about your hot, fiya ass," Roxy butted in once again but bringing up a good point.

"Aw, babe, I'm sure you did. But word of mouth never gives someone real justice. Let ya girl find out about me on her own. How about that?"

"And what's there to find out? I mean, for real, though, I really don't get down with girls, and that shit I said earlier was just a joke." Carla stared at me erotically, taking in every inch of curve I'd been blessed with. Feeling her eyes undress me from the swimsuit, my knees slightly buckled from the intensity of her sizing me up.

"Oh, well, in that case, let me not waste not another minute of my time—or yours. I'm out, shorty. Do you. Happy Birthday, Jazz." With that, she turned and walked in the other direction. She didn't give me time to take back my words or even take a cop. Feeling like I'd put my foot in my mouth, Carla left me standing, looking salty, stupid, and at a total loss for words.

"Guess you better be real next time, babe." Jazz smacked me on the ass. "Come on, let's get in the pool." She danced around, seeing a few people getting a game of water volleyball started. Watching Carla move on socializing with chicks on the boat had me slightly irritated and pissed off. To prevent myself from looking like a fool, going over to address my standoffish performance, I took Jazz up on her offer and followed into the already jam-packed pool.

"I'm gonna have to pass on that. My hair didn't cost a car note, so it won't handle the water." Roxy looked deflated as she plopped back down onto the sun chair.

"Damn, that's fucked up," I shook my head. "You should've done better knowing we were coming to Miami . . . duh." Yeah, I could've cut my girl some slack and not knocked her for having a bottom-grade, nappy weave—but let that be a lesson to her for keeping me and mine outta her mouth.

"Bitch, whatever. I got you, trust." Her words were cold, but not enough for chill bumps to pop up. Roxanne didn't scare me or intimidate me in the very least. As I watched her get up and storm off, it was clear I had pissed her off once again. Well, so be it.

Chapter Eighteen

Roxy

Mike Mike had my mind fucked up. I couldn't shake how badly things had gone with us. I'd been working on having him eating out of the palms of my pussy walls forever and lacing my purse with money to blow. But instead, he threw serious shade my way and set Sable up to show me what I was truly missing. Instead of me enjoying the presents and upgrades like Jazz, my bitterness grew stronger. In the beginning, I had felt bad for fucking Mike Mike, being a home wrecker to my best friend. But since being on this trip with her uppity ass acting like her shit don't stink—I was truly starting to hate her. If my hair wouldn't have napped up instantly upon hitting the water earlier, I would've jumped in that pool and smacked her up. Real friends didn't put friends on front street like that. Yeah, I was fucking her man, but behind her back . . . in private. Being disrespected in public was so embarrassing. As Sable and Jazz chopped it up with their newfound game-time friends, I crept back to the room for some alone time.

Suspecting ole boy from the party bus was going to be on here too, I hadn't seen him around the deck. If only I could catch a nut, my mood would ease up and relax. Having no other choice and needing to release the built-up stress, I grabbed my travel bullet from my purse and slid underneath the covers. Placing the vibrating gadget on my clit, waves of pleasure shot throughout my body. Starting to twist and turn, I pushed the volume up to the max, pushing the red plastic play toy inside of me. Spreading my legs into a perfect "V," my juice box was leaking on the sheets. I was nearing an orgasm. But Sable's phone started ringing and kept ringing, making it hard for me to concentrate on coming. I knew it was probably Mike Mike constantly stalking calling her. She'd been ignoring him, making it perfectly clear this trip and these gay bitches were far more important than him. Since my feelings with that nigga were straight raw right about now, the ecstasy I was experiencing flushed itself away, replaced by self-pity. Mike Mike had a way of making me feel less than worthy.

"Aaah, fuck her, Mike Mike. Why her? She ain't shit and don't give two shits about you, apparently." He couldn't hear me, and since the boat was so loud, I doubt others did either. Snatching the bullet from inside me, I tossed it across the room. Aggravated and annoyed, I'd gotten caught up with him once again, losing my much-needed relief.

Jumping up and sliding the crotch of my swimsuit back over my slippery pussy, I crashed the bar, popping the cork of the courtesy 1800 and tilted it back. Hearing her phone set to send him to voicemail, and he calling again enraged me. I was a bad bitch, top of the line, who sucked his dick like a pro, and he was treating me like scum. Setting the bottle down, running across the room, I snatched up her purse, sifting the Android out immediately. Seeing his picture flash up on the main screen of her phone brought about mixed emotions. He was looking so fine, so sexy, so likable—but so not mine. But the truth was staring me in the face. He was blowing her up, checking to make sure she stayed in line. I was nothing to Mike Mike, so fuck him for that.

"Guess you're looking like the fool now, huh? Pretty Princess Bitch ain't trying to answer," I spitefully spat into the phone.

"What the fuck? Where's Sable?" Mike Mike shouted into the phone out of breath, huffing and puffing. I'd never heard him sound so angry. He had me shaken and wasn't even asking for me. "Where's that rotten, bottom-feeding bitch?"

"Whoa, Mike Mike, huh? *Now* she's a bitch?" His harsh words for his precious girl caught me by surprise. "Yesterday, she couldn't be topped." Something in me said to hang up, erase the call, and go back to my girls. But Mike Mike was my magnet, and anything that dude talked about was golden. Plus, I was nosy.

"Look, I ain't got time for that crybaby shit right now, yo. Where's Sable? Put that ho on the phone." My ears hadn't heard him wrong. From the sound of it, li'l Miss Thang's throne had been compromised.

"At the pool party, and she's been ignoring your calls, duh." I made matters worse. "She doesn't even know I'm in here answering the phone to you. How about that?"

"What motherfucking pool party?" He wasn't screaming by now, but the agitation in his voice hadn't disappeared. I didn't care, though, especially since, yet again, Sable was the topic of our conversation when he should've been apologizing for the spiteful shit he'd said to me.

"What else do you think goes down in Miami but partying, Mike Mike?" I naively asked, looking out the window at the crowd starting to clear out. The Captain's Party was set to begin in a couple of hours.

"Y'all scummy hoes down there living right off my money, huh? I'm gonna kill that bitch. That's my word."

"Oh, you ain't about to drag me into what you two got going on," I yelled back at him, not feeling like I should be part of the attack. "You sponsored her, so what the fuck?"

"That bitch is a thief, and when I catch up to her, she's gonna pay." He'd caught me off guard. I wasn't expecting those words.

"Thief? Huh? What are you talking about, Mike Mike?"

"She stole my stash—about fifty thousand to be exact. I ain't into sponsoring no gay trips, and you can bet that. I want that tramp's head on a platter."

Even though he wasn't yelling and seemed to be calmer, the anger and hatred in his voice were clear and evident. On my end, I was blown back. Sable had been out here stunting and showboating when all along, she stole it from her man. Oh, hell naw. I couldn't blame her, though. He had done her like trash—well, before I came into the picture, and had she not left him broke, he wouldn't have aimed to change.

"That serves your ass right. You and everyone else thinking that girl don't have foul stinking shit like us all. And she got down on you," I mocked him, laughing hysterically, taking another swig from the 1800 bottle. "Good for ya dumb ass."

"Zip your lips, Roxy. It's time for you to prove your loyalty. How much do you love me, girl?" Turning his suave game on, I started to melt into his game plan like putty. "You want to be number one so bad, well, here's ya chance."

I melted. "You know I love you, baby. You just keep playing with my heart." I kept it real, not wanting to ruin the moment or miss my opportunity.

"Well, it's time for all of that to end. Sable has fucked up with me for the last time, and there's no way I'm allowing her to get back right. Now, are you sure you're ready to be with me?" My heart was starting to beat fast. I've been waiting to hear him ask me that since the first time I dunked on his dick.

"You know I'm ready, Mike Mike. I've been ready. So, now, what's up?"

"I can't have no thieves or liars in my camp, Roxy. Sable is going to get taught a swift lesson for fucking with my money, baby. You know that, right?"

"Yes . . . of course, and she deserves one." My personal thoughts could stay just that—personal. I wasn't about to go against the grain or disagree with him just because I had another belief in mind. This wasn't my plight to have out with him. Sable had made her bed to sleep in.

"Promise me that you'll never cross me like her rotten ass and that you're dedicated to the team. I've had my share of ghetto bunnies. And with Sable, and I'm not up for taking any more losses. Are you 100 percent down with me, or what?"

"Baby, I swear that it don't get no realer than me. I'll never go out like Sable. You can trust that. She's down here clowning, acting like you don't exist and shit." Jumping ship like a snitch, it was easy to rat out my longtime friend and spill the beans on her questionable mannerisms. "You've got my word, Mike Mike. I'm down for you and only you. I'm your new number one."

"Those words are like magic to my ear, Roxy. That's precisely what I wanted to hear. Hold on a second." Hearing him having background conversation asking for directions to his gate, he got back on the phone and continued to butter me up. "Yeah, baby, back to our chitchat, a nigga hates to be so rude," he said, sounding sincere. I'd never heard Mike Mike act so sweet. This must be the type of love and affection Sable was accustomed to.

"It's okay, Mike Mike. I'll hold on for you." I kept caking with him, loving the mood he was creating. Continuing to sip straight from the bottle, I was buzzing off both the liquor and him smooth-talking me heavy. At this point, the *Sunrise* and its party atmosphere meant nothing to me.

"Will you do anything for me?"

"On demand, baby, and you wouldn't have to ask twice."

"Good. I need you to confirm Sable stole my cash. Have you seen it? Do you know where it is? Can you find it?" Mike Mike didn't waste any time going in on me and testing my word.

"Ummm," I tried thinking, but the liquor had me floating. "She's been spending big. I know she probably has it."

"Where the fuck is it?" He screamed like *I* stole it in the first place.

"Okay, damn, let me look." Running through the room, I was searching hard for the Nike duffel bag she had aboard the boat. "She only brought one bag, so I know it's here." Huffing and puffing, working hard to please Mike Mike, I had to find this bag and his money.

"Hurry up. I'm about to have to hang up in a second," he yelled, back to his usual bossy self. No doubt, this dude had split personalities, but it didn't dry up my thirst.

"There's a safe here, but it's closed. I wouldn't know where to start with the combination." Sitting down beside it, I knew this was the only place it could've been. I looked all around, and if I were hiding stash money, it would be here.

"A safe? Fuck. What type of combination keypad does it have?"

"Huh? Um, its square, and you press the numbers in. Is that a good enough description?"

"Damn, okay . . . let me think." Giving me two different five-digit combinations, I could hear the frustration in his voice as someone in the background asked him to power off his handset. "Gimmie two seconds, sweetheart," he told her, then directed his attention back to me.

"Where are you at, Mike Mike?" I questioned, kind of getting jealous because he was around another girl calling her sweetheart. I wouldn't be taking the outright disrespect like Sable.

"Never mind that. Push in 21707, and don't fuck up. After this, the safe will lock up, and she'll know someone has tampered with it because the hotel management will have to be notified."

Taking my time to push in the code exactly as he told me, I couldn't believe my eyes when the lights flashed green. "Mike Mike, it's open! It worked, it worked!" Pulling it open quickly, I snatched the bag out and shook it unwrinkled, thinking the money would drop out. "How did you know?"

"That was the due date of our first baby. Now, is my money in that safe or not, Roxy? Tell me what the fuck is going on."

Baby? What the fuck did he mean, baby? Sable didn't tell me that she had been pregnant. I wonder if Jazz knew. I dared not to say anything else about that to him. This wasn't the time, and there was no reason to make him upset.

"I'm still looking, babe, probably so—" I cut off as I unzipped the compartment seeing more money than I'd ever touched in a lifetime stuffed inside. "Oh my God, baby, you were right. That bitch. I've got the money in my hands."

"That's my baby." His tone got calmer. "I knew I could count on you to do everything right. Now put everything back in place just how you found it."

"But why, baby? Let me out this snake and blaze her. I could be on the first plane smoking back to you in no time," I whined, not wanting to part with the cash so soon. I'd just got my hands on it, and already, it was gone. Wanting to take a few stacks for my troubles, I didn't ask him again, knowing he wasn't going back on his word. Stuffing everything back in the safe, I left it cracked open, just in case I decided to take a few for my troubles.

"Do as you're told. I'm gonna handle her when I get down there."

"You're coming? You're on the plane? Oh shit." Everything in my life was glowing. Sable was about to be replaced, and for once, I'd be put on the pedestal before her and in front of her. I'd finally top that trick.

"Listen, Roxy, listen. Stay cool and act like you haven't talked to me. Exactly where are y'all at now?" I could hear the same lady rushing him off the phone, but he was still holding her off.

"On this party boat called the *Sunrise* off South Beach. It gets back at 8:00 a.m. We're staying at the Clevelander," I blurted out, anticipating the moment everything with us would finally be official. Tired of fucking in back rooms and short stays, my kids and I were finally getting ready to be legitimately set up straight.

"Cool. I need you like never before. Prove yourself, baby, and remember to play all your cards the same. Don't tell Sable or Jazz I'm coming. We've never talked. You got it?" He continued to repeat himself, but he didn't have to. I wasn't a slow learner, and when it came to street life, I caught on quickly.

"Mike Mike, I know my role, baby. I ain't shit like Sable, and I ain't never turning on my team. That female left you broke, and you can trust when you get here, I'm tag teaming to fuck her up. Until then, I'll play it cool. I got you." Giving him a spill, I tried to show my love and keep reminding him that it was unconditional.

Out of all the things I poured out to him, the only thing he could focus on was being outsmarted and done foul. "No one gets down on Mike Mike. You can trust a nigga got stash boxes like I got hoes. I'll check for your ass in a few. This creepy cracker flight attendant is lurking again." Hanging up, I reflected on his last comment, which had me shaken. If he thought he had hoes, after today, they'd be dismissed.

"I'm finally one up on you, Sable." I victoriously shouted out into the cabin suite even though she wasn't in here. Deep down, I was excited and happy. Mike Mike was finally going to make good on his word and send her packing—maybe even dead—for stealing his cash.

Everything in my life was about to go ten times better than it had ever gone before. No more knockoffs, bad weaves, and eviction notices taped to my window. Mike Mike was known for getting a bitch off craps. I'd seen so with my own eyes when it came to Sable. Picking up my bullet from the floor, then taking a few swigs of 1800, I leaned back and resumed my sex session, this time, with thoughts of how Mike Mike would whack this up once he got down here and fucked Sable's world up.

Mike Mike

Roxy was just as dumb as I thought she'd be. Never in a million years could she be my wifey with the fucked-up track record she was rolling with, but she fell into my hands like putty with the mere mention of us being together. I needed her help to lead me to Sable, so until then, whatever I had to do to keep her on my team was fair game. She'd already proven to be an asset by confirming my now ex-girlfriend was the for-sure culprit. I couldn't wait to see the look on that bitch's face once she saw me in the flesh to collect what was mine. Having backup money in more than one place, of course, a broad will never have full access to what really makes Mike Mike, Mike Mike. And once this straight shot landed, I'd be beating her into the ground, literally, once and for all.

Leaning back in my chair, counting the hours until my dream could become a reality, I rubbed at my still sour, bubbling stomach. Whatever drug Sable snuck me with was still fucking me over, but I was fighting through it. Damn, I couldn't wait to lock my hands around her throat. That undercover whore was going to regret fucking me over and biting the hand that has fed her most of her rotten, no-good life. Her time was coming.

"What up, doe, my nigga? Have you talked to that slimeball bitch, Roxy?"

Mike Mike had just taken his second shower for the day. He was trying to get his life together. His body worn out from the last twenty-four hours, the drug dealer fought to stay stable minded. "Naw, guy, why would I be talking to her? You the one that's been giving the ho the dick lately, so she your headache now, not mine."

Lenny laughed at the statement and the person who was saying it. "Say what now?" Mike Mike hawked up a gang of thick mucus that was continuously forming in his throat.

"Come on, now, I ain't no fool. You and her fucking around is the worst-kept secret in the damn hood. So, naw, guy, I been stop running up in that rotten-womb trick. Matter-of-fact, all us have."

"Whoa, hold up, Len." Mike Mike was finally feeling better after spitting out the last glob of what had him bent.

Lenny was amused once more. "Dawg, once you started hitting Roxy, she thought she was about to take ya girl place. That bitch had her ass on her shoulders. So, yeah, she marked her pussy as damn near off-limits."

Mike Mike hated that what he thought was his deceitful business, in fact, wasn't. Despite sneaking around, he was not discreet. However much he crept, apparently, he was not. Here his boy Lenny was blowing him out of the water. "Look, man, I just need you to come my way. I got some shit on the table, and I need to put it in full motion."

"Oh yeah?" Lenny eagerly pondered, smelling the impending opportunity to make some money in the air.

"Yeah, my dude. And before you ask, yeah, it's a come-up for you in the long run. So swing by my crib. Time is ticking." Mike Mike had just about read his homeboy's mind. A hustler out in the streets, he'd learned a long time ago that nothing motivated a nigga to move faster than cash on the barrelhead.

Chapter Nineteen

Carla

Ole girl was acting like she didn't want to get in my zone and wasn't down with the bisexual world, but I knew that was some straight bullshit. No girl plays that much and isn't willing to give it up, but I could tell off rip she wanted to play games. With a body as banging as hers, I'd be willing to only partake in them for a little while. Time was money, and already, I'd had more money pile in tonight than any other night this year. Being a skilled pimp in my game, I could easily replace Sable, but I liked the thrill.

Going into the main ballroom of the boat, I checked the décor, stage, and setup to ensure everything for tonight went successful as planned. A few acts were already rehearsing, and the live band was starting to get their equipment prepped. As always, my crew ran like a well-oiled machine. Taking off the snapback hat I was wearing to wipe the sweat from my brow, I frowned. Even though business looked butter smooth, something heavy was eating at me.

Pulling out my iPhone, I scrolled through my missed call log and messages to see if any were from Gianna. The last call was last night before I swooped her up on a booty call. I shook my head, knowing I'd pissed her off royally. "Damn, baby, pick up," I spoke into the receiver as her phone kept ringing but to no avail. The voicemail picked up again. Swiping the call to end, I tried to gather my composure. Gianna's uncalculated behavior had me feeling uneasy. I knew her like the back of my hand, and she couldn't be trusted. Gianna was the type of bitch you needed to keep tabs on—a real nutcase. I needed a blunt to calm my nerves.

Chapter Twenty

Sable

The crowd at the pool party was dwindling, and we'd kicked back in the late-evening sun drinking margaritas and playing around in the water for a few hours. Neither Carla nor Roxy had ever resurfaced, so my mood had gone bittersweet. Taking this as an opportunity to talk with Jazz alone about what was more serious than any of them, I wasted no more time.

"Have you talked to your cousin yet?" I questioned Jazz again, wanting to stay consistent because, at one point, this boat ride and vacation would conclude. I'd found it odd she hadn't brought him up.

"He called me earlier, so everything should still go as planned. You're worrying too much about something I already told you I'd take care of." She blew me off again, refusing to hook me up with his name or number. Something was telling me to lay off and come up with another game plan . . . just in case. Jazz didn't seem too reassuring.

"All right, girl, I won't bring it up again. It's just that if I don't get up with him for a new identity, Mike Mike won't have any problem tracking me down. That just can't happen." I kept it real. "If he finds me, you'll be burying your girl, and I ain't holding you up on that."

"Trust me, I know. Your problems have become my problems." Jazz's last comment was snide and hurtful since she held all my darkest secrets, and she was tighter with me than Roxy. Above and beyond all that, she'd created problems that weren't even on my plate by encouraging me to steal from my deranged, unstable-ass boyfriend.

I let her words be the last of that topic, and the final time I'd share a heartfelt moment with her. As many times as I've been her shoulder when some anti-gay activist ran up on her, having her crying and hating the world, she had some nerve to act like *I* was intruding on *her* personal space. I wasn't about to trip or blow it out of proportion, though. Hopefully, she'd just come through when it counted for sure.

"The real thing you need to be concerned about, though, is Carla." Here she went again changing the subject. I swear to God if she didn't come through, I was going to kick her ass. I'd blown hella money, making her birthday unforgettable and her wardrobe ten times better. If I've wasted my get-right money on her lying ass, it was going to be hell to pay, for sure. I had to let it go and move on, for now, anyway.

"Um, well, since she hasn't come back, maybe I have blown it with her. You know how us girls get."

"Naw, she's probably teaching you a lesson for playing hard to get. You heard Tyrell. She gets pussy and money. It's nothing for her to be pressed so hard on you."

"Then there's no reason for me to be pressing so hard for her." I got cocky, pointing at my body to prove the point.

"Miami breeds bodies. Look around. I suggest if you're truly feeling her, not to stunt for us—well, Roxy's old hating ass anyway. I already know what's up."

"Whatever. We'll see what's up. Come on, let's go back to the room to get ready for the next event on the agenda."

"I already know what's up, girl. I'm just waiting on your slow-acting ass to catch up. We can bounce. Ain't no way my ass gonna show up late to a drag queen show." Getting up, we made a beeline for the room. I was ready to blow a blunt and chill out for a few before heading to the Captain's Party. The sun had beat me down, and I was a little more than salty my woman crush hadn't come back to check for me.

Jazz

I was so tired of being caught up in the middle of drama. Between the rocky relationship of Mike Mike and Sable, and the low-key cheating shit with Mike Mike and Roxy, and now this pop-up girl, Carla, everyone seemed to have something crazy going on that I had a hand in. You'd think with it being my birthday, the light would be on me. Coming to Miami was turning out to be a bust. And trying to help my girl was starting to look like it was going to blow up in my face. Once again, I had to deflect the topic and pray on the inside that my cousin wanted to look out for her. Paradise truly wasn't what I expected it to be. Craps out.

Roxy

The 1800 and uncountable nuts I let loose to the thoughts of finally being a moneymaker's girl had put me out cold. Hearing laughter and the door lock being rammed back and forth woke me up. I leaped up from my come-induced sleep to Jazz and Sable, trying to get in. With the bullet and bottle in hand, I slammed the safe shut, tossed the toy into my bag, and flew to open the door. I'd have to find a time to get back for my pain and suffering payout before the money made its way back to Mike Mike. I didn't look at it as stealing—after all, Sable would take all the blame for any stolen dollars.

"Damn, my bad. I was in here drinking, trying to get right for tonight. I didn't want anyone to walk in on a bitch drunk and passed out," I half-lied, really bolting the room down while I searched for Mike Mike's stolen cash.

"Oh yeah, my bad earlier when I came at you about your weave. I know it's hard out here without a sponsor." Sable tried to throw shade my way again, snidely looking innocent like she'd done nothing wrong.

"Don't worry about it, friend. Sometimes, it is what it is." I took her under-the-belt shots now because later, I would laugh at her demise. Mike Mike was going to take her out of the game, and with pride, I'd be the one to help him. She looked at me oddly but didn't reply to my comment. Remembering what my boo asked of me earlier, I had to keep cool and play my position.

"Well, give me that bottle. I need to get where you're at." She snatched the 1800 and walked toward the closet. Then she proceeded to get drunk, tilting it up, spilling some over on herself and the bathing suit I'd claim in a few hours.

Chapter Twenty-one

Sable

The main ballroom for the Captain's Party was just as decked out and pristine as the cabins were. I hadn't felt the least bit of distress or regret spending out of what was now my private stash. I had to admit that being the boss of our clique for this trip had my ego swollen. Florescent lights danced throughout the dimly lit ballroom, immediately sucking me into a trance. Rainbow-colored balloons, centerpieces, and banners were draped strategically throughout, representing gay pride and unity. A few tables had flyers or poster boards propped up, advertising a particular performer or group.

Tonight's itinerary included a drag queen show, something my virgin eyes had never experienced. Unlike many custom ship ballrooms, the *Sunrise* had a stage and runway with two stripper poles on each end . . . not to mention projection screens running real-time club footage. Two cages surrounded the dance floor and another stripper pole in the center. Already crowded just thirty minutes into the party, it was apparent Tyrell hadn't lied when he said this spot would be turned up. The freaks were out and all-girl or not, the vibe hypnotized me. Everyone was dancing with all guards down. Jazz's crew knew how to party.

Roxy and I hit the bar for a couple of waters and to scope the club out. Jazz had caught the eye of a stud first thing through the door and got sidetracked. Truthfully speaking, everyone was dressed to impress, rocking the latest fashions and kicks. A few studs had caught my eye too. Even though Roxy's mood had slightly improved, she still wasn't showing any interest in being here, which was cool as long as she didn't attempt to ruin our energy or kill our vibe. Carla was heavy on my mind. I kept scanning the scene for her but was coming up dry. It was hard for me to admit I was acting so pressed over a chick, but I was digging the thought of something fresh and new.

We grabbed up our drinks headed fast in Jazz's direction as we saw the chilled bottle of Moët on the table. I needed the water to bring me down some from my high. The blunts and shots had taken over early. Jazz and I had gotten white-girl wasted at the pool. Walking across the room, I felt as if I were being watched, so I moved with grace. My goal was to leave an air of mystery. I was starting to lose my cool, knowing Carla was close by. She had to be.

"Ladies, this place is bananas. It ain't a G-spot in here that don't want to get licked," Jazz said, giggling, as we walked up to sit down. "The lesbos in the 'D' don't get down like this," she remarked, looking across the room at the stud that'd checked for her earlier.

"Yeah, it is," I replied, turning to lock eyes with none other than Carla. Standing across the room, she'd attracted me like a magnet. Her style was fresh . . . fire-engine red studded-out blazer, white-collar button-up, denim True Religion jeans, and a pair of navy polo boots. Her appearance was everything of a manly thug, but I knew underneath that red and white snapback Miami Heat's hat was an impersonator. I couldn't help but smile and nod, letting her know she had my approval. Returning the gesture melted me inside, knowing I'd met my match.

"Good, then let's enjoy," Jazz shouted, breaking my thoughts but not my stare. It was the truth. I was curious, and tonight was going to be the chance for me to find what I had been secretly seeking. Jazz happily poured us each a glass of Moët. I began to sip and seductively dance for my stud like eye candy.

My girls and I were tearing it up on the dance floor. Pulling out all of my best moves, it was a celebration for Jazz's twenty-second birthday and a liberation victory to be from up under Mike Mike's lock and key. The DJ had the crowd going crazy playing all my favorites—Jeezy, Drake, and J. Cole, just to keep the list short. All of the newfound attention had my ego slightly swollen. No doubt, I was looking good and dominating the crowd. I was truly feeling myself. The attention added had me on a new high. I tried not to focus in on Carla, but either my mind was playing tricks on me, or the thought of having something new seemed very intriguing. Never having any interest in chicks before tonight, I was entering dangerous and unknown territory. And from the stares coming from ole girl, she definitely didn't care about me claiming not to be into girls earlier. Fuck it. The night was young, and I was in it for the long haul, so, hey, it was whatever.

"*Shorty, I'm only gonna tell you this once, you're the illest,*" Nicki's song, "Your Love," rang out through the speakers. Every time the beat banged, so did my body.

"*Sunrise* is the truth," I shouted to my girls as I was gigging to the song.

"So, you trying to get Carla to come over here, or what?" Jazz asked, whispering in my ear as I danced back on her. I was in the zone, and from her slanted red eyes, so was she.

"Yeah," I answered back, taking a sip of my drink, not even caring about being real tipsy. I couldn't have a chance at playing behind my girls' back, so fuck the cat being out of the bag. "Ole girl been watching my every move since we walked over here." I grinned, feeling myself never losing my beat with the music. "It's gonna be on."

"Whelp, that explains why you out here freaking yourself, touching and popping all that booty. I heard that, boo. You better do it." Jazz high-fived me and started getting busy to the beat too. A femme walked up behind her, and she immediately started doing her thang. I secretly wished I had the guts to just go with the flow and live my life without limits or boundaries. All that jaw jackin' at Wet Willie's was just a front to make Carla's girl jealous.

The buzz dominated my mind. No longer was any part of me thinking rationally. I was lifted off the weed, and the bottomless liquor was making my body want to dance, so I was moving seductively. Yeah, I intended to get some attention, and it was most definitely working. A few random girls came over to dance, and I was very appreciative with my suggestive moves. They thought I was dancing for them, but I was just trying to entice Carla more . . . and it was also working. Each time a chick ran her hands across me or pulled me in closer for a more intimate dance, Carla's expression hardened. She looked jealous, and that shit was turning me on. As she stood at the head of the room with her hands firmly in her pockets, I desperately wanted her to end this game of cat and mouse. If she approached me again, I'd be more than willing to give in.

"Her fine ass got you hooked, huh?" Jazz quizzed, noticing my stare down with the Carla. "Welcome to our world. You can't continue to front like you don't want to try it," she said, kissing me on the cheek. Smiling back at her without hesitation or rejection of her words was all the confirmation she needed to know that I was bicurious.

"Well, don't be rude. Go see if she wants to dance." Jazz's commands didn't stop. Trying to nudge me in ole girl's direction, she walked off, pushing up on another stud that was standing nearby. My homegirl was undeniably in her element. She wanted me to be like her, but bossing up on a girl had to be something totally different than leaning on a dude.

Focusing back in on my chosen stud, she grimed me, continuing to stare my chocolate body up and down. In the zone, I continued to move for her, belly dancing, licking my lips, letting her know I was available and ready to go full throttle. For some reason, I couldn't back down, even though Mike Mike was a faint thought in the back of my mind. As she nodded at my seductive suggestions, adjusting her snapback hat to mask the blush engraved on her face, I was sure she was on her way over. All of a sudden, leaving me hanging and caught up in my feelings, Carla winked, disappearing into the crowd.

"Welcome to the stage, a veteran and the one who makes all this freaky shit possible," and the room erupted with applause and screams. "Yeah, y'all know how the *Sunrise* does it. Come on, baby, let's show these ladies how you get down." As the beat of a music intro came on, Carla mysteriously appeared in front of a thin cloud of smoke. Seconds later, she had the entire crowd, including me, mesmerized. When Carla made her way through the crowd, she found me and showed all the way out. Out of the corner of my eye, I noticed Roxy with her cell out, recording, but I was too all in to care.

Chapter Twenty-two

Gianna

"Oh my God! Oh, hell to the fuck naw!" Hyperventilating, I leaned over the rail, trying to let my lungs gather some oxygen. Carla might as well have driven a knife straight into my heart with her bare hands. The ballroom walls had started to close in on me. I couldn't breathe. I couldn't speak. I was dizzy with fury. Sitting through my so-called devoted woman caressing and serenading someone other than me was pure punishment. I couldn't take my eyes from the heart-wrenching pain as I witnessed another person who claimed they loved me betray me in a way that couldn't be repaired. Sneaking on this boat to see her behind-the-scene behavior was stupid. Point-blank period. She'd shown me her true colors time and time again, but I ignored them.

If it hadn't been clear at Wet Willie's earlier that I'd become old news and replaceable to her, shit was sparkling bright right now and crystal clear. I watched Carla seduce ole girl from only a few feet away. Disguised in a wig, I was inconspicuous. Had she not been stunting for that newbie and trying to impress her like she'd done me months ago, maybe the supposed love of her life would've stood out amongst everyone else in the room, wig or not. It had been hard not to run up on the stage and do them both in. Having learned my lesson earlier, ole girl was a true match, and I had to catch her totally off guard. That was a given.

Lighting a laced blunt, one of the many habits Carla hooked me on, I trembled as I blew the poisoned smoke into the ocean breeze, trying to scheme on a plan of revenge. It was wrong for coming here in the first place, but I had, and now both they asses had to pay. Starting to pace back and forth, I opened my purse to assure myself the pistol was still in place. Pulling the universal key I used to unlock the doors to clean cabins, I made a dash for what I'd found out was Sable's room. Knowing Carla wouldn't have another bitch laid up in her room, they'd definitely be heading to Sable's at one point during the night, and without question, I'd be waiting and hiding, and once they got there . . .

Chapter Twenty-three

Sable

"Hey, ma, can I kick it with you for a minute?" Carla coo'ed, easing up behind me, kissing the nape of my neck. Her lips were soft and slightly wet. Sensations shot up and down my spine. I nodded and took her hand, once again, following her lead. Roxy saw the hookup and dipped her own way. Watching her exit the door, I assumed she was fed up with all of Jazz's and my over-the-top gay behavior.

"So, were you feeling my show for you tonight, or what?" she probed, walking me over to what I assumed to be her private booth.

"You seemed to know I would like it, putting me on blast and all," I blushed, not knowing what else to say.

"See, I know you better than you think. All that stunting shit at the pool . . . Please tell me you've gotten it out of your system." She stared at me, intently.

"Yeah." I bit at the corner of my lip, all of a sudden shy. I'd never been this way before, but Carla was shaking me up.

"I hope you're really ready." Carla reached over to rub my back. Leaning in, she kissed my neck once more, making my body jerk. Her touches were making my heart skip beats, and my body became timid. Everything in the room started to slow down.

"So, that's how you feeling?" she asked in tune with my body's movements, making sure her lips stayed on my ear a little longer. This time, when she waited on my reply, her hand rubbed alongside my side, and her chin rested on my neck. She swayed to the beat. This chick had the impression of a dude on point and was turning me on for real.

"Well, you making me feel that way," I responded, not even giving a fuck about holding back. She had gotten my vagina wet, so I was ready to let her explore. I started to grind, encouraging her to touch me even more. I got lost in the beat of the music and the smell of her cologne. I moved close up on her neck and kissed it gently. This was new. I was drunk and high. "Can we go back to your cabin? I know you've got a private one." Fuck it. I wanted all in. I was about to live a new life anyway. Maybe it would be with girls, and Jazz and I could do this all the time.

"I'd be a fool not to. Let me give you what you been missing," she whispered, leading me out of the party.

I didn't tell my girls I was leaving. I hastily sent Jazz a text message on our walk to Carla's room. She replied that she was getting some head anyway and peace out, so I had no worries in the world.

"You sure you ready for this? I can tell this is your first time," she asked, stopping outside room 296. "I'm honored to be your first."

Out in the open, she started to rub her hand up my thigh. The word to describe me was speechless. My mouth couldn't utter any words. A woman had her hand close to my hookup, and I hadn't given her the business yet. What I really wanted was more. She needed just to open the door. From that point, I guess it would be on.

Chapter Twenty-four

Roxy

I wasn't going to miss my opportunity to get in on the come-up out here partying and playing with Jazz or Sable. I'd had enough of being fake, friendly, and putting on a phony façade. The only thing on my mind was cracking open the safe again and collecting me a few stacks. What was supposed to be an all-girls' getaway to Miami was slowly turning into the dismantling of best friends. It was time, though. I'd outgrown those hoes, and being gay just wasn't my forte. My kids and I were about to live right, starting with the stacks I was about to snatch off top.

Swiping the plastic key to open the door, I called out to Jazz and Sable, making sure I was here alone. Running to my side of the room, I gathered all my belongings, throwing them into my luggage. Once Mike Mike got here, and pandemonium broke out, there wouldn't be time to be thorough and detailed. Making a beeline for the bedroom closet, I opened the flimsy white door and kneeled on the floor. Entering the same code Mike Mike told me earlier, the lights flashed green, and I snatched the door open. "Bet. Hmmm, let's see. One stack, two stacks, three stacks, four." Peeling them out of the bag and setting them on the floor beside me, I didn't care if

I was greedy. Sable was gonna take the blame and beat-down, so who cared in love and war?

"Yeah, bitch, put your motherfucking hands in the air, purple slush-pouring whore, before I make this thang sing."

Startled, I felt a lump instantly develop in my throat. Slowly, I turned my head to see ole girl from Wet Willie's. It was Carla's crazy bitch-ass girlfriend. Standing with a pistol pointed down in my face, she was pissed. With no other choice if I wanted to live, I did as I was told. I dropped my head and raised both hands. "Ay, yo, you've got the wrong one, baby. It's Sable you're checking for. She's with your girl right now. Not me," Out of desperation, I looked back up, trying to talk some sense into her.

"Naw, shut the fuck up. I owe you for pouring that slush and popping off earlier. You already know I ain't forgot." She stared me dead-on before smacking the spit out of my mouth. My face bounced back and forth, and I was ready to attack.

I quickly tried to stand up from the floor, but she moved with more speed, kicking me in the abdomen. I bent over, grabbing my stomach. This trick was straight deranged and taking her aggression out on the wrong person.

"Didn't I say put your motherfucking hands up?" she yelled, stomping up and down like a child having a tantrum.

I slowly started to raise my hands, crying in agony as my stomach needed constant pressure to try to relieve the excruciating pain that was shooting through my entire body. "Okay, okay."

"Good. Now, turn around and move fast. With all your whining and shit, somebody might've heard you." This chick was on the crazy tip, and it was apparent my fate was looking bleak. Not wanting to take a shot to the back of the head or back, I tried hard to think of a way to grab the gun and shoot her punk ass first. "Turn the fuck around."

Testing my strong arm and trying my faith, I dove for her and the gun in an attempt to save my life. Going out like a sucker was never a credit I thought I'd have to roll with. To my dismay, I never had a chance. This bitch had come here with a master plan. That's what I get for getting drafted into some gay-bullshit with my so-called girls.

"I told your ass—I warned you," was all I managed to hear. Then everything went black.

Chapter Twenty-five

Jazz

The sun was peering down onto the boat as some passengers were already starting to unload the *Sunrise*. Having knocked boots all night long with the hot stud from the Captain's Party, my legs were wobbly, and I was hungover. I couldn't wait to get back to our hotel room and crash. I was done. Listening to the annoying sounds of my cell, I found it on the floor next to one of my shoes. Reaching to pick it up, I rubbed my eyes before looking at the screen. Looking down to see it was my fam, I was happy he was up and at it, making good on his promise. "Hey, cuz," I barely answered, leaning over on the rail. Wanting to make sure we got to talk in private, even though I was dog-ass tired, I held up for a minute.

"Happy Birthday, baby," he sang into the phone, being the first to tell me on my official day. Even though Miami had gotten off to a rocky start, my birthday morning had started just right.

"Thank you," I weakly found the strength to sing back.

"So, did y'all have a good time or what? A few girls on the strip last night complained about not getting on board, so I figured that joint must've been slapping." He had way too much energy for it just to be eight in the morning.

"Hell yeah, you know me, cuz. I'll make me a good time," I giggled.

"I know that's right. Low key, you keep more hot hoes than me. You're gonna have to hook me up with one.

Just make sure they ain't hot and hype like the two you brought down here. I can't handle no short fuses like that in my calm, reformed life."

"Whatever . . . You're in this hot-ass city fronting like a workingman when we all know your ass is a menace to society." I paused, waiting for a response. Since there was none, I continued, hoping this would play out for the best. "Speaking of which, what's up on that stuff for ole girl? She keeps asking."

"Listen, cuz, I'm going to keep it straight 100 percent boogie about ya girl. Under normal circumstances, I wouldn't fuck with her on business, but 'cause you're family, I'll look out." His words were like music to my ears.

"Yes! Yes! This is a great birthday present, fam. You had me worried not responding to my texts last night. And I couldn't tell what you thought about her from earlier."

"Yeah yeah yeah, yo' ass owe me one. And I'm gonna need you to have a serious talk with your girl about discretion. If she gets caught up with old dude she dipped on, my name better never come up."

"Fa'sho. You already know, cuz, and please believe I appreciate the favor." I felt a swarm of relief. I couldn't wait to break the news to Sable. She'd been on me heavy about introducing her to my cousin, and the time had finally come.

"It's a favor for you, but business with her. I've got her new life in my glove compartment, but I'm gonna need five Gs up front first."

"Oh, that's what's up. It ain't gonna be a problem. I'm about to get back to the room and hook up with her. We'll be out ya way in a few." I was ecstatic, knowing I was about to save the day.

"Cool. Hurry up, though, so we can clear this crowd. You know a nigga gotta punch a clock."

"All right, then, I got you. Let me go get my girls, and then we'll be out."

Hanging up, I no longer walked with little energy to our cabin. Damn near running full speed, I couldn't wait to break the news to Sable. I'd already called her a few times this morning but had failed to get an answer. I couldn't wait to hook up with her and find out about her night with Carla too. Hopefully, her first experience with a female had been a great one. Easing up closer to the cabin, I saw the door was cracked, and the lights were already on. Roxy and Sable must've already been up shuffling to get dressed. Good for me not having to wake up their cranky, hungover behinds.

"Good morning, bitches," I yelled, pushing the door wide open, walking in. Unexpectedly, there wasn't a sign of life in the room. Both beds were still made, the television and radio sets were powered off, and the glasses we took a toast in before leaving for the Captain's Party still sat on the bar, half-empty. Shit seemed strange. "Hey, Sable, Roxanne," I whispered out loud, pondering where they were. No one responded. I knew Sable had hooked up with Carla, but as far as I knew, Roxy hadn't gotten lucky. Maybe she'd hooked up with the dude from the party bus and hadn't checked in. "Oh well, I might as well get my stuff together. They should be here in a minute."

Moving toward the closet to pull out my bag, I let out the loudest, shrieking, call-of-death scream I could. My eyes weren't prepared for the sickening image before me. Next to the wide-opened empty safe, Roxy laid sprawled out with her legs and arms twisted like a rag doll and a bright red puddle of blood gushing from her head. What in the fuck!

Breathe, Jazz, breathe. Oh my God, what should I do? What happened? Sable, answer this motherfucking phone. My heart was rushing, and my head was now pounding. Almost throwing up at the sight of my girl down like that had my nerves shook. Calling Sable's phone back-to-back, I ran around the room, tossing my clothes and belongings into my duffel bag. She better answer, and quick, because things had gone really bad. Please tell me Sable ain't find out about her and Mike Mike and bugged the fuck out. With one best friend unconscious or dead, and the other missing in action, I was the only one left standing, innocent and curious about what had really gone down. My battery was going dead, and Sable still wasn't picking up. Thankfully, my cell rang when it did.

"Um, hey, cuz," I tried to mask that I was out of breath and had been crying. I was confused and fucked up in the head. My homegirl was dead for all I knew. My hood instinct kicked in. I couldn't and didn't wanna be questioned by no damn police, especially this far away from home. I had to get it together—and quick.

"What the fuck is taking y'all broads so long? If I'm late to work again, this punk gonna report me to my probation officer . . . and I got no time for violations," he spat into the phone.

Not wanting to put him in the middle of this tricky situation, I knew that he was three strikes into a three-strike deal. If he didn't play by the rules this time, the judge wasn't cutting him any slack or sympathy. But I had no one else to get me out of this bullshit. Instantly, I'd regretted introducing him into my girl's and my drama. I had to think of something. I wanted him to help me, but I didn't know just what the hell had happened my damn self. Suddenly, my line finally clicked. Thank God, it was Sable.

"Okay, cuz, we coming, we coming. Just hold tight." I swiftly hung up on him, clicking over to the sounds of Sable asking what was so important that I had been blowing her up.

Chapter Twenty-six

Sable

"Baby, wake up. Your phone keeps fucking vibrating, and I can't get no sleep," I heard her screaming.

I was woozy and could barely lift my head from the pillow. It took me time to get my mind right and put together where I was at. This sure wasn't Mike Mike, and I was far from my city. "Oh, good morning." I opened my eyes to look at the first lady I've ever slept with. I didn't know how to feel or what to think. Maybe it was the booze or the Miami heat that had me do this impromptu freaky bullshit. In a matter of forty-eight hours, my entire life had been turned upside down. *Damn, I gotta get my shit back together. All of this madness and chaos ain't me.*

"Go turn that thang off and let me give you a great morning," Carla said as she leaned in, giving me a quick but awkward peck on the lips.

Mustering up enough energy to reach into my purse and grab my phone, fifteen missed calls and twenty text messages stared me in the face . . . all from Jazz. What the fuck was wrong? "I don't know what popped off last night, but my girl Jazz has been blowing me up." Sitting up, rubbing the crust from my eyes, I decided it would be best just to call her back.

"Straight-up? Well, hit Light Skin up and see what's going on," she sat up now, checking her own cell. I had to remember to get her number, knowing I'd want seconds and possibly thirds before my trip ended. With Mike Mike out of the picture, I was single and ready to mingle.

Scrolling down and hitting call, it didn't take but two rings before Jazz hysterically answered, screaming my name into the phone in tears. "Hey, what up, doe sis, what's so important? What's wrong? Whoa whoa whoa . . . Calm down. I can't understand a word you're saying." I was on my feet by now, searching all over the room for my panties and bra.

"Girl, Roxy's knocked out, dead, or something. Lots of blood is by her head! Oh my God, Sable. Please hurry—the money—get here." I barely made her chopped-up words out. Through the screams and sobbing, I thought I heard her say the word "money," but I didn't second-guess it being mine.

"What the fuck! Damn. Okay, try to relax. Chill. I'm on my way to you." I slid the phone to end, finally finding all of my clothes and getting dressed. "Carla, come on. Something's wrong with my girl Roxy, and I think it's all fucking bad."

Carla jumped up. Panicked, she quickly slid her jeans and button-up on, not missing a step. It wasn't for her concern for Roxy but for what had popped off on her boat. "Hurry up, ma, we've gotta go."

Running out of the room where I'd shared many nuts with Carla, we ran with lightning speed up the passageways of guests unloading. Ignoring the stares, rude remarks from us bumping them, and the people looking to say what up to her—we finally made it to my VIP cabin.

"What's going on here?" Carla bolted in first, scanning the room. "Oh shit! What the fuck. Oh, hell naw."

"What? What?" I rushed in behind her, scared to look but needing to anyhow. Sprawled out was Roxy, and shit was looking bad.

"This is how I found her. I ain't been over there to check her pulse or see up close—fuck that." Jazz's usually pretty and vibrant face was stained and blackened from the runny makeup.

"Okay, calm down. I'll call emergency so they can get an ambulance out here. One of y'all go check on her." Carla looked over at us, then pulled out her phone.

Since Jazz was a crying mess and had already proven she wasn't stepping a foot near Roxy, I took the high road and went to check on my girl. She looked terrible, I couldn't even lie. Her legs and arms appeared to be limp or broken, blood was pouring out of her head, and her face was black and blue. Whoever got ahold of my girl must've truly had it out for her ruin. Hesitating to lean down, I put my ear close to her mouth and nose to check if I could hear faint breaths, and thank God, I did. "She's not dead, y'all. Carla, tell the ambulance to hurry."

"Oh my God, she looks like it." Jazz was tossing her clothes into her luggage, not the least bit concerned with our friend's condition.

"Come over here, Jazz. Roxy needs us." I couldn't believe she was getting ready to bail. Our girl was unconscious and had taken an ass whipping, and Jazz was too concerned about getting off the damn boat. "We riding on that ambulance," I spat, turning back to the one girl down. Grabbing Roxy's hand, I held it tightly. "Stay strong, girl. I'm here, and I've got you."

"You do you. I'm not celebrating my birthday like this, for one. And if you were laid out on the floor like that, trust, that bitch would leave you for dead." She zipped her duffel bag and threw it onto her shoulder. "You've got bigger things to worry about. You're so worried about that backstabbing bitch that you haven't noticed the empty fucking safe." Jazz pointed toward what instantly broke me down and shattered my world.

“Oh, hell to the naw! Where’s my fucking money?” I shouted, dropping Roxy’s hand flat and looking around the room. “Where’s my bag?” There wasn’t a Nike bag in sight. The room was starting to close in.

“Yeah, the money is missing, and my cousin came through.” Jazz broke me down even more. I’d doubted my girl, and not only did she not lie about her cousin, but he’d also already gotten me a new life. Now, I was the one who’d come up short and had no idea who took my money or did this to Roxy.

“All right, the ambulance is on the way,” Carla cut in, shaking her head in disbelief. “No shit has ever gone down on the *Sunrise* like this or any of my events. Man, what the fuck,” she shouted, pulling out her phone. “I’ve gotta call my partner on this one. We gotta do some damage control.”

“Yeah, this obviously wasn’t a paradise trip for real. What am I going to do now, Jazz?” I stood helpless, homeless, and without a penny to my name. Things couldn’t get worse.

“Get your shit and let’s go. Maybe my cousin will look out under the circumstances, but I can promise you nothing. All I can say is, I’m out.” Jazz started walking toward the door.

“Okay, but what about Roxy . . . just leave her?”

“This probably ain’t the best time to tell you, Sable, but I can’t let you sit here and nurse her fake friendship ass. She’s been fucking Mike Mike for months.”

My expression went cold as anger boiled inside of me. How could my girl be fucking my man? How could she be sitting in my face being a liar and deceptive-ass slut? I’d fed her, clothed her, and even brought Pampers and milk for her snotty-nosed, brat-ass kids. Chicks these days had no loyalty or respect for the game. Turning around and staring down on Roxy, I thought of all of my lonely nights with Mike Mike. This bitch had been the reason for my extra beatings, extra neglect, and extra denial during my relationship. I can't stand a copy-cat-ass-gotta-have-it-'cause-I-do-ass bitch. Get your own and quit coming for mine. Not being able to control my anger and hatred anymore, I took my turn to whip up on Roxy's foul friend ass. Taking my Red Bottom heels off to keep my balance, I picked one up and proceeded to bang bruises all up and down her body to match her already battered face. "Yeah, you sleazy home wrecker, show this body to that nigga now."

"Hey, Light Skin, get your girl," Carla barked at Jazz, who was standing as a spectator, nodding in approval.

"Nope, you fucked her last night. And besides that, Roxy is probably getting her Karma. That ain't got shit to do with you or me. So fall back. Fall all the way back."

I wasn't looking for either one of them to say or do anything. I had this, and old, funky, dog-headed ho Roxy was mine. Dropping my shoe, I hawked up a big glob of spit, landing it directly on her face. I wanted to keep beating her ass, but time would not permit it. Instead, I had other plans for her.

"Okay, baby, that's enough. Get your stuff, and let's go." Jazz finally leaned over and reached for my arm. I snatched back and stared at her with discontent.

"Don't put your fucking hands on me. How you gonna know some shit like that and keep it from me?" I got grim with her, planning to take her out once I finished with this dirty ball I'd once called my homegirl.

"It wasn't even like that, but whatever. I'm about to be out. So beef or not, bitch, let's go. We can talk about that later. I can't be detained by no damn police."

Ignoring her, I picked up Roxy's arms and started to drag her. This bitch was getting ready to come up out of this room and into the ocean. Fuck her and any so-called friends out here on some grimy shit. "Open that door," I screamed as they side-eyed me like I was crazy. "This backstabbing whore about to go swimming—period."

Chapter Twenty-seven

Sable

Momentarily, there was an eerie silence inside the cabin. No one could believe what I was attempting to do to this shifty female. Nonetheless, at this point in the game, I could care less about what these people thought about me and my actions. Not only had my money seemingly vanished, but also now I find out that this low-down, conniving, so-called friend of mine had been fucking Mike Mike on the regular for months. Naw, I didn't give two hot shits that Roxy was already fucked up and half dead. She still was going to suffer even more when the murky water of the ocean filled her lungs. Grabbing both of Roxy's legs by the ankles, I sneered, "Yeah, whore, since you like having these bitches up in the air, wide open for someone else's man, keep that same energy now." Once more, I demanded someone open the fucking door before they'd be next on my bitter revenge agenda.

Not knowing what else to do but comply, Jazz did as I had ordered. My back was turned, yanking on Roxy when I heard my girl yell out. "Oh shit, what you doing here?"

Carla looked around, dumbfounded, not knowing what was up. In turn, I did the same thing—and was left with a dry throat and speechless. My broken heart raced. I felt dizzy, weak all of a sudden. I dropped Roxy's ankles, taking a few steps backward. My nightmare was now a reality.

"My sweet, sweet, unpredictable Sable. I've been missing you the last few days."

"What?" I barely mustered up the courage to speak.

"Yeah, now, bitch, where's my motherfucking money? Run my fucking shit right damn now." Mike Mike was standing less than ten feet from me with all intent on stretching me out across the floor next to a visibly injured Roxy. He wasn't the least bit concerned about his side piece fuck buddy's condition. She was expendable when it came to his funds. Hell, we all were, and shit was about to get real.

"But—" I tried to say something and was once more cut off.

"Naw, no buts, ya sneaky trick slut. Y'all foul-mouthed carpet munchers got all of ten seconds to run me my bread or each of y'all cunts gonna feel something hot. Now, fuck around and think I'm bullshitting. Sable, you already know how I get down. So a nigga ain't taking no damn shorts either."

"Whoa, hold up. Who in the hell are you? This *my* damn boat," Carla bossed up, acting as if she were a man and could go toe-to-toe with one. "And I suggest you watch your mouth with all of them derogatory statements."

"Watch my mouth?" Mike Mike hawked on the carpeted floor, giving her a "fuck-you-bitch" expression. "Look, you wanna be a man, freak? Your best bet is to fall all the way back and stay out of my business before you have problems that once-a-month bleeding pussy ain't equipped to handle—ya feel me? So stay in your lane before I kick ya period on."

Carla was pissed he was being so disrespectful with the name-calling and threats on the boat she owned. Her first reaction was to run up, but she knew better than to try Mike Mike. She might have dressed like a man, strapped on, and fucked like a man—but toe-to-toe, balls-to-balls, the female I'd just spent the night with was no damn man. Carla knew she had no-win. Mike Mike looked and talked like he hadn't come for any games or foolishness, and since he was at least fifty racks lighter in the pocket, I couldn't say that I blamed him.

Searching the room for an escape route other than straight past my living nightmare, Jazz held on to my arm, trembling in fear. Praying the sirens would get closer, hopefully, I could get spared from the pain Mike Mike was hell-bent on putting down on me if I didn't produce the missing cash. My heart was working overtime. Mustering up the courage to speak while stalling for time, I stared him dead in his eyes. "So, you been fucking Roxy, huh? My own best friend! Is *that* how we doing it now?"

Mike Mike's expression changed. It was like the devil himself entered the cabin and had taken over his body and soul. He hated being caught up in his own shit. Like any other man, he tried flipping the script. "Look, Sable, I don't give two fucks about what you talking about right about now—just run my bread—and quick." He took three steps closer as I took four steps backward, almost tripping over Roxy's body. "If I have to beat my money outta you, then so be it. Now, this the last time I'm asking your stanking ass. Run me my goddamn money—all of it."

"Wait! Wait!" Jazz selfishly intervened, hoping to just make it safely off the boat and to her cousin. "Mike Mike, the money is gone. Someone stole it. It's gone. We came back in here, and it was missing, and Roxy was like this—fucked up."

"Say what?" Mike Mike shouted as he rushed across the room, knocking me to the ground. He was furious. That was the last thing he wanted to hear.

I know for a fact he'd hustled hard to stack that money after we'd taken a few serious hits with his pill addiction. Like I was pissed for various reasons, now, he was too.

Our buried emotional baggage throughout the years was now out on the surface. The things we were saying as we fought were raw, and they were real. As we struggled on top of Roxy's mangled body, at one point, Carla tried to yank him off me, prying his hands from around my throat.

On the verge of passing out, I caught a glimpse of Jazz running out the door. I gasped for air as my eyes rolled to the back of my head. The last thing I heard before being out cold was Jazz's voice telling someone that there was a fight in Room 217 and to hurry and get there.

Chapter Twenty-eight

Gianna

Hailing a cab outside the gates of the dock, one pulled up, and I wasted no time climbing in. "Miami International Airport," I instructed him as he pulled away from the curb. Going into the Nike duffel bag, I pulled two hundred-dollar bills from the rubber band, "as fast as you can go, please."

"Oh, yes, ma'am. Now, *this* is a tip." The Indian man pushed his foot on the gas pedal, accelerating to almost ninety miles per hour.

Gianna looked out the window, smiling. She was on the highway cruising, about to go experience her next journey and write the next chapter of her life. With about forty-five thousand to her name, clear free, she had plans of living her life right. Once at the airport, she'd buy a one-way ticket to the fastest flight out of this hellish city. Maybe she'd visit Detroit where the fine-ass nigga that had just boarded looking for some chick said he was from. Gazing out the window, she saw a few police cars and the ambulance floating and cutting through traffic up the other side of the highway. Knowing they were going toward the *Sunrise,* she smiled even wider, locking the dude's number in her cell.

Even though she hadn't gotten to harm Sable physically, taking revenge out on her girl had been just as good.

She had pistol-whipped her ass two good times before slapping her a few more times across the face after she went down. *She's nothing to me and deserved what she had coming for pouring that purple slush all over me.*

Finding the money had been a bonus, and the reason I couldn't fight back the urge to jump out of the bedroom closet and confront her ass in the first place. After knocking her out cold, I searched the bag and came up on the jackpot. Stuffing in the other four stacks she'd taken out for herself, I zipped the bag up, grabbed my belongings, and rushed to get the fuck out of Dodge. Ditching the *Sunrise* keycard and pistol in the ocean after walking out the door, I never looked back and never fucking planned to. Fuck Carla and all *Sunrise* had to offer. I was about to live my best life . . . courtesy of the next bitch.

Chapter Twenty-nine

A Few Months Later . . .

Carla

"I can't believe after all of this time, everything is done—finished. I put so much time into building my name, brand, and this business. Now, just like that, some random bitches from Detroit have ruined it. Damn!" Carla and her partner removed the last of their personal items. Sadly for them, all things considered, the sheriff's department acted. Under court order, they padlocked the federally seized *Sunrise,* bringing an end to Carla's reign as the Boat Ride Czar of Miami. Just as she stated, they'd have to rebuild their business and brand. That was, *if* they could.

Jazz

I wonder what's going to become of Sable. It seems as if we were just hanging out, drinking, and having the time of our lives. Then bam! Roxy's dead, and my home-girl is locked up. And here I am, a stranger in a strange place, missing home. Jazz was terrified to go back home for fear of Mike Mike's certain wrath for her involvement in the entire situation. She knew the last time she saw him, he wanted them all dead. Wisely, she decided to use the documents her cousin Tyrell had gotten for her girl and relocated to parts unknown.

Mike Mike

Once the Princess of Detroit DLA, an injured Sable was transferred to prison awaiting sentencing. The charge was for the first-degree murder of Roxanna, a.k.a. Roxy. After several autopsy reports, it was determined that the fatal blow that killed her once-best friend came from the blunt force trauma of a nine-inch heel of a shoe. Sable's ultimate fate was sealed. She was now broke, alone, locked up, and destined to spend years behind bars for killing a backstabbing bitch that "had it coming." Sure, I could have gotten her a lawyer but chose not to do so. My funds were not totally on craps. Of course, I could have chosen to keep money on her books, but I opted not to do that as well. Instead, just as she ducked out on my black ass intending never to see me again, I gladly returned the favor.

With constant contentment, I lived in the moment of Sable's once-celebratory words she'd vowed when leaving me facedown in my vomit. "*I'd rather be dead than to deal with you again.*" Now, she was getting her wish. I was leaving her for dead. Yeah, I'd faced the fact that I was out of 50K. Not stupid on the way the game went, I knew that stash was gone forever. But I did find some peace knowing my once-pampered princess was out of her freedom. That brutal truth gave me some small sort of contentment that I enjoyed. In my eyes, as long as Sable was locked up behind bars for life, the jealous part of me that was always lurking in our damaged relationship was good with it. She'd never belong to another man again. I was never shy about my feelings. I'd always made clear . . . If I couldn't have her, no other man could. And I was good with that—period.

Gianna and Mike Mike . . . sitting in a tree . . .

After traveling here and there, courtesy of the come-up lick she'd hit, Gianna never thought about Carla or her old life once. Bored of recklessly spending money, she finally decided to visit Detroit. The slick thief decided to hook up with the guy she'd met on the Miami dock after creating havoc on the *Sunrise*. Corresponding with him from time to time, she was ultimately won over by his sweet-sounding voice, boss demeanor, and the memory of his thugged-out swag. With nothing else on her agenda, she flew into Detroit Metro, where he was eagerly waiting to pick her up. The next couple of days were seemingly magical. The two hugged up in a VIP booth of a crowded strip club, popping bottles. It was easy for all to see, Mike Mike and Gianna were feeling each other. Since Sable's untimely incarceration, Mike Mike was in the market for a new princess to spoil, and he felt Gianna fit the build. The more the couple drank, the drunker they both gleefully became.

In the zone playfully talking shit, Mike Mike started to tease his new friend about her being too soft to handle these Detroit females that were in the club throwing shade her way. As the loud music bounced off the walls, they popped another bottle, which a white-girl-wasted Gianna then generously volunteered to pay for. Two glasses into that bottle, tired of Mike Mike talking shit about how bad the bitches were in his hometown, she started slurring, telling him a straight-up gangsta move story about a few stupid-ass Detroit hoes she'd gotten over on a few months back on some boat. The more an overly intoxicated Gianna talked—the more Mike Mike sobered up to make sure he was hearing her cocky tale correctly.

The bottom line . . . Karma is a bitch.